SACRAMENTO PUBLIC LIBRARY
828 "I" STREET
SACRAMENTO, CA 95814

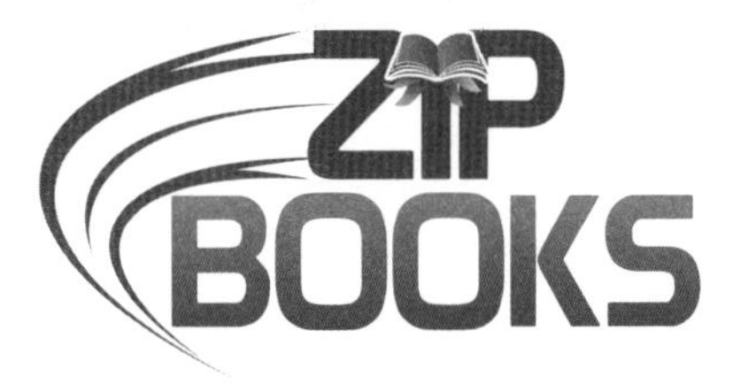

This item was purchased for the Library through Zip Books, a statewide project of the NorthNet Library System, funded by the California State Library.

the PAPER & Hearts SOCIETY

BOOK ONE

LUCY POWRIE

HODDER

HODDER CHILDREN'S BOOKS

First published in Great Britain in 2019
by Hodder and Stoughton

1 3 5 7 9 10 8 6 4 2

Text copyright © Lucy Powrie, 2019

The moral rights of the author have been asserted.

All characters and events in this publication, other than those clearly in the public domain, are fictitious and any resemblance to real persons, living or dead, is purely coincidental.

In order to create a sense of setting, some names of real places have been included in the book. However, the events depicted in this book are imaginary and the real places used fictitiously.

All rights reserved.
No part of this publication may be reproduced, stored in a retrieval system, or transmitted, in any form or by any means, without the prior permission in writing of the publisher, nor be otherwise circulated in any form of binding or cover other than that in which it is published and without a similar condition including this condition being imposed on the subsequent purchaser.

A CIP catalogue record for this book is available from the British Library.

ISBN 978 1 44494 923 0

Typeset in Wilke LT by Hewer Text UK Ltd, Edinburgh
Printed and bound in Great Britain by Clays Ltd, Elcograf S.p.A.

The paper and board used in this book are made from wood from responsible sources.

Hodder Children's Books
An imprint of
Hachette Children's Group
Part of Hodder and Stoughton
Carmelite House
50 Victoria Embankment
London EC4Y 0DZ

An Hachette UK Company

www.hachette.co.uk
www.hachettechildrens.co.uk

To Mum & Dad, for giving me life. (Literally.)
And in memory of my maternal grandparents,
Nan and Grandad. I wish with all my heart you
could be here to see this.

With freedom, books, flowers and the moon, who could not be happy?

OSCAR WILDE

Chapter One

Tabitha Brown's heart thudded in her chest as she read the Instagram caption on her phone. *Best night with my favourite girls!*

She didn't want to look, but she couldn't help but scrutinise every inch of the picture – Jess, her blonde, crinkled hair flowing down her shoulders, with her arms round two other girls, all three beaming into the lens. They looked like the *best* of friends.

You really shouldn't be looking, Tabby thought. *There's absolutely no reason to.*

But still she did.

She was sprawled out on the lawn in her gran's back garden, a book open by her side – *Solitaire* by Alice Oseman – and prescription sunglasses over her face.

Gran's garden wasn't huge, but she'd made the most of the space: there were pots teeming with flowers on the patio, beautiful clematises climbing up the side of the wall and dahlias spread open in bright, pink bloom; they'd only just begun to flower. Tabby's favourites, though, were the almost-black cornflowers, a shock of vivid blue every few flower heads catching her eye. Gran had sent her a packet a few years ago, which she'd grown back home in Cheltenham. Then, they'd reminded her of Gran; now, they reminded her of home, so many miles away, being packed up. Soon, she'd have a new home here to think about.

She opened the comment box and took a deep breath in. *They weren't your favourite girls before*, she typed, but deleted it a second later.

'Tabby?' Gran's voice floated through the back door. 'Are you coming in for lunch?'

'Just a minute!' she called back, slipping her phone in her pocket and picking up her book.

Gran stood at the kitchen counter, cutting the crusts off a slice of bread. *She refuses to acknowledge I'm old enough to eat my crusts.*

'What were you doing out there, love? I thought the point of being outside was that you actually spent time doing something other than being glued to that mobile of yours.'

'Nothing really,' Tabby said. Her phone burned in her pocket.

'Well, don't spend too much time on it,' Gran said, wrapping her arm around Tabby's shoulders. 'I don't want you beating my high score on Candy Crush, do I?'

The surface of the kitchen table was covered with old TV magazines, bits of paper and empty medication boxes. Gran kept promising she'd tidy them up, but so far hadn't attempted it; one of these days, Tabby was going to take matters into her own hands. For now, though, she pushed everything to one side to make room and sat down.

'What have you got planned for the rest of the day?' Gran asked, joining her.

'Not much.' Tabby patted her book. 'Finishing this, I guess.'

And stalking Jess's Instagram.

'You could go out for a run. I see you brought your trainers with you. Why not pop out for a bit?'

'No, I really just want to get on with reading.' *I don't run. Not any more.*

'You didn't bring many books with you. I thought you'd have come with half your bookshelf in your suitcase!'

'What's with all the questions, Gran? There wasn't enough room to bring them all, and Dad made me clear loads out anyway. Apparently, I could have taken up an entire removal van with my bookshelf.'

'Well, you'll have to go to the library then. You brought your library card, didn't you?'

'I really am fine. Honestly.'

Tabby hated to get snappy, but she was content staying here, inside her blissful cocoon for ever, where the only irritation she had was Gran waking her up with One Direction blaring from her (old-school) CD player every morning. ('You do know they've been split up for years, right?' Tabby had asked, and received a sharp reply that yes, Gran did in fact know and it would be nice if Tabby never, ever mentioned 'Wayne' leaving because she was still highly emotional about it. Tabby hadn't bothered to correct her.)

Gran gave her a pointed look. 'It's either go to the library tomorrow or come to Zumba with me. Your choice! But if it's Zumba, I expect you to put the maximum amount of effort in. I saw you slacking last time. Rose and I could run rings around you and we have a combined age of a hundred and fifty-five.'

'All right, I'll go to the library. I'll leave you and Rose to OAP Zumba.'

Gran got up and placed her hands over Tabby's shoulders. 'If you change your mind, I've got some spare Lycra you can borrow. Hot pink, I think it is – perfect for your complexion!'

Tabby swatted her away, and their laughter mingled around them as Gran kicked her leg up in the air in an imitation of a Zumba move.

'You'll dislocate your new hips if you're not careful!'

'I'm invincible,' Gran replied. 'Don't you worry about me!'

Tabby felt the vibration of her phone inside her pocket.

Jess: So youve decided to run away early? Good luck with that

Jess: You may be able to leave but youll never get away from the fact that youre a complete loser

'Got a secret admirer?' Gran asked.

'No.' Tabby laughed it off. 'It's just one of those adverts asking me if I want a super summer saving on my phone bill.'

Palms sweating, Tabby put the phone back on the table; it clanked down harder than she'd intended. 'What would you say to a cup of tea?' *I've perfected the art of distraction.*

'I'd say you were the best granddaughter in the whole world.'

I don't know about that.

Chapter Two

It is a truth universally acknowledged that any book lover in want of a good book will always find one in a library.

The library was in the centre of the Dorset town where Gran had lived all her life, and now Tabby was moving here too. She was used to visiting for the Easter and summer holidays, for Christmases and birthdays, but it would be different living here. She felt she had to pay more attention to where everything was.

It was just like any other town: charity shops and too many coffee shops, the usual high street chains and big names; but there were also the well-stocked library and a gorgeous independent bookshop, Woolf and Wilde. Gran had taken Tabby there once when she was younger and let her pick out whatever book she'd wanted.

She'd chosen *The Lion, the Witch and the Wardrobe* and her dad had read it to her in the car on the way back home. She'd spent the next week bashing into the back of her wardrobe, trying to find her own way to Narnia, but to no avail.

There was a familiarity in walking through the sliding doors of the library: the smell of books old and new; the vastness of the shelves. Tabby felt like she'd known it all her life.

She headed to the YA section, scanning the shelves for books she hadn't read before. There was a method to it: start at the top and move your way across, and then reverse back along the row to the beginning and move down to the next shelf. You had to keep your eyes skimming back and forth just in case you missed a book, and then right at the end do another quick scan to make sure nothing had escaped your attention.

Once she'd picked up a few books – *Anna and the French Kiss* by Stephanie Perkins, *One Italian Summer* by Keris Stainton, to name a couple – it was time to peruse the classics section. *Please have it, please have it, please have it*, Tabby prayed, thinking longingly of her bookshelf at home. Yes. There, nestled amongst the P section was *The Bell Jar* by Sylvia Plath.

'You and that book are attached at the hip. One of these days I swear I'll catch you reading it in your sleep,' Mum had taken to saying whenever she found Tabby reading it. Which was *very* often.

It wasn't just a book any more – it was Tabby's lifeline. She lived and breathed it; it comforted and soothed and explained exactly how she was feeling even when she couldn't understand those feelings herself.

Tabby tried to pull it out from the shelf, but it wouldn't budge. It was as if something was caught in it, making it too big to come out easily.

She looked over her shoulder to check if anyone was watching, and then leant in closer. Prising her hand between the book and the back of the shelf, she managed to wiggle it out.

It was a well-thumbed copy with a different cover design to hers at home; the protective plastic covering the surface clearly hadn't done much to protect it over the years, but that didn't matter. *What's important is the inside.*

Tabby opened it to find a crumpled-up piece of paper jammed inside, stark white against the yellowing pages. She unfolded it, smoothed out the wrinkles and read:

JOIN THE BOOK CLUB!

Know your Jane Austen from your Brontë sisters? Got what it takes to survive *The Hunger Games*? Love nothing better than sharing recommendations and having bookish adventures?

We are a group of friends aged 15–17 who LOVE
talking about books and **WE NEED YOU!**

We're getting bored of having the same bookish
conversations over and over again and need
fresh blood (in a non-Dracula way, of course!)
to make our book-filled hearts sing.

Come and help us show the world
how cool books really are!
(No literary snobs, book haters or ADULTS allowed)
(Chocolate will be supplied)

First meeting: 2.30 p.m. Saturday 20 July @ the park
Message Olivia @bookswithlivs on
Instagram for more details

Tabby tucked the poster back into the book and snapped it shut. *Maybe this is a sign . . . I'll think about it.*

'I bet you'll have read all those books by tomorrow night,' Gran said as they sat down to eat dinner. 'But I suppose it's better than you watching that *Strange Thing* constantly.'

For the five billionth time . . . '*Stranger Things*, Gran. It's *Stranger Things*. And I don't watch it constantly, but you do *complain* about it constantly.'

She loved her, really. She could take Gran's cluelessness about anything that happened after 1960 if it meant she got to hug her every day and lose herself in the warm home-cooked meals and lavender smell of her jumpers.

Now that they were moving here, she'd get to see Gran as much as she wanted, and just the thought made her feel the happiest she'd felt in a long time.

Mum had been looking for a new job for a while. When one came up at the hospital in the town she'd grown up in, it had been a no-brainer: they all wanted to spend more time with Gran now she was getting older, and it had always been Mum's dream to move back.

So Mum and Dad had packed Tabby off early to stay with Gran for a bit while they packed up the rest of the house. She hadn't minded – she'd be able to spend loads of time like this with Gran.

Tabby considered her next words carefully, wolfing down a third helping of roast potatoes to give herself time to think. She had to act casual so Gran wouldn't get too enthusiastic.

'I found something at the library today.'

'Another book, by any chance?'

'Ha, ha. No, it was a poster actually. For a book club.'

Tabby pulled the poster out from the copy of *The Bell Jar*, which she'd been carrying around ever since she got back, and slid it across the table to Gran. She lifted it closer to her face and her eyes wrinkled as she smiled.

'Oh, that's wonderful! You're going to go, aren't you? A book club! What a marvellous idea. You know, I was talking to Shirley round the corner the other day and she says she's been really enjoying that *Fifty Shades of Grey* book and is going to lend it to me. Do you want it afterwards? Isn't that the kind of thing you talk about at book clubs?'

Where did I get her from? 'No, Gran, you're a bit late to the party with that one. I think I'll pass.'

Tabby could swear her grandmother was going through puberty all over again. Just last week, she had been adamant about going for a slow jog around the housing estate, hoping to bump into Mr Helstone who lived over the road. Gran was particularly impressed by his obsession with growing his own veg, which she regularly dropped into conversation, despite having an intense dislike of courgette.

'I don't think I'm going to join. It's not really my thing.'

Gran paused, a fork full of peas hovering mid-air. 'Not really your thing? Tabby, you were reading before you could talk. How is a book club *not* your thing?'

'I just don't see the point in joining something.'

Gran reached across the dining table and grabbed Tabby's hand. 'These kids sound like they're as obsessed with books as you are, and we need to surround ourselves with people who are just as passionate about the things in life that we are. Take Mr Helstone and his veg, for example. Now, there's a passionate man. He's made many friends at the local competitions he attends. Just goes to show: it's never too late to find your people.'

'I'll think about it,' Tabby said, mainly to stop the impending talk of Mr Helstone's carrots. *The last thing you need is to get close to people. It only ever ends in disaster.*

Gran looked exultant. 'No, don't just think about it,' she said, tapping the poster in front of her. 'I can't believe I'm saying this, but get your phone out and message this girl now. I know what you're like: you'll keep putting it off. And if you don't do it, I'll create my own Insta*gran* account to do it myself and then you'll be sorry.'

Tabby saw the hope in Gran's eyes. *It's impossible to say no to her.*

@WhatTabbyDid *Hi, is this Olivia who left the book club poster in the library?*

@bookswithlivs *Yes, that's me! HI! Are you interested in joining the club?! :D*

@WhatTabbyDid *Only if there are spaces left. I'd hate to take up somebody else's if you've already had lots of interest*

@WhatTabbyDid *And don't worry, I'm not a book hater or an adult ;)*

@bookswithlivs *Haha! We would LOVE to meet you!*

@WhatTabbyDid *So I'm okay to come on Saturday?*

@bookswithlivs *YES! I'm soooooooo excited about it. We're meeting by the big tree at the far end of the park. Are you oaky to meet us there?*

@bookswithlivs *Oops!! Typo! I meant OKAY, obviously!*

@WhatTabbyDid *Haha, sounds lovely. See you there x*

Chapter Three

The park was packed, even for a Saturday afternoon. Tabby had to dodge around screaming kids and their sun-lounging parents, being careful not to tread on any stray fingers, either human or chocolate, on picnic blankets. The *last* thing she wanted was squished melted chocolate over her white Converse. That wouldn't make a great first impression.

She took a deep breath in, steadying her pounding heartbeat. Her nerves weren't helped by the heat of the day, the sweltering July sun threatening to turn her pale skin from practically translucent to tomato red.

She was filled with the overwhelming temptation to turn around and not look back until she was at Gran's again, when it would be too late to change her mind.

I can't do this. I can't join a club full of teenagers who will all know each other and will be far more confident than I am. I'll make a fool of myself!

But there was something about the oak tree at the far end of the park, raised on a slight hill and keeping watch over the area, that called to her. Large roots cascaded down like sea monsters diving head first into the ocean, their tails left behind, and the afternoon sun hit the boughs and cast long shadows. It dawned on her that she was too close to walk away now, especially as she'd spotted the outline of two figures underneath. Could one of them be Olivia?

PLEASE try to act normal. Please remember how to interact with other people. Please don't do anything stupid or awkward or embarrassing.

'Um, hi.' Tabby walked over to the pair, not wanting to get too close in case she had the wrong people. They didn't look up. Tabby knotted her hands behind her back and bit on her bottom lip, raising the courage to speak again. 'Is this the book club?'

The girl, her dark, straight hair flowing past her shoulders, jumped up, showing a mouthful of braces as she beamed wide. Despite her excitement, she seemed composed and in control, something Tabby definitely didn't feel. *I'm just a hot mess.*

She stuck out her hand for a handshake but withdrew it and pulled Tabby into a quick hug. *Woah.*

Although surprising, Tabby found it strangely comforting to be greeted with such warmth. 'Sorry, we were deep in conversation there! You must be Tabby. Thanks for coming! I'm Olivia. You know, the one you spoke to. Or wrote to, I guess. It wasn't really speaking, was it?'

Her voice rose at the end of each sentence; Tabby could practically see the exclamation marks floating in the air between them.

'Honestly, when you messaged me, I was over the moon. Are you from around here? I don't think I've seen you before; I would remember. I've got the kind of brain that recognises faces easily, even if I've only met somebody once. I'm sure I haven't seen you before!'

The boy she was with cleared his throat. He had his hands stuck casually in his pockets and looked amused. *His hair makes him look like he should be in an indie band*, Tabby thought. His light brown fringe was swept to one side, just touching the top of his tortoiseshell glasses, which slipped down his nose as he moved. Tabby noted that his glasses formed part of his look, unlike her plain rectangular frames that she kept meaning to replace.

'I'm Henry.' A dimple appeared on each of his cheeks as he smiled and added, 'Nice to meet you.'

Wow. A normal-length sentence, spoken slowly. Tabby had almost forgotten what that was like.

'Nice to meet you too,' she said, but there was a buzzing awkwardness all over her body, and she was regretting ever coming.

'We're just waiting for the others to arrive and then we can get started,' Olivia said. 'It's not like there'll be an initiation or anything serious like that. We won't make you run through the park naked or prank call someone or drink alcohol until you're sick, but I thought it would be nice to introduce ourselves, especially as the rest of us already know each other. Unless anyone else turns up today, you're still our only new recruit. Can you *believe* that? Who wouldn't want to join a book club?'

'Such a shame,' Tabby said, feeling her mouth run away from her brain. 'I signed up in the hope that we'd all be running around the park naked while reading.'

Why did I say that?! Oh god, I'm blushing.

'One problem with that: there'd be nowhere to keep a bookmark and Olivia gets very upset if anyone dog-ears the pages,' Henry said, laughing.

'Too right I do!' Olivia said. 'You're a nightmare when it comes to borrowing books. Never again, I swear!'

Henry directed a shrug at Tabby as if to say, 'What can I do?' and she smiled back gratefully; at least there hadn't been an awkward silence after her stupid comment.

'How many others are there?' Tabby asked.

She imagined twenty other people turning up, crowding around and overwhelming her. There may not be any new recruits, but Olivia and Henry didn't seem like the kind of people who had very few friends.

'Well, there's my best friend Cassie. And then there's Ed, who is a best friend but not quite as bestest as Cassie. So . . . two. Two more. But at least we're amongst friends! I said "friend" a lot there, didn't I?'

Oh. Maybe twenty people would be better than four best *friends.*

'We're going to have so much fun, Tabby. I've already got *loads* planned; there's going to be so much book talk that your ears will bleed. Have you read any Jane Austen, by the way? I love her. She's the best. Please tell me you love her just as much as I do: that would make me *so* happy.'

'Livs . . .'

'Yes, Henry?'

He lowered his voice in a mock whisper. 'I think you might be scaring Tabby.'

'Oh no, it's fine,' Tabby replied. 'I've just never been around other people who love books like I do. It's a lot to take in.'

'You'll get used to us, I promise,' Olivia said. 'Actually, I'm not sure if *I'm* even used to us yet . . .'

You're being nice to me now, just like Jess was, but you'll get fed up with me and then that will change. It can't last.

'So, how did you find out about the book club?' Henry asked. His voice was deep but had a gentleness to it that was the total opposite of Olivia's. Tabby had to lean closer to him to listen properly.

'It's funny, but I left a copy of my favourite book at home so I went to the library to borrow it. When I found it, the poster was lodged inside.'

'Olivia spent so much time putting those together, but Cassie wasn't convinced anyone would actually be interested. She'll be pleased to see you. Serendipity, hey?'

'Certainly seems like it.' *I bet it turns out to be more like bad luck.*

Henry opened his mouth to respond when a squeal erupted from Olivia. She promptly ran down the hill and collapsed into the arms of a tall girl with dark hair cut into a neat bob. She had brown skin and wore red lipstick, rings all over her fingers, and a denim jacket covered in patches and enamel badges. Tabby was instantly jealous of her black Dr. Martens boots, with red roses interlaced up the sides.

Intimidatingly cool. She looked down at her own distressed jeans, with one too many rips, and the floral top she'd scrubbed to get a stain out of that morning, and wished she'd made a little more effort.

Tabby watched as Cassie took a chocolate bar out of her pocket and handed it to Olivia, who lit up as she saw it.

If they're handing out chocolate bars, they've got to be good people. Right?

'Don't take too much notice of Livs,' Henry said. 'She's been going on about this book club idea for months. It's turned into her baby, so expect mega levels of excitement.'

'Ha. Thanks for the warning.' *Argh, why can't I think of anything to say?!*

Olivia and Cassie were joined by an out of breath boy with short but curly blond hair, cut close at the sides. He wore a cheeky grin on his face, which played host to a collection of freckles, dark against his white skin. Tabby couldn't help but feel secretly happy that he didn't look like he'd be winning a fashion prize soon either. His bright orange shirt was more of a practical choice . . . practical if he was ever lost and needed to be instantly found.

'Got any food?' he asked Olivia. 'I had to roll out of bed for this. Didn't even have time for breakfast. You could've brought me a chocolate bar too, Cassie.'

'Ed,' Henry said. 'You do know it's quarter to three, don't you?'

'Exactly.'

He stopped as he noticed Tabby and narrowed his eyes, squinting up at her. She took a step back without realising she was doing it, almost bumping into Henry, who politely seemed not to notice.

'I've got cookies,' Tabby said with a shrug, pulling the packet out of her bag. She'd bought them earlier to take back to Gran who was partial to a chocolate chip cookie or two. But this would make a good first impression, and Gran would never need to know. She handed them over with a small, shy smile.

'I like this queen who bringeth beauteous biscuits,' Ed said, taking the packet from Tabby.

She blinked. *How am I supposed to respond to* that?

'He likes Shakespeare,' Henry informed her. 'Another thing you should probably ignore.'

'Is there anything I should *not* ignore?' she asked.

'Me?' Henry grinned. 'Okay, but on a serious note, Olivia's right: you'll get used to us. We've known each other for such a long time; to us, we're normal. To everyone else? Probably not.'

'How *did* you meet?' They seemed a ragtag bunch – mismatched, yet somehow fitting together.

'We all went to the same primary school and one Christmas we were cast in the play. To cut to the chase, the school had to rewrite their safety procedures after that, because during rehearsals Ed touched part of the set while the four of us were on stage. The entire thing collapsed, trapping us underneath. Instant friendship. Ed was very upset about the rips in his white tights, if I remember rightly. See what I mean about normal?'

What have I let myself in for?

'It's time!' Olivia called. 'Now we're all here, we can get started. Take a seat!'

She grabbed hold of Cassie's and Ed's arms and pulled them down so that they were sitting in a loose circle; Ed was focused on unwrapping the biscuits from their packet.

'Everyone,' she said, 'this is Tabby. Tabby, this is everyone!'

'Hi,' Tabby said weakly. 'It's nice to meet you all.'

'This is the best day of my life,' Ed said. 'Just when I was beginning to get fed up with these losers, somebody new arrives, *and* she's bearing biscuits. I'm Ed.'

There was something infectious about the grin that had been stuck to his face ever since he'd arrived; Tabby couldn't help but grin back. He handed out the cookies to each of them and gave the spares back to Tabby.

'So what are you doing here?' Cassie asked, flicking her hair over her shoulder. 'It's a bit strange joining a club as the *only* new person. I'd *hate* for you to feel like you're not wanted.'

Tabby's grin disappeared. *So much for 'pleased to see you'* . . . 'I like books.'

What more was there to say? But Cassie didn't seem satisfied, raising a single eyebrow.

Olivia finished her cookie and cleared her throat. 'Enough of the chit-chat . . . Let's get going.' She clapped her hands together. 'Starting a book club has basically been my dream ever since I realised that book clubs were a thing, so thank you so much for coming. I'm a teeny tiny bit excited, as you can probably tell.' Henry laughed under his breath. 'We're going to be like the Three Musketeers but with five of us and books, not swords! I'm just so, so glad you all wanted to be a part of it.'

'Did we?' Cassie muttered. Olivia gave her a stern look and carried on.

'Shall we begin by introducing ourselves? Tabby, you can go first. I'm sure we're all *dying* to hear more about you.'

Tabby's stomach lurched. She wasn't sure what to say, didn't know how to begin. This was way too awkward. *Never again*, she promised herself. *As long as I get through this next part, I never have to see them again and can hide for the rest of the summer. Simple.*

But it wasn't simple. How was she supposed to introduce herself? It was like one of those embarrassing back-to-school activities where the teachers made you say an interesting fact about yourself and the only thing you could think of was that your favourite colour was purple, or that you once got chased by a pigeon.

'I'm Tabby.' *Yes, they already know that, genius.* 'Uh, my favourite book is *The Bell Jar* by Sylvia Plath.' A nervous giggle. Where did that come from? 'I love her poetry too. It's not the cheeriest, though.' She hadn't been able to stand cheery recently.

'Oh, that's so cool and sophisticated!' Olivia said. 'Are you in school or sixth form or . . .?'

'I'm fifteen – going into Year Eleven in September.' *Leave it at that, Tabby. They don't really want to hear about you. The less they know, the better.*

'Same age as Olivia and me,' Henry said, smiling at her. 'Cassie and Ed are old compared to us.'

'Older and *far* wiser,' Ed said. 'The knowledge in my little finger is more than all of your brains put together.'

He demonstrated his point by wiggling his little finger in Cassie's face, who shot him a look of disgust.

'You say that,' Olivia said with a giggle, 'but really we know that all your knowledge consists of is weird facts about cats, food and Shakespeare.'

'But what about cats dressed as Shakespeare, eating? That would make a great YouTube channel.'

Cassie rolled her eyes. 'Is it my turn yet?'

'Will you stop being so grumpy?' Ed muttered under his breath, which earnt him a death stare. What was Cassie's problem?

Cassie ignored him. 'What's that book I'm reading that you lent me, Livs? I can't remember the title.' Olivia responded with something Tabby couldn't make out. 'Oh yeah.' She nodded her head. '*Fangirl* by Rainbow Rowell. It's good so far; I like it. But mostly I like reading graphic novels because I'm an artist and I'd like to write and illustrate my own books one day.'

'An "artiste"?' Ed teased.

Cassie rolled her eyes again. 'As I was saying, *Edward*, Noelle Stevenson is probably my favourite graphic novelist. *Nimona* is a work of genius. But I doubt any of you are that interested in graphic novels, so I don't know why I'm here really. Are any of you really going to read them just because I said so?'

'Yes!' Olivia replied, her voice rising. 'That's the whole point of the book club.'

'Brilliant.'

Tabby felt what little spirit she had dampen.

'Well, I'll introduce myself next then. My name is Olivia,' she said, turning to Tabby, 'and I moved here from the Philippines when I was five. I remember feeling homesick for days, but my mum read to me each night until I felt better and ever since stories have been the most important thing in my life. My parents are both journalists and they've always encouraged my sister and me to love words as much as they do.'

'I remember,' Henry said, 'when we were little kids and you'd carry a notebook everywhere with you so that you could write your own stories, and then you'd copy them up into tiny books and hand them out to the whole class.'

Olivia laughed. 'I thought I was straight out of *Anne of Green Gables*! But now, instead of writing stories, my dream is to be a book editor and help everyone else to tell their own stories.'

Tabby had never met anyone her age before who had such a good idea of how they wanted their future to look. She didn't know what she wanted for dinner that night, never mind what she wanted to do for a living.

'And my favourite author in the whole wide world is Jane Austen,' Olivia continued. 'If I could raise the dead, I would raise her.'

'Not creepy at all,' Ed said. 'And I thought *I* was the weird one.'

She poked her tongue out at him. 'That's completely normal. And you're telling me you wouldn't raise Shakespeare from the dead if you had the chance?'

'No, because Shakespeare would be too cool for me and would show me up.'

Tabby heard herself say, 'But what if you raised Shakespeare *and* Jane Austen? I think the world would implode if both of them were writing at the same time. *Romeo and Juliet* crossed with *Pride and Prejudice*. Can you imagine it?'

She felt a warm sensation fizzle inside her as Ed and Olivia laughed and agreed with her, like she was being accepted.

'The ultimate showdown,' Ed said. 'Jane would never stand a chance.'

'Hey!' Olivia protested. 'You know that's not true.'

'Okay, okay, my turn to introduce myself,' Ed said, clapping his hands together. 'My name is Ed, I have graced this planet for seventeen years now, and I am loved by many. I was born in a hospital on a hot day much like this one and have since been the apple of my mother's—'

'You're just showing off now,' Henry scolded, pushing Ed's shoulder playfully. 'We get one new person and suddenly you're the life and soul of the party.'

'I am *always* the life and soul of the party,' Ed said, widening his eyes and leaning in close to Tabby. 'Don't believe a word anyone says about me. They're just jealous of my wit and charm.'

'What wit and charm?' Olivia teased. 'I've never seen evidence of either.'

Tabby patted Ed's shoulder. 'Jealousy,' she whispered to him, and he put his hand out for a high five. *Who am I?* she thought. *I never make jokes like that, no matter how awkward.*

It won't last. It can't last.

'Finally!' Ed called. 'I have an ally!'

'You won't have any allies if you don't do us a favour and get to the point. Tell us your favourite book or let someone else have a chance.' Cassie had her death stare down to a T.

'All right, all right . . . You guys already know this, but for Tabby's benefit, my favourite book is *A Game of Thrones*. George R. R. Martin. I know, I know. I bet you're wondering how I didn't land the part of Jon Snow in the series when I'm so good-looking. They said it would be too distracting, that I might break TV screens from all the beauty.'

'You wish,' Cassie muttered. The rest laughed.

Tabby was pleased she'd taken her turn early. Now she could blend into the background, turn into a chameleon and act as if she wasn't there. As Henry took his turn, she let his voice wash over her, tuning out to the other sounds of the park: the screams, the laughs, the car engines stopping and starting as people parked outside to pick up and drop off kids.

'. . . and it's not a fiction book, but my favourite poetry collection is *Birthday Letters* by Ted Hughes.'

'Seriously?' She may have zoned out, but Tabby was fully conscious again now. Had Henry really said what she thought he'd said?

'Yes?'

She'd only spent the entirety of the year so far reading anything to do with Sylvia Plath. And Ted Hughes had been her husband. They'd had a tumultuous, controversial relationship, but Tabby had never met anyone before who knew about either of them, let alone had read any of their works.

And the poems in *Birthday Letters* had been written about Sylvia Plath. This was too good to be true.

'I've never met anyone else who knows about *Birthday Letters*.'

He grinned. 'Neither have I. That's so cool. What are the chances?'

'Great,' Cassie said, clearly not finding anything great at all. Tabby had noticed, out of the corner of her eye, that she'd been on her phone for the past five minutes. 'Anyway, I'm off – I'm meeting Yaz and Georgie in town. We have to discuss our college art projects for the start of September.'

Olivia frowned. 'But we've only just got started. Did you really have to organise that for today? We need to plan our next meeting. Like, decide stuff about the regularity of meetings and who's going to host each one and—'

'You know I only came for you, Livs,' Cassie said. 'I've got better things to be doing. I've got no interest in making new friends or living the "best bookish life *ever*" when I'm perfectly happy with the friends I've got.'

I must have said something wrong. I shouldn't have come. I'm ruining their friendship group and I've only been here half an hour.

'Charming,' Ed said, the grin lost from his face. 'If you didn't want to be here, you shouldn't have come.'

'Point duly noted, Edward.' And with that, dusting the dirt from her bare legs, Cassie walked away.

'Should I follow her?' Olivia looked shell-shocked, as they watched Cassie head for the exit.

'Just leave her to sulk,' Henry said. 'You can't let her ruin your day.'

Tabby's chest was beginning to tighten up and she pushed back against the sensation. *Not here, not now. Please.*

First came the tightness in her chest, then the light would start getting too bright, the only sound her own breathing, becoming more ragged by the second. She'd feel like she was drowning, feel like somebody had cut off her oxygen supply, feel like the world was crashing down around her.

Olivia sighed. 'Let's just hope the next meeting is better. Let's get ice cream? I hear Brain Freeze are testing new flavours today.'

'Actually, I've got to be getting home,' Tabby said, getting up and walking away from the circle before she had a full-blown panic attack. Her voice was too quiet, barely above a whisper. She turned back. 'Nice to meet you, though.'

All she could think about was wrapping herself up in her duvet at Gran's and not emerging for a month. Or maybe ever again.

'Wait!' She felt a hand grab hold of her arm and spun around. Olivia's smiling face was next to hers. *Too close.*

'Are you okay? Please don't leave on account of Cassie. I really didn't expect her to be like this today. She's had a tricky time of it, but she's lovely, I promise.'

'I'm fine,' Tabby said. *Now please let me leave.*

'Can I add you on Facebook?' Olivia asked, taking out her phone and tapping away.

'Sure,' she said, and sent herself a friend request when Olivia passed her phone to her. She heard the familiar buzz of a notification alert in her bag.

'Are you guys coming for ice cream or not?' Ed called. 'My stomach is grumbling like a very angry bear that's just woken up from hibernation. Do you really want to irritate that bear further?'

The perfect opportunity to escape. She pushed a semblance of a smile on to her face. 'Thanks for today, but I really have to get back. My gran's having a barbecue and I don't want her to have eaten all the sausages by the time I get there. I am partial to a good sausage. Ha, ha!' *Why are you lying? And why, oh why, did you have to mention sausages when you've already embarrassed yourself by expressing your disappointment at not running through the park naked? This isn't an episode of* The Great British Bake Off*!*

Tabby's mortification threatened to squeeze the air in her lungs tighter and her vision started to blur. *I've got to get out of here. Now.*

'At least someone is concerned about food,' Ed said, coming over with Henry to join them.

'You've already eaten a load of cookies, so you really can't complain you're hungry,' replied Olivia.

'Will we be seeing you for the next meeting?' Henry asked, smiling down at Tabby. *He really is so tall.* 'We'll have to message you and let you know the details, once we've sorted everything with Cassie.'

He's only asking me to be kind. He doesn't want me there. He's plotting an excuse in his head, trying to let me down gently.

'That would be nice,' Tabby said. It was the second lie she'd told that day.

Olivia: Hi Tabby! I hope you had a good time at the book club meeting! I'm really sorry about Cassie. She isn't usually like that, I SWEAR! I hope you'll come back again – we'd love to have you! Did you have a good time at your barbecue?! You were missed at our ice cream extravaganza!

Tabby: Hi Olivia. I had a great time, thank you. On both counts. :)

Olivia: Ahhh YAY! That's amazing news! Are you okay if I add you to our group chat? I made it especially. That way we can talk about our plans!

Tabby: Sure :)

Olivia added Tabby Brown to the group chat.

Olivia: Hi Tabby! Welcome to the group!

Henry: I hope this is better than the other group chat where you spammed us with pictures of dogs in other animal costumes. Otherwise I think Tabby will be leaving in a hurry.

Ed: RULE NUMBER ONE: ONLY PICTURES OF CAKE ALLOWED

Olivia: Noooooo Ed!

Cassie: why am i in this?

Ed: YES OLIVIA CAAAKKEEEEEEE

Olivia: Ed do you ever think about anything other than cake?!

Ed: Doughnuts

Olivia: Doughnuts ARE cake

Ed: They are most definitely not. They are completely separate things

Henry: I think Olivia might be right on this one.

Ed: FIGHT ME

Olivia: We NEED to discuss a name for our book club. It is VERY important so that we seem more official.

Cassie: official for what?

Olivia: Well nothing but that's not my point!

Ed: DANGEROUS READERS

Olivia: Can you please take this seriously?

Ed: I AM

Olivia: . . .

Cassie: you guys are sad

Ed: Just because you don't appreciate my talent

Olivia: ANYWAY, we need to have another meeting next week so we can start this book club properly. Is everyone free on Wednesday? Who would like to host?! VOLUNTEERS PLEASE!

Cassie: you know i can't

Olivia: Henry?!

Henry: My sister's been ill all week so unless you want horrific toddler disease, the answer is no, sorry :)

Ed: I VOLUNTEER AS TRIBUTE

Olivia: Thank you!!!!

Olivia: By the way, do any of you own a bonnet?

Chapter Four

Legs sprawled over the sofa, phone in one hand and TV remote in the other, Tabby flicked through the channels without glancing up. Until she felt her phone vibrate. It was the Tuesday after the book club meeting, and she'd spent the weekend coaching Gran through her OAP yoga homework. ('I don't think downward dog is really that downwards, Gran.')

Olivia: Hi again Tabby!! I just wanted to send you a quick message to check you're okay??? I saw you'd read the messages in our group chat but you haven't replied and when I spoke to Henry about it he said you were probably feeling overwhelmed because we can be pretty FULL ON so I'm sorry if we're all confusing and random but I'm sure you'll catch up in no time and then everything will be PERFECT. :D

Olivia: WOAH that was a long message. But I hope you're okay and it really was so amazing to have you at the book club!

Olivia: Did you want to come to our next meeting on Wednesday??

'That sound goes right through me,' Gran said. 'Who are you texting now? It can't be your mum, she'll be at work.'

Tabby peered at her over the screen and sighed. 'You say that like the only person I'd be texting is Mum.'

'The only person you *do* text is your mum and you know it. Even I have more friends on the Facebook than you.'

'It's just "Facebook", Gran. And it's a wonder you have any at all when you send so many game requests. I'm surprised they haven't all unfriended you by now.'

'You've got such a cheek on you, honestly. I know what you're doing; stop changing the subject and tell me who you're messaging.'

'Okay, fine,' she said, and put her phone down on the arm of the sofa. 'It's the book club.'

Gran clapped her hands together with glee. 'I told you you'd enjoy it, didn't I?' She bent forward from her position in her armchair to snatch a Werther's Original from the packet on the coffee table.

Tabby half shook her head. 'Well, you're not completely right. I enjoyed *some* of it. It was nice to be able to talk about books, but I can't help but feel I made an idiot of myself.'

'If these people have any decency, they'll accept you for who you are. You think too much about things, that's your problem.'

But I'm not thinking too much about this. Why would Cassie have been so against me being there if I was wanted? I can't go back, no matter what Olivia says. I'll just ignore her message and I won't have to see her or the others ever again. We can forget this happened.

Olivia's message was still playing on Tabby's mind, though, as she stared up at the ceiling in the spare bedroom that night. She shuffled from one side to the other, on to her stomach and then on to her back, but she couldn't get comfy.

She lifted her phone up from where it was charging on her bedside table and found Olivia's messages again. The next minute she found herself clicking on her Facebook profile, and Olivia's face appeared, a stack of books centre stage as her header photo.

She scrolled down further, taking in the book quotes Olivia had shared and the pictures of her with her family – her mum, dad, trips tagged to the Philippines along with what looked like her younger sister, and a very cute little dog – as well as statuses with book recommendations and links to her other social media accounts.

The girl was clearly obsessed with books. No, not just obsessed. She lived and breathed books.

There was also an abundance of illustrations, most captioned with things like, Ahhhhh look how EXTREMELY gifted @cassie.artx is! Is there really no limit to her talent?! or Don't forget to check out @cassie.artx's display in the town hall this week, celebrating the absolute best of the town!

She pressed on the link to Olivia's Instagram account, which revealed itself to be . . . even more book photos. And group pictures: Olivia and Cassie with their arms round each other, grinning into the screen (*Cassie's actually capable of smiling?* Tabby thought. *I doubt she'll be smiling at me like that any time soon.*), and one of the four friends posing in front of a huge banner saying, 'Literary Festival'. Henry was crouching slightly to fit into the frame, next to Olivia, who had hopped on to Cassie's shoulders and had her arms up in the air; Ed, meanwhile, was using a printed-out picture of William Shakespeare as a mask to cover his face. The caption read: Who needs the Famous Five when you can have the Famous FOUR aka US? (Even if Ed is pretending to be camera-shy when we know he is the complete OPPOSITE usually!!)

No, this settles it, thought Tabby. *They're too close to each other; I can't invade that.*

The photo, however, did reveal that they were tagged – @TheIncredibleEd and @cassie.artx, but no Henry – and

Tabby couldn't resist the urge. Luckily, they were public accounts.

One quick look won't do any harm, will it?

Cassie's account was filled from top to bottom with amazing sketches. In one, a scribbled 'My Favourite Books' gave way to tiny versions of her favourite books: *Nimona*, the graphic novel by Noelle Stevenson she had mentioned at the meeting, but also another graphic novel called *The One Hundred Nights of Hero* by Isabel Greenberg and *Jane Eyre* by Charlotte Brontë. In another, a girl, the spitting image of Olivia, lay on the floor reading an open book. The attention to detail was incredible – Cassie had captured Olivia to a T, from the look of concentration on her face to the tiny quirk of her lips where she was smiling down at the book. It must have taken her ages.

Tabby clicked on another picture, this time not an illustration, where only a pair of feet could be seen poking out under a mountain of books.

@cassie.artx *when @bookswithlivs decides to organise her bookshelves and buries herself under a pile of books. i don't know why i put up with her*

@bookswithlivs *Because you'd be lost without me!*

@cassie.artx *@bookswithlivs true. sometimes.*

@bookswithlivs *@cassie.artx <3 <3*

@TheIncredibleEd *Why wasn't I invited?!?!*

@cassie.artx *@TheIncredibleEd because you can't organise anything to save your life*

Tabby didn't know what she'd expected, but it wasn't this. *How can someone as friendly as Olivia and someone as grumpy as Cassie be best friends? Best friends who are polar opposites just don't work. It's impossible.*

Ed's account showed selfies with a rather photogenic cat interspersed with ice cream cones and pancake stacks from various cafes tagged in Dorset. She clicked on a selfie he had taken with Henry, trying to fit the last piece of the puzzle, but there was no tag again. Henry obviously wasn't on Instagram.

Tabby scrolled to the bottom of Ed's photos, taking her back years and years to when Instagram had only just formed. In one photo, heavily filtered, he had his hair stuck up with gel and was doing a peace sign with his fingers. Tabby stifled a laugh, aware that her gran was sleeping, and zoomed in to get a closer look by pinching the screen.

It really was hair gel overload. *Wait. Wait. Waiiitttt.* She blinked. Blinked again. Why was the heart below the photo now red? Had she . . .? *OH NO. Oh noooooooo.* This was bad. This was really bad. She'd liked the picture!

What if he sees it and thinks I'm weird and tells everyone? I know it shouldn't matter because I'm not going to go again, but then I'll be guaranteeing *I'll never be invited back to the book club.*

Tabby tapped it again so the heart returned to black and white. *Phew.*

There's no way he'll see it, right? And I'm definitely, under no circumstances, seeing them again.

But . . . Okay, maybe there was an appeal. Not a Cassie-shaped appeal or an appeal sparked by Tabby's desire to be as awkward as possible, but an appeal that she could pretend her life was normal, that she could start over, forget.

And you do need friends, she thought, the picture of Jess with Kat and Rach invading her mind. *If she can move on, so can you. All you need to do is pretend that everything is okay.*

Ed: How much pizza is it possible to eat in one day and would you have a pizza hangover in the morning?

Act as if nothing happened, Tabby.

Tabby: Are you asking for a friend?

Ed: OF COURSE I am

Ed: (I secretly hate pizza)

Olivia: LIAR

Henry: Why is it that every message you write is about food, Ed?

Ed: . . . not EVERY message is about food

Ed: I once sent a picture of Cassie crying when she was reading The Fault in Our Stars.

Cassie: i was not crying

Ed sent a picture

Cassie: i was not crying and i will murder you with my bare hands if you send that picture again

Ed sent a picture

Cassie: good luck sleeping tonight edward

Cassie removed Ed from the group chat

Henry: Do you two ever stop arguing?

Henry added Ed to the group chat

Ed: Okay you hooligans are keeping me up. Night everyone

Olivia: NIGHT THE BESTEST FRIENDS EVEERRRRR!!!!

Cassie: oh thank god I can finally stop listening to ed

Henry: Don't make him cry again, Cassie

Ed: I HEARD THAT! Well read it. STOP BULLYING ME

Olivia: DON'T FORGET TO COME UP WITH NAMES FOR THE NEXT MEETING TOMORROW PLEASE! AND BRING SUITABLE FOOTWEAR!

Ed: Suitable for what?

Olivia: My lips are SEALED!

One more meeting won't do any harm, Tabby thought. *I'll stay out of Cassie's way, I'll try to have a laugh, and it'll pass the time. That's all. One more meeting.*

She opened up Olivia's private message to her and typed out a response.

> Tabby: Yes, I'll be at the next meeting, but only if that's okay with you. Could you send me the address please? :)

And if she changed her mind in the morning, she could always say she was ill or had been abducted by aliens or Gran had forced her to do Zumba. It was as simple as that. She opened the notes app on her phone and wrote:

1. *Try to act casual and not like the awkward being you are.*
2. *Don't mention anything about Before.*
3. *At least attempt to make them like you. Not that it really matters.*

Oh whhhyyyyyyyyyyyyyy am I doing this to myself, whyyyyyyyyyyyyyyyyyyy?

Chapter Five

Feral butterflies gnawed at Tabby's stomach as she walked up the street towards Ed's house. It wasn't far from the park where they'd had the first book club meeting, so it had been easy enough to find, but as she got closer all the houses began to look exactly the same. Long stretches of terraced villas bordered the road, with parked cars running the length of it. *Why did I think this was a good idea?*

She'd been told to look out for the house with the red van outside and she was relieved when she finally spotted it ahead. Words were etched into the dirt that covered the back window – on closer inspection it looked like 'Ed <3s Shakespeare' over and over again – and someone had stuck stickers all across the back bumper, their colours so faded from the summer sun that they were unrecognisable from their original forms. Tape covered a corner of the back window, keeping out rain from a deep crack.

Tabby rang the doorbell before she could chicken out.

The next minute, the door opened and Ed's face appeared. As he revealed more of himself, Tabby could see he was holding the fluffiest cat she'd ever seen in his arms. It was the same one she'd spotted on his Instagram.

'You made it!' he cried, gesturing with his spare hand for her to come in. 'Did you get here okay? Oh, this is Mrs Simpkins. She's the love of my life. Do you like cats?'

Not how she'd expected to be greeted, but she'd run with it.

'Fine, thanks. It was surprisingly easy. And yeah, I guess I do.' She reached out and stroked Mrs Simpkins on the head, thinking, *Who names their cat that?!* but pulled her hand back quickly as the cat hissed and tried to swipe at her.

'Now, what did you do that for?' Ed said in the kind of voice people usually reserved for young children. Was he talking to her? He put Mrs Simpkins down and watched as she trotted up the stairs, the bannisters of which were adorned with fairy lights.

'Sorry,' Tabby said, feeling small. 'I don't know what I did wrong.'

'Oh, not you,' Ed said light-heartedly. 'Don't worry; I'm not sure what's got into her today. Usually she's perfectly behaved, but she sprayed all over Henry's legs before you arrived. He had to borrow a pair of my shorts! She's an angel normally.'

'Oh god, poor Henry.' Tabby tried not to laugh, but it was too difficult to fight against it.

Ed started walking down the hallway, to a door at the far end, but then stopped and grabbed Tabby's arm.

'The hair gel was too much, wasn't it?' He sleeked his hair back with his hand, grinning. It took her a moment to cotton on. 'I have to admit that thirteen-year-old me didn't really have a clue when it came to cool hairstyles.'

KILL ME NOW. 'I wasn't stalking, I promise!' *Obvious lie.* 'I was just . . . Well . . . I was curious and then I accidentally clicked on the like button . . .'

A vision swam in front of Tabby's eyes: *her phone being grabbed out of her hands, feeling out of control as hostile laughter filled the air, not being able to see who had taken it. But she had her suspicions.*

'Why didn't you text me to say you weren't staying after school?' Mum said when she'd got home.

Tabby shrugged, trying to keep her composure. 'I left my phone in my locker. It's okay, I'll pick it up again in the morning.'

But it only turned up again a week later, Sharpie scribbled on the back: 'Tabby is a freak'.

She recognised the handwriting, and when she opened it up all the apps had been rearranged.

Jess is the only one who knows my passcode, *she thought.*

Ed came back into focus. 'Don't sweat it. I'll just believe you've got a massive crush and want to marry me because you're so attracted to boys with spiky gelled hair. I get it. I'm irresistible.'

'What can I say?' Tabby said, beginning to relax in his presence. *He's not like they were.* 'You're absolutely right: irresistible.'

'Come on, crushmeister,' he said. 'Let's go and join the others.'

Passing a small cupboard door to their right, Tabby couldn't help but think about Privet Drive. Like he read her mind, Ed bashed it and said, 'That's where my good friend Harry Potter lives.'

'. . . Mum's bad again. I don't know what to do about it.' Cassie's voice floated through the door at the end of the hall, and then Tabby heard a loud sigh.

'Is there anything we can do to help?' She guessed that was Henry; his voice was the deepest.

'I don't think so, but thanks. Just got to keep soldiering through, haven't I?'

The conversation stopped as Ed pushed the door open and led Tabby into the kitchen. The sight of Cassie, Henry and Olivia sitting at a kitchen table, mugs of tea and coffee in hand, made Tabby feel a mixture of warmth and nerves.

The kitchen wasn't exactly modern in design – it resembled Gran's, the more she thought about it, with its wooden units and lived-in feel. The difference, though, was that Gran's units weren't covered head to toe in photographs and various arts and crafts that looked like they'd been done by primary school children. In fact, these ones probably *had* been done by primary school children. When Tabby took a closer glance at the one nearest to her, she found in untidy writing the words: 'My school holiday by Ed Eastfield age 8.'

What do I say to them? Is 'hello' too simple? Am I supposed to be pally with them when I've only actually met them once? WHY IS THIS ALL SO COMPLICATED?

'Look who I found hanging out on the doorstep,' Ed said, breaking the ice for her. (Tabby decided, then and there, that she really did love Ed for that.)

'Great,' Cassie mumbled, clanking her mug on to the table too loudly to be undeliberate.

'Hi, Tabby!' Olivia said. 'Were you okay after last time? You missed out on the *best* ice cream at Brain Freeze!'

'Yeah, I was fine, thanks. Gran wanted help with her barbecue, that's all.' *Try to be light and breezy; act like Cassie never said a thing.*

'I'll pop the kettle on,' Ed said, and went over to a sink at the far end of the kitchen. 'Tea? Coffee?'

'Is that okay?' Tabby fiddled with her hands in front of her body, worried she'd give the wrong answer. *What if this is some sort of test and I fail it?*

'Of course,' Ed said.

'Tea with lots of milk then, please.'

His happy expression changed quickly, now aghast. '"Lots of milk"?' he echoed. 'Who even are you? What's the point in having tea if you're just going to fill it up with milk? I am *horrified*. We can't be friends. "Lots of milk"! Imagine!'

'Ed's a tea purist,' Henry explained. 'Ignore him.'

Olivia cleared her throat, ignoring their conversation. 'Can we please focus on the matter at hand?'

'Let's move into the living room,' Henry said. 'We can't discuss anything properly here.'

Olivia squealed, jumping up and rushing to block the door. 'No! You absolutely *cannot* go in there, not until I say so.'

'Right, sorry,' Henry said. 'I forgot.'

Tabby couldn't help but stare at Henry's legs on full show in a pair of shorts that really were far too short. She averted her gaze when Henry's eyes met hers, but when she looked back she found him grinning.

'Did Ed tell you what happened? I'm never going to live down being peed on by a cat, not for as long as I live.' It was kind of nice that he was so comfortable in his own skin not to be shy in Ed's short shorts.

'Oh, stop fussing,' Ed said. 'You'll give Mrs Simpkins a bad reputation.'

'She did try to bite or scratch me. I'm not sure which,' Tabby pointed out. 'I think that reputation might be deserved.'

'We need to start an anti-Mrs-Simpkins club,' Henry said. 'We can't be victimised like this.'

'Bullying Mrs Simpkins is *not* allowed and I won't stand for it. She's my baby!'

'She's a cat,' Cassie said, her tone flat. 'An aggressive cat. Like I'll be if you keep going on about her.'

'Grouchy,' Ed sang, but Henry shut him up with a look and shook his head.

Olivia banged her hand against the table. 'Are you lot listening or shall I just talk to myself over here?'

They all scrambled to take their places around the table. Ed passed Tabby a mug of tea.

Dipping into her bag, Olivia picked out an A5 hardback notepad, red with gold foil swirls embossed on the cover. 'This,' she said, 'is our book club scrapbook, and in it we are going to document every single memory in shelfie and written form so that when we are old and wrinkled and Ed smells like boiled cabbage we can look back on it and remember all the bookish fun we had.'

'I love it already,' Cassie said, dripping with sarcasm.

'Shut up, Cassandra, and listen.'

'My name is not Cassandra.'

'It is now,' Olivia said, and poked her in the shoulder with her pen.

'It's *not,*' Cassie said, but this time the grumble was replaced with a barely detectable smile.

Olivia opened the cover of her scrapbook, placing it on the table, and smoothed out the first page. Leaning over it, she turned back to the others. 'Right! First on today's agenda – which, by the way, I'll be taking at every meeting – is our new book club name. Suggestions, please!'

Ed pulled out a tatty piece of paper from his back pocket. 'I had a think about this last night and—'

'No!' Olivia cried. 'I want to make it very clear that names involving food, violence, swearing, illegal activities or your cat are not acceptable.'

'But doughnuts aren't just food. They're a way of life.'

'Can't we just be the "Book Club"?' Henry asked. 'Surely a name isn't that important.'

'*Not important?!*' Olivia parroted. 'How are we ever going to establish a brand identity if none of you are taking it seriously? I am very ashamed by your lack of bookish spirit.'

'How about "Bookish Losers" then?' Cassie pretended to inspect one of her fingernails. 'Because that's what we are.'

'We're trying to lead our best bookish lives!' Olivia practically screamed, throwing her hands up in the air.

Cassie grabbed the scrapbook from Olivia and scowled down at it. 'Excuse me, but writing "Cassie complains" on the agenda is unfair. You don't *have* to make me look bad like that.'

'No, don't rip it out!' But it was too late: Cassie had ripped the page from the scrapbook and was tearing it into tiny pieces.

'That's such a waste of good paper,' Olivia scolded. 'And it's going to take me even longer to write it out again, thanks to you. Honestly!'

There was a crunching in Tabby's ears and she turned to find Ed munching his way through a packet of Love Hearts next to her. 'Want one?' he offered, holding the packet out to her. 'I always think it's a good idea to bring snacks with you, just in case you get a bit peckish. And there's something very charming about Love Hearts.'

'That's it!' Tabby said, excited, while Ed looked nonplussed. 'What about the Paper & Hearts Club? We're all here because we love books. And that combines the two.' Tabby couldn't help but feel a burst of pride. Until . . .

'I'm going to be sick,' Cassie said, rolling her eyes. 'There is no way I'm being part of something called that.'

'Oh, so you want to be a part of it now?' Ed said, rolling his eyes back at her. 'I thought we were all losers to you.'

'Whatever.'

'I like it!' Olivia said. 'But it doesn't sound unique enough. We're not just any old club. We're . . . a society!'

'The Paper & Hearts Society?' Henry said. He nodded consideringly. 'That could work.'

By this point, Olivia was jumping up and down. 'So the Paper & Hearts Society it is! Eek! This has made me more excited than I thought possible!' She took a second to update her scrapbook; Tabby used the time to gulp down her tea, grinning as Ed pulled revolted faces. She stuck her tongue out at him in response. 'And now on to the second point on today's meeting agenda: how the Paper & Hearts Society will run.'

'Just so you know,' Ed said, 'I'm not running anywhere. A slow walk, maybe, but definitely not a run.'

Olivia cleared her throat. 'As I was about to ask: would we like one big group read for the Paper & Hearts Society, or more general book discussion and activities?' She tapped her pen impatiently against her scrapbook.

'Hypothetically speaking,' Cassie said, 'if I was to join in with this book club, and I'm not saying I am, I refuse to read anything that Ed recommends because Shakespeare bores me and if there's anything *Game of Thrones* related, I will take all one thousand plus pages and commit murder with them.'

'See!' Olivia said. 'You're getting into the spirit of it now: connecting themes with the books. I *knew* you'd like this, Cassie.'

'I think it might be a good idea to *prevent* murder actually, Livs,' Henry said.

Olivia shrugged and smiled to herself as she doodled hearts in the margins of the scrapbook.

'You're only saying that,' Tabby said, 'because it's one of your tactics to reach the Iron Throne: tell everyone else not to commit murder so that you can get in there first.'

She felt a thrill of satisfaction as Henry chuckled at her joke.

'How am I ever going to win now you've revealed my plan?' he said, playing along.

'It's always the quiet ones you've got to watch out for.'

'Soooo, any thoughts? Anyone? *Please?*' Olivia said.

'I'm only doing a group read,' Ed said, 'if it means we can read something with cats in. Preferably cats who can dance.'

'You are *unbelievable*,' Olivia said, and she turned to Tabby and Henry. 'Can I get some sense out of you two, at least? Group read or general activities? Save me, please!'

Henry shrugged. 'I don't mind,' he said. 'But I think it would be more fun if we shared recommendations rather than forcing each other to read something we know we're not all interested in.'

'Right, that's that decided then!' Olivia said, putting her pen down. 'And it leads very nicely on to our first activity as the Paper & Hearts Society. Are you ready?'

'As we'll ever be,' Henry said.

'We are going to have a Jane Austen dance party! A Jane Austen dance party! How excited are you?!'

'A what?'

'Well, Henry, I'm glad you asked. I believe that Jane Austen is the greatest person to have ever lived, so I am always looking at ways in which I can bring her to life again.'

'That's the second time you've mentioned bringing Jane Austen back from the dead now, Livs,' Henry replied. 'I think you might have a problem.'

'What I mean is that we're going to have a Regency dance! Like they have in *Pride and Prejudice*, aka my favourite of Jane Austen's books.'

They followed Olivia into the living room. The two sofas and coffee table had been pushed to one side and laid out in a pile on the floor was a crumpled bonnet, a waistcoat, a long and voluminous dress and a very large top hat.

Cassie had clocked them at the exact moment Tabby had. 'I am not dressing up,' she said, backing away. 'No way. And my allegiance lies with the Brontë sisters and *only* the Brontë sisters. I won't go messing about with Jane Austen.'

'But, Cassie, please!' Olivia wailed. She reached down to pick up the bonnet, thrusting it into her arms. Cassie resisted, putting her arms behind her back, and Olivia reacted by yanking it on top of Cassie's head herself.

'This is the worst idea you've ever had,' Cassie grumbled from beneath the bonnet.

Twenty minutes later, Tabby had to sort of agree.

She was currently facing Ed, who had squeezed himself into the dress and was having trouble breathing under the many layers crushing him from all sides.

'You shouldn't have worn it over your normal clothes,' Tabby tried to say, but he wouldn't hear it.

'None of you want to be faced with my hairy legs!'

'The dress is touching the floor, Ed,' Henry said, the top hat sitting on his head. 'Nobody would see them anyway.'

'I don't trust you not to lift it up and look at what's underneath.' Ed shuffled about so that the dress was sitting better on his body. 'And don't even think about laughing because I'm wearing a dress. I won't put up with your ridiculous gender rules!'

For the first part, Olivia had decided that her role would be as instructor, explaining the moves as they acted them out; that was the part Tabby and her two left feet weren't looking forward to. Olivia's phone speaker was at its maximum and she'd come prepared in typical Olivia style with a printed list of instructions, as well as a YouTube tutorial she'd found on Cassie's phone and was now watching.

'Go!' she called. 'Right foot forward, Ed! No, Cassie, don't go backwards! Yes, Henry, that's perfect! A true Mr Darcy! No, hold hands and spin around in a circle! Now you split apart and cross arms.'

Olivia was unimpressed. 'No, no, you're doing it all wrong. I'm going to have to join in and show you how it's done.'

'Dibs on partnering with you!' Ed cried. 'We'll be the best.'

Thanks a lot, Tabby thought. *Is there really something that wrong with me that you don't want to be my partner? PE classes where nobody would partner with her, sitting in the middle of the coach on the way back from a cross-country competition on her own . . .* She shook the thoughts away.

'No, Ed,' Olivia said. 'Cassie needs me more than you. Don't you, Cassie?'

'Do I?'

Olivia patted her on the shoulder. 'Yes, of course you do.'

'Who am I going to dance with?' Ed cried. 'Look how attractive I am! Why won't you dance with me?' He turned on Henry. 'Come on, you can't turn me down. I'm an amazing dancer!'

'I *can* turn you down, actually,' Henry said, 'because you turned down Tabby, and for that you can dance on your own.'

'Me?' Tabby squeaked. *He can't mean me, surely?*

'You may have inferior taste in books,' Henry said with a smile, 'but I don't mind partnering with you. As long as you don't force me to read Sylvia Plath.'

He'd remembered! 'We'll see who has inferior taste,' Tabby said. 'If you'd ever read any Sylvia Plath, you'd realise how very wrong you are.'

'Or how very right I am. I think you'll find that *you* are wrong.'

'Fine,' Ed cried out. 'I've got a better idea.'

And with that, he disappeared out of the door and left them staring in his wake.

When he returned, he had a doughnut in his hand, and began to dance a very odd-looking waltz with it, icing dropping to the floor.

'You cannot be serious,' Cassie said from underneath her bonnet.

'I think he is,' Olivia said. 'Okay . . . I'll count us all in. One . . . two . . . three! Dance!'

Tabby stared down at her feet as she tried to work out the moves Olivia was calling out while dancing. It felt so awkward. She'd never make it on to *Strictly Come Dancing.*

'This is the most ridiculous thing I've ever done,' Henry said. Tabby realised how close they were; it was one thing hanging out with a guy . . . it was another thing dancing, hands together, bodies touching. Admittedly, it was Regency dancing and not like they were grinding up against each other at a nightclub, but she was still super aware of herself. And of him.

Ed wandered past them with the doughnut in his hand, his face a mask of forced concentration, humming under his breath to the music. Henry and Tabby started giggling, and then they couldn't stop.

'Now we join the two up!' Olivia called. 'Pairs dance and then we'll dance as a group. A nice challenge for us! Ed, *please* can you abandon the doughnut now?'

'But it's the only thing that cares about me!' he exclaimed, although there was a munching noise a moment later and suddenly the doughnut had disappeared.

Tabby was doing well until suddenly she wasn't. Her foot buckled underneath her in the exact moment they'd all crossed arms, and her knees gave way under the sharp discomfort. Closing her eyes, she braced herself as she felt herself falling, pulling the other unknowing dancers down with her, letting out a strangled mewl as she reached the floor. The air was knocked out of her as she was hit by the weight of three grown humans.

Olivia was the first to get up, and she scrambled to stop the music. 'What happened?! Are you okay, Tabby?' She leant over the remaining pile and reached her hand out to help them up; other than Henry's top hat being flung to the other side of the room and Ed's dress ripping the length of one side, they seemed fine. Physically, that is.

'*Somebody* wasn't paying attention properly, clearly.' Cassie took Olivia's outstretched hand and got back on her feet, glaring at Tabby. She let go of Olivia's hand, but the two still leant against each other.

'I'm fine. I'm so sorry,' Tabby choked out. *It's really not that hard; I should have been paying more attention; if I can't even do this right, then how am I ever going to make friends I can actually keep? A failure, Tabby. That's what you are! Jess was right. You're a loser. Don't cry, don't cry, don't cry. Just hold it together.*

'It wasn't Tabby's fault.' Henry's voice came out firmer than she'd heard it before. 'It was mine. I slipped. End of.' He pulled her up from the floor.

Why was he protecting her? It *was* her fault, she knew it. Every word out of Cassie's mouth had been true. *He must pity me. And for good reason.*

Henry turned to Olivia. 'I'm exhausted after that. What's next, Livs?'

'Put the hat back on, Henry. It is *selfie time.* Or actually, *shelfie* time! Get it?' she said, laughing at her own pun.

She pulled them so that they were all squeezed in together, Tabby squished between Ed and Olivia who, as the shortest and the one with her phone out, was at the front.

'Say . . . Jane Austen!' Olivia said, clicking the button. She didn't show the others the result, but turned to look herself, shielding the screen from prying eyes, and tapping away at it.

'I don't think that was my best angle,' Ed said, trying to look over her shoulder.

The notification alert went on Tabby's phone.

***@bookswithlivs** Introducing the Paper & Hearts Society, the best book club in the entire universe! I love you, @cassie.artx, @TheIncredibleEd, @WhatTabbyDid (and Henry who still REFUSES TO GET INSTAGRAM) <3*

'I'm blinking!' Ed protested. 'That's so unfair!'

'First rule of the Paper & Hearts Society: no complaining about blinking in shelfies.' Olivia said. 'Okay, maybe that won't be an official rule. But speaking of, who wants to be the next meeting host? You'll have to come up with an idea even better than a Jane Austen dance party.'

Ed pretended to stroke an imaginary beard. 'I think I might have just the thing.'

'Great!' Oliva grinned.

She moved on, putting her phone away and turning to the bag at her feet again. Her whole face lighting up, she brought out a DVD case with Colin Firth and Jennifer Ehle smiling from the cover in Regency costume. 'It is a truth universally acknowledged that every Jane Austen dance party must be accompanied by a Jane Austen viewing party. Tabby, have you seen this? It is my favourite thing ever!'

'No, I don't think I have,' Tabby said.

Tabby sat next to Ed on the sofa. 'You shall be a *Pride and Prejudice* virgin no more. Are you ready for your life to change for ever?' Olivia said.

Tabby nodded, but there was one thing she had to do first.

She opened up the Instagram app, found the picture Olivia had taken of them, and screenshotted it. She took out the original caption before uploading it to her Instagram story with a GIF of a fluffy cat in the top corner to represent Mrs Simpkins.

***@WhatTabbyDid** The perfect afternoon!*

A simple caption. No clues as to who they were or what they'd been doing. But the smile on her face in the photo said it all. You couldn't tell that Cassie was anything but nice or that Tabby was internally cringing and externally aching from her accident.

They say a picture can tell a thousand words, but Tabby didn't need thousands. She didn't even have to send a separate message to Jess – she was always on Instagram anyway, and the message was clear.

I'm not as worthless as you think I am.

As Olivia went to find Ed's TV remote – which, apparently, Mrs Simpkins usually stole and hid upstairs – and Ed and Henry went back into the kitchen to make another round of teas, Tabby was left alone with Cassie. She was unsure what to say, and spent more time looking at the floor than anywhere else.

A moment passed and then Cassie looked over her shoulder quickly, towards the half-closed door. 'What's your game?' she said in a deep, ominous timbre.

Tabby stopped dead. 'What do you mean?'

'You heard me: what's your game? Why should I trust you? You come pushing your way into our group, trying to make friends when we don't want you around. Why are you even here?'

'Don't tell me you actually thought I'd invite you,' Jess said to Tabby, laughing across at Rach stood next to her. 'Why do you think I'd ever want you at my party? Nobody wants you there. In fact, nobody wants you at all.'

Tabby blinked at Cassie, then shook her head. 'I'm here because I like books. That's it. I promise you, I'm just being myself.'

Before the others returned, Cassie shot Tabby one last warning glance. 'Don't get on the wrong side of me, Tabby. If you so much as make Olivia, or any of the others, *frown*, you'll regret ever joining us. I won't stand by and see you break our friendship group up piece by piece.'

It was no good protesting any more. *I'm really not here to split apart your group. I just want to make friends!*

But Tabby knew that, to Cassie, there was nothing more important than her friends.

And she was most definitely not included in that list.

Why is it that wherever I go I find trouble?

Three Reasons I Love Jane Austen by Olivia

Everyone underestimates her as just some silly woman author who wrote romances but in reality she was far more than that and it just goes to show that you should never, ever underestimate a woman.

In the First World War, soldiers read her books as a form of escape in the trenches, so despite being dead for one hundred years by that point, she was still offering a valuable contribution to the war effort and comforting people through the hardest of times.

Elizabeth Bennett is, hands down, the best fictional character ever to have been written. She refuses to bow to the pressure put on her to marry, is incredibly devoted to her sisters and delivers hardcore comebacks to Mr Darcy whenever he's being a proud fool.

Henry: Hey, are you okay after your fall? I'm sorry how Cassie acted after it. I don't think it was fair she treated you like that

Tabby: There's no need to apologise. I messed up the dance moves, she was right. I'm not upset about it. And I was lucky to only come away with a tiny bruise. :)

Henry: Sure?

Tabby: Yes :D

Henry: At least we're not actually living two hundred years in the past and have to do that regularly. Can you imagine?

Tabby: I don't want to! I'm sure Olivia thinks I'm a disgrace to the name of Jane Austen. I bet you're regretting partnering up with me now

Henry: When the other option was Ed? No. Way.

Tabby: Good point! Although maybe next time I'll consider a doughnut for a partner. That did look rather fun

Henry: Replacing me already?

Olivia changed the name to 'The Paper & Hearts Society'

Olivia: TADAAAAAAAAA!! New and official name!!

Chapter Six

'Gran tells me you've got some new friends. That's so great, love!'

Tabby sat cross-legged on the sofa, her phone out in front of her face so her mum could see her properly in the FaceTime camera. They'd finally managed to find time for their weekly call; Mum was wearing the dressing gown Gran had bought her last Christmas and her blonde curly hair was tousled from just getting out of the bath. Tabby missed her so much. She was surrounded by cardboard boxes and balancing on the end of their sofa, bare of all the usual cushions and hidden under layers of as yet unused bubble wrap.

Tabby had never gone so long without seeing her mum before and longed to be snuggled up on the sofa with her watching Saturday-night TV talent shows and painting each other's nails with the most ridiculous shades of nail varnish they could find.

Tabby shrugged. 'Yep, I guess.'

But they're not really my friends. I heard Cassie: she doesn't want them to be friends with me. She'll find out what I'm really like.

'It's good for you to be getting out. I think Gran was worried you were becoming a vampire, never going out in the day. What's that book . . . *Twilight*? You're not really a vampire, are you?'

Tabby rolled her eyes overdramatically but couldn't help but smile. '*Twilight* isn't cool, Mum. Other books do exist, you know.'

'Well, what *is* cool then?' she said, throwing her hands up in the air. 'I've got it. Do you remember when we bought you the DVD of *The Princess Diaries* when you were eleven and you were so obsessed that you made your dad and me call you Princess Mia for a month? You were a super-fan!'

'I was not!' Tabby said. 'I just liked it, that's all.'

'You so were and you can't deny it. You were so disappointed when you visited Gran and she hadn't turned into Julie Andrews!'

'Okay, fine.' Tabby held her hands up in surrender. 'Maybe I was. But that's between us!'

Mum grinned.

'I miss you and Dad,' Tabby said. 'Even though Gran does give better hugs than both of you put together.'

'Not long now! We'll be there before you know it, and then you'll be starting at your new school and you'll be wishing the summer holidays were back again.'

'True,' Tabby said. *School.* Just the thought of it filled her with dread.

'Oh, I forgot to tell you. I saw Jess the other day and she was asking after you. Isn't that nice!'

Tabby felt a shiver run down her spine. 'Yes, that's lovely.' She slowed her speech down, trying to act casual, as she asked, 'What did she say?'

'Oh, I think she wanted to know where you were, what you were up to. She'll be missing you, I bet! Who's she going to train with now?'

Change the subject. 'I got invited to a party down here.'

'A party?' Mum wrinkled her nose. 'But you hate parties, love.'

She was giving Tabby that knowing look, the kind that could only mean one thing: *I know you're going to regret this, but I'm not going to be able to talk you out of it.* As usual, Tabby ignored it.

'Well, *hate* is a bit of a strong word.' But Mum wasn't wrong: she *did* hate parties. The crush of people, the pressure when choosing what to wear, the loud noise and alcohol and buzz in the air. The memories they brought back . . .

But there was something different about this party.

She'd been watching a TV quiz show with Gran last night, who had kept shouting out absurd answers to make Tabby laugh, when she'd looked down at her phone to find a message.

Ed: HEY GIRL, HOW ARE YOU? I'm having a summer party in a few weeks and I'd love you to be there. I know I'll see you before but I've sent you a Facebook invite anyway with all the details and I absolutely promise Mrs Simpkins won't bite you if you come (that was a one-off!)

Ed Eastfield has invited you to his ANNUAL SUMMER PARTY!

There were fifty other people invited, lots of whom had already RSVP'd, but there were only three people, minus Ed, that she knew: Olivia, Cassie and Henry.

A party would be fine. She could handle it. It would be GREAT.

'I'll be fine. You don't need to worry about me.'

'Mum, can you come and pick me up? I can't do this any more – I can't stay here.' Her heart was racing out of her chest and even the cool of the front garden, away from the noise and heat of the party, wasn't enough to calm her down. 'Please . . .'

'If you're sure,' Mum said. 'But maybe you should let me speak to this girl's parents first to check everything will be okay there.'

Tabby bit her lip. 'Well, actually, it's Ed's party. And he said that his parents are fine with it; there's no need to fuss.'

He hasn't technically said that, but he wouldn't have a party without it being okay, would he? And what Mum doesn't know can't hurt her.

'A boy?' Mum said.

'Yes, Mum, a *boy.* Girls and boys can be friends, you know. We don't live in the Dark Ages. In fact, all five of us, boys *and* girls, get on perfectly. They've invited me to the next book club meeting tomorrow and I bet not once will any of us bring up the fact that it's weird that we're friends *and* different genders.'

The other end went quiet until Mum reluctantly said, 'Well, if you're sure . . . I trust you, Tabby. But let me speak to Gran about it, okay? I hate being so far away from you.'

Tabby passed her phone over to Gran, who spent what seemed like an age talking to Mum.

Tabby had nothing else to do while her phone was in use; she'd already finished her latest book, *Unconventional* by Maggie Harcourt, a contemporary story about comic conventions and fandom, with amazing fictional book references, and she didn't want to start another until she went to bed that night. She couldn't turn the TV on because Gran would shush her and it was too hot to go outside and not sweat all her make-up off within ten seconds.

Her mind began to wander. *I move as far away from her as I possibly can, try as hard as I can to push her out of my mind, but she won't go away.*

Tabby wanted to shut her eyes and wish as hard as she could that Jess would be erased from her life for good.

Gran *eventually* got off the phone, taking five minutes to figure out how to hang up the FaceTime call. She'd been pressing every button she could see except the huge red hang-up one, so that when Tabby retrieved her phone she found many disgruntled, accidentally-taken selfies on her camera roll. One was so close she could see crumbs of the custard cream Gran had been eating around her mouth. She sent it to Mum to make her laugh.

It was still bugging her that Jess had been asking after her. She opened up her messages and started a new one to Jess.

Tabby: Why were you asking about me?

The response was almost instant.

Jess: can't a friend ask how her friend is doing any more?

Friend. The word cut Tabby to the core.

Jess: so who was that on your Instagram? bought yourself some new friends?

Tabby: Nobody.

Jess: they don't look like nobody to me.

Tabby: Honestly, they're nobody. Just some losers I met who like dressing up in weird outfits and being huge nerds. I'm only using them because I don't have any other friends here. They're convenient, that's all.

Just like I was convenient to you, Tabby thought. *Someone to be friends with and then throw away when you don't need me.*

She still remembered the scene in the school changing rooms, as they were all getting ready to head to the cross-country tournament.

Jess perched on the end of the wooden bench, rubbing lip balm into her lips using a small, handheld mirror.

Tabby was lacing up her trainers as Jess turned, narrowing her eyes and smirking. 'You can't seriously be wearing those old things,' she said, indignant. 'You'll make us a laughing stock.'

'But I don't have any others,' Tabby said. She looked down at the shoes on her feet, the laces tatty and muddy but still functional. They were comfy, she could run in them – and run fast. What was the problem?

'Oh, that's a shame,' Jess said. 'It's just that I heard some girls from another school laughing at you when you went to collect your prize at the last competition. I'd hate for you to be embarrassed like that again.'

Then it dawned on Tabby. This is all because I beat her last time. *But there was still a little voice in her head that said,* Maybe she's right. I'll embarrass the whole school because I look too scruffy. Everyone will laugh at me.

And Tabby still couldn't shake the feeling that, deep down, everyone was still laughing at her.

Ed: Do any of you own a hula hoop? Asking for a friend

Olivia: I do!!!! I'll private message you. MUST KEEP THE SECRETS

Ed: Don't give it away!!!!

Olivia: Hey Tabby!! Have you read *The Upside of Unrequited* by Becky Albertalli? I just finished reading it and Cassie's already borrowed it and I don't let Henry borrow my books any more because he just destroys them, so I was wondering if you might like to borrow it? No pressure!!

Tabby: Are you sure? That would be so lovely. :)

Olivia: Of course! I'll bring it to the meeting tomorrow!

Tabby: Thank you! :D

Chapter Seven

Tabby was late getting to Ed's house and it was starting to panic her. As soon as the bus stopped at the stop closest to his, she jumped off and power-walked up the street, all the while thinking, *Cassie will be there before me and she'll tell them that she thinks I'm up to something and I'm a fake and a fraud and I'll never, ever be a good friend and . . .*

Gah! Why did her brain have to work like that? Why couldn't she just have a day off from the irritating voice? Just one day. That was all she was asking for.

'Hey, Tabby!'

She turned around to find Henry smiling and waving at her, his tall frame instantly recognisable, the sun glinting off his glasses – turning the glass green, like the aurora borealis, matching his simple green T-shirt and dark denim jeans.

Reversing her course, she met him halfway.

'Hi,' she said, when really she was thinking, *Thank god I've got someone who might stick up for me. He did last time. Will he do it again?* 'Are you ready for round two of the Paper & Hearts Society?'

'Am I ever,' he said. 'I think Ed's been losing sleep over this. And that's saying something because the thing Ed prizes most in the world, other than his cat and doughnuts, is sleep.'

Tabby was trying to concentrate on what Henry was saying, but all she could think about was how she'd be received by Cassie.

'What do you think?'

'Huh?' *Oh god, I've missed everything he was saying. FOCUS, PLEASE, TABBY.* 'Oh, sorry, I was just thinking about how pleased I am that I'm not the only one who's late.'

You did not just say that. PLEASE say you did not just say that. She felt herself turn red and looked quickly away from him.

'Me too, actually,' Henry said. 'I kept trying to get away, but my mum's working at home today and she wouldn't let me leave until I'd finished all of my summer maths homework. Never mind the fact that there are weeks and weeks left until September. And I hate maths.' He shrugged, as if he'd said enough.

'That is the one good thing about moving to a new house and school,' Tabby said. 'No homework.'

'Enjoy it while it lasts,' he joked.

As they got closer to Ed's house, passing the red van parked outside, something alarming became apparent. Thrown haphazardly over the front door was a big sheet with giant gold stars stuck to it, and from behind it came the sound of giggling. Lots of giggling.

She exchanged a look with Henry, who was fighting to keep his face straight. 'Now's your last chance to run away before the mayhem starts,' he murmured.

'Surprise!'

Tabby jumped back as Ed sprang out from behind the sheet, knocking it to the ground and spraying Tabby and Henry in a sea of glitter and tiny stars. He had a yellow tie around his neck, a stick in hand, and started dancing round, humming under his breath.

'Ed,' Henry grumbled, shaking the glitter out of his fringe. 'This stuff will never come out.'

'Relax a little, man,' Ed said, handing Tabby a stick. 'Now is a time for magic, not moaning.'

Tabby held the stick in her hand, looking it over as if it were an alien object. She had no clue what was going on but thought it best just to go along with it. Ed seemed to know what he was doing . . .

'Come in! My *casa* is your *casa*, or whatever the saying is. I never paid any attention in Spanish.'

'Um, Ed?'

'Yes, Tabitha?'

'What is this?' She held the stick up in the air between the tips of her fingers like she was too scared to hold on to it tightly.

'It's a wand, silly! Now don't just stand on the doorstep. We can't have all the neighbours finding out we're wizards, can we?'

He'd finally lost it. Tabby knew it. *What's he going on about?* She followed him into the house.

In the living room, they found Cassie and Olivia rolling with laughter on the floor. Cassie had a hula hoop in her hand; Olivia was trying to throw a beach ball into it. Just as Tabby thought it couldn't get any weirder, Ed lunged through the air for the ball.

'Ed!' Olivia scolded. 'I was going to score then!'

Tabby turned around to shoot Henry a questioning look. 'Quidditch,' he explained. 'You have read *Harry Potter*, haven't you?'

'Of course I've read *Harry Potter*,' she said. 'Who do you take me for?'

'My favourite is *Half-Blood Prince*. That ending . . . I'm still not over it.' He was smiling down at her.

'Are you serious?' She looked him dead in the eyes. 'The best is so obviously *Prisoner of Azkaban*. The book and the film.'

Henry scoffed. 'Just another example of your bad taste.'

Olivia's scream as Cassie tackled her, wrestling the ball out of her hands, stopped their conversation mid-flow.

'Stop, stop! I surrender!' Olivia's body creased with a fit of giggles. 'Harry would never be treated this way!'

Cassie, however, stayed put, leaning her elbow on Olivia and poking her in the side until Olivia managed to grab the beach ball back.

Tabby thought she'd walked into an alternative universe. One where Cassie had a humorous side.

'Why *are* you all playing Quidditch and waving sticks about?' She didn't think anyone at Hogwarts played Quidditch with a half-flat beach ball.

Olivia shot to her feet, smoothing out the fluffy pink bathrobe she was wearing. 'It's a *Harry Potter* movie marathon!'

Ed had disappeared out to the kitchen, where he now returned laden with five popcorn boxes, kernels falling on to the floor with every step he took. He leant down into one of the boxes, stuffing his face into it and emerging with a mouthful.

'Ed, that is so disgusting.' Cassie snatched the remaining boxes out of his hands before he could get into them too, scowling at him while she did. She had a witch's hat atop her head, the point almost touching the lampshade on the ceiling, and a lightning bolt scar drawn on her forehead in Sharpie.

'There's still chocolate in the kitchen,' Ed said, 'if anyone wants it.'

'You'll get it, won't you, Tabby?' Cassie said, narrowing her eyes.

'Y-yeah, sure,' she said.

'I'll come with you,' Henry offered.

'Because Tabby's too much of a wuss to do anything by herself?' Cassie said. Tabby noticed Olivia dig her in the ribs.

Tabby put the makeshift wand down on the sofa with a pat, hoping Ed wouldn't get offended if he noticed. *Does he seriously expect me to carry it around with me all day?*

'Don't Ed's parents mind us being here?' Tabby asked, following Henry into the kitchen. 'We created so much mess and noise last time; my parents wouldn't be happy with that.'

'His mum's at work and she's very easy-going,' Henry said. 'And his dad isn't around. His parents split up a while back. He spends most of the time here with his mum, but he goes to his dad's sometimes too, when his older brother's not home from uni. They can't stand each other. I don't think Daniel can understand why Ed still finds their divorce difficult, even though so much time has passed.'

'Oh, that can't be easy.'

'It's not. I wish he would talk about it more often; he bottles everything up.'

Tabby and Henry each reached for the bowl of broken up chocolate that Ed had placed on the counter at the same time. Tabby snatched her hand back quickly as their fingers touched.

'I suppose you're like a second family to him; he's lucky to have you.'

'We're lucky to have *him*. And he's lucky to have you too. Things have been confusing and difficult between us all for a while.' He raised an eyebrow mid-smile. 'I think you, Tabby, might just be the thing we need.'

And maybe you're the people I need, Tabby thought, but she berated herself a second later. *Henry will change his mind once he gets to know me better. He'll learn what a terrible person I am.*

She wondered what Henry meant by *confusing and difficult*. Outwardly, they seemed so perfect, so put-together. Unbreakable. She was about to ask, but he'd already moved on.

'I bet your friends at home don't do this.' He laughed and the mood turned lighter. For a moment, anyway.

'Not quite.' *Understatement of the century.* Jess wouldn't be caught dead anywhere near *Harry Potter*, and the only interest they'd ever shared was running. But even then, once they'd both made the cross-country team, that wasn't enough.

I wasn't enough.

'You must be missing them. I hope they don't think we're replacing them.'

Tabby laughed airily. 'Oh no, they don't think that. They're really happy I'm here. They keep asking me to text them every night with updates. I think they're jealous; they'd love to be part of a book club.'

If by 'book club' you mean making fun of me because I like reading.

Ed's voice rang down the hall, breaking them apart. 'Are you two coming or what? We're getting too excited to contain ourselves down here!'

Henry twisted his mouth into a crooked smile, raising a single eyebrow. 'Time for magic.'

Olivia stood in front of the TV, crouched over, wand in hand. 'You tell him, Harry!' she screamed at the screen, staring into the eyes of a very baby-faced Draco Malfoy. 'Slytherins are evil!'

Cassie picked a piece of popcorn from her bowl and flung it in Olivia's direction. It bounced off her shoulder, landing on the floor. 'We're not all evil. That's just a stereotype invented by Gryffindors who have too much time on their hands.'

'Yeah, right.' Ed's comment earnt a glare from Cassie. His mouth was filled with popcorn, his words muffled. 'Name one Slytherin that did something moral or useful.'

'Says the Hufflepuff!' she retorted, neck arched in defiance.

'See! You are evil! Stop being so discriminatory towards Hufflepuffs! What have we ever done to you?' He made puppy dog eyes towards Henry and Tabby who sat on the sofa, craning their heads around Olivia's body to see what was happening on-screen.

'They haven't even been sorted yet,' Tabby said half-heartedly. She really did want to watch it.

'It doesn't matter! Slytherins will always be the enemy to us Hufflepuffs.'

'If you're going to talk through it all,' Henry said, 'there's no point in watching it. We've got three movies to get through yet.'

Ed took his cue and shut up.

Tabby felt like she was having an out-of-body experience. It felt a bit surreal, sitting down for a *Harry Potter* movie marathon. Seeing the excitement on Olivia's and Ed's faces made her realise just how nerdy people could be, and how it really wasn't that weird to be excited about fandom and characters and the intricacies of the Wizarding World.

Tabby smiled across at Ed as they watched Olivia mouthing along to most of the lines.

'It's a tradition,' Henry explained. 'We've done it ever since Olivia's tenth birthday, when our parents let us stay up for an entire night to watch all of the films. We couldn't move the next day, we were that tired. And we had to wipe Ed's tears away with our sleeves at the end of *Deathly Hallows*. I've never seen anyone cry so much in one go before. We have to be careful now.'

'You're telling me you don't cry at the ending?' Tabby teased.

Henry let out a breath of laughter. 'Of *course* I do.' He leant in closer, briefly putting a finger to his lips and lowering his voice. 'Don't tell anyone, but I cry more than Ed, Cassie and Olivia combined. I don't stop for days.'

A roar erupted from Olivia. She had her Gryffindor scarf around her neck and was running around in circles, screaming, 'Gryffindooorrrrrr!' while the Sorting Hat sorted Hermione and she left the Hogwarts stage.

Tabby leant over to within reaching distance of him to make herself heard. 'Is it always like this?' she asked, feeling exhausted just at the sight of Olivia, who still refused to sit down. Every now and again she would reach for her bowl of popcorn and shove a handful into her mouth, instantly returning her gaze to the TV. It was a choking accident waiting to happen.

Olivia was just as excitable when she insisted on taking selfies with each of them once *Philosopher's Stone* had finished, and then Ed joined in to conduct a mini photo shoot. There were poses and props and way too many pouts on Ed's part, and then Olivia pulled out the Paper & Hearts Society's scrapbook and handed it to Cassie to doodle in while they watched the next film.

'It has *got* to look professional,' Olivia said, 'and I do not trust Ed to do that.'

'I'll have you know I am a wonderful artist,' Ed replied, 'and I could take Cassie down any day.'

Cassie responded by raising a single eyebrow, her head already in the scrapbook.

Olivia turned to Tabby. 'Wh . . . house . . . in, Tab-abby?' She spoke through a mouth of popcorn, the chewed up kernels sticking to her braces.

'What was that?'

'What Hogwarts house are you in? Surely you know! It's a *Harry Potter* rite of passage!'

'I've never done the quiz,' Tabby admitted. 'I don't feel like any of the houses really fit me.'

Not brave enough for Gryffindor, not smart enough for Ravenclaw, too much of a pushover for Slytherin, and not nice enough for Hufflepuff. I'll never fit in anywhere.

'Tabby, you need to do the quiz. It's a crime not to know!'

She shrugged. 'Maybe one day. Luna Lovegood is my favourite character, though.'

'My first crush was on Luna Lovegood,' Cassie said, still looking down at the scrapbook. 'At first I wasn't sure if I wanted to *be* her or wanted to *marry* her, but then I realised that I really was too Slytherin to be her, so it must have been the latter.'

'Better than that Pete guy from college you kept going on about,' Ed moaned. 'Your taste has got so much worse.'

Cassie rolled her eyes. 'Did I ask you for relationship advice? Anyway, you know I wasn't seriously interested in him.'

Olivia got up suddenly and left the room.

Is she okay? Tabby wondered. Excusing herself to use the toilet, she followed Olivia out.

She found her standing in the kitchen, pouring herself a glass of water from the tap.

'Is everything okay?' Tabby asked, wringing her hands awkwardly at her side as she drew closer.

Olivia turned around, putting her glass down on the counter. 'Absolutely fine,' she said breezily, but her smile looked fake; Tabby knew because she'd never seen someone smile as much as Olivia and this one was more like a grimace. 'Just needed a glass of water, that's all. Gotta keep hydrated!'

Tabby recognised the tension in Olivia's voice. *Is it possible that Olivia feels just as uncomfortable as I do?*

'Hey, I have that book in my bag for you.' Olivia seemed to shake herself away from her thoughts. 'I'll go and get it.'

She went into the hall and came back with her red and white polka dot rucksack, placing it on the kitchen table and unzipping the front pocket. She handed the book – *The Upside of Unrequited* – to Tabby.

'I hope you enjoy it,' she said. 'I love how Becky Albertalli writes about LGBTQ+ relationships. That's one of the things I want to focus on if I become an editor one day. Have you read *Simon vs. the Homo Sapiens Agenda* or seen the film *Love, Simon*?'

Tabby shook her head. 'I've heard of it, though.'

She noticed that the spine of the book was in immaculate condition, as if it had never been read. 'How *do* you manage to keep the spine this neat?' she asked.

Olivia grinned and took the book from Tabby's hands. 'This is what I do.'

She opened the book cover up slightly and began to read; the pages were only open a crack, and the spine hadn't budged.

'But *how* can you actually read it like that? It's impossible!'

Olivia handed the book back. 'It's a skill I have perfected over many years. You get used to it. Try it when you read it.'

'Is that a ploy to make sure I don't crack the spine?' Tabby asked.

Olivia laughed. 'You can't be any worse than Henry. Don't worry about it.'

'It's too bad then that Henry asked if he could borrow it from me afterwards so that he can avoid your anti-spine crack procedures,' Tabby teased.

'So cunning. Speak of the devil,' Olivia said, as Henry poked his head around the kitchen door.

'Are you two coming back in? Ed's threatening to swallow a Golden Snitch to see if he can cough it back up and survive.'

'We were just having some bookish bonding time,' Olivia said, linking her arm in Tabby's. 'But maybe it would be a good idea to get back to Ed before he chokes to death.'

'Agreed,' Tabby said.

The vibration in her pocket was the first thing that alerted Tabby. The second was the damp spreading across her chin, like a snail trailing down it. *OH GOD.* She'd been asleep.

It took her a moment to groggily collect herself, wiping away the drool from her face and waking up her muscles.

Her glasses had slipped down her face so she pushed them back up, everything coming into focus. She couldn't believe she'd fallen asleep on Ed's sofa, with all the others around her. They'd probably been laughing or taking pictures. She hoped there wasn't a moustache drawn on her face.

They are not your old friends, she told herself firmly, but her hand still crept up to touch her top lip.

'You're awake.' The voice was soft, non-urgent.

Tabby twisted her neck round to look at Henry, trying to contain her embarrassment. Her eyes were sticky and seemed to have a mind of their own as they tried to close again.

'I don't usually fall asleep, I promise.'

The room was pitch-black except from the glow of the TV screen. She'd definitely watched the start of *Prisoner of Azkaban* because they'd filled themselves up with pizzas as they were watching, but now the credits were rolling and she had no clue where she'd been for the middle and end. Well, she did, but just thinking about it brought a blush to her cheeks.

'Your phone's been buzzing non-stop.' Henry nodded down to it in her lap. 'I wondered about waking you in case it was urgent, but you looked so peaceful.'

She clicked on the home button of her phone, the glare of the light stinging her eyes. The time read 21:43.

Jess: SO much fun last night!! I'll tag you in my story xx

Jess sent a picture.

Jess: Sorry wrong chat xxx

Huh. Tabby clicked on the picture. Jess, Kat, Lexy and Rach filled the screen, pouting overdramatically into the lens as they stood in a living room Tabby didn't recognise. The random people in the background holding cups were a giveaway – they were at whatever party Jess had managed to schmooze her way into this week.

Wait. Is that my dress?! My favourite dress, the one Mum bought me for my fifteenth birthday, which I thought I'd lost. It was red and off the shoulder with a skater-style skirt, and Tabby had been over the moon when she'd unwrapped it, squealing into Mum's ear as she'd hugged her.

'Maybe it's got stuck behind the back of your wardrobe again,' Jess had told her. 'I'm sure it will turn up at some point.'

And turn up it had. *She didn't have to be so blatant about it,* Tabby thought. The more she stared at the picture, the more her heart began to race.

Wrong chat.

'Tabby, are you okay? You've gone all pale.' Henry was trying to read the expression on her face, but she deliberately drew away from him.

She remembered what Olivia had responded with earlier. 'Absolutely fine.' Tabby couldn't add the breezy edge to her voice, though.

I'll never get away. I'll be seventy years old and Jess will still be following me everywhere I go.

'You were like Sleeping Beauty.' Ed got up to switch off the TV and turn on a light, illuminating the room just enough that they all started rubbing their eyes.

If only I were Sleeping Beauty and could fall asleep and forget. Wake up in a thousand years when none of this will matter any more.

'I should probably get going,' Tabby said, pulling a mask of calm tight over her face. 'It's getting late and I'll end up falling asleep again if I'm not careful.'

Even to her the laugh she let out sounded fake, forced. *Stay composed, just until you get out of here. Nothing's wrong; you've had a good time. Let them believe that.*

'If you don't want to go back on the bus,' Ed said, 'I can always take you home in the van. It won't exactly be a road trip and I can't promise you won't be sitting on a squashed sandwich, but it's an option.'

She was about to reply when Olivia jumped up from her position on the floor and let out a high-pitched squeal.

'Jeez,' Ed said, covering his ears with his hands. 'What was that for?'

'I just had an idea. Please ignore me! Go back to normal. Nothing to see here!' She perched on the sofa next to Tabby, who thought she must still be in some kind of weird dream. 'But I really should be getting home because I *need* to write this down.'

'I'll walk you back,' Cassie said, pulling on the tie of Olivia's dressing gown, also known as her stand-in wizard robes.

'I only live around the corner. It's not like I've got to get back to the Outer Hebrides,' Olivia said, but she didn't refuse. She put her arms around Cassie's neck and leant on her shoulder. 'If you *really* want to protect me, though, then I won't say no.'

'If you did live in the Outer Hebrides,' Cassie said, poking Olivia on the end of her nose, 'I would fully expect you to walk by yourself.'

Tabby noticed for the first time that maybe there was a different kind of closeness between Olivia and Cassie that she hadn't quite spotted before. *Is that why Olivia was acting so strange earlier?*

'Very valiant of you.'

They all bustled around to collect their bags and belongings. Olivia had Cassie's witch's hat perched precariously on her head. Their limbs hung looser, their voices mere murmurs compared to their earlier outbursts.

It was beginning to unnerve Tabby just how used to

them she was getting, how much she was beginning to like them and feel like maybe, just maybe, they might like her too. Although it was obvious Cassie would need longer to convince.

Ed waved them off, closing the door behind him, no longer decked in magical stars. Henry, Tabby, Cassie and Olivia were left to make their way home.

'Did you enjoy that, Tabby?' Olivia asked. Much to Cassie's chagrin, Olivia had linked her arm through Tabby's and had a spring in her step. Even tired Olivia had more energy than Tabby ever had. 'Other than the bits you were asleep for, of course.'

'I'll never live that down,' she groaned.

'Oh, don't worry – if Cassie had started snoring,' Olivia turned to her, 'it would be enough to shake the whole foundation of Hogwarts and everyone would think another war was coming.'

'That is most definitely not true,' Cassie replied.

'Your snoring is so loud that it would drown out the entirety of the Hogwarts choir.'

'Now you're being ridiculous.'

Olivia giggled. 'No, I've got it! Your snoring is so loud that it would have the power to convince Voldemort's nose to grow back.'

'Has anyone ever told you how annoying you are?' Cassie said.

'You often tell me,' Olivia replied. 'But I choose to ignore you.'

A ringtone went off, and Cassie pulled her phone out of her denim jacket. Henry and Olivia exchanged a glance. Tabby felt the atmosphere change.

'No, no, I'm coming home now,' Cassie said, the phone tight to her ear. Her voice had turned the softest Tabby had ever heard it, as if she were talking to a child. 'I won't be long, I promise. I'll make it back as quick as I can. Yes, I love you too. Very much. I'm going to go now so I can start walking home, okay? But if you need anything else, please ring.'

As soon as she'd hung up, Olivia put her arm around Cassie's shoulders. Cassie leant her head against Olivia's shoulder and gave her a quick hug. It was a gesture that spoke a thousand words.

'Okay?' Olivia asked.

'I'll be fine. Just the usual. One of my aunties is staying for the next few weeks, so I don't have to worry too much. It's great, except when you're bursting for the loo first thing in the morning and she forgets that we only have one bathroom between the three of us.'

'You didn't tell me that,' Olivia said, frowning.

Blink and Tabby would have missed it. But for a moment Cassie had looked shaken, and Tabby had no idea what was going on.

'At least there's someone else there to look after her, though,' Olivia said, switching to a reassuring smile. 'Does that mean you'll get more drawing time this weekend?'

'Here's hoping,' Cassie said.

They got to the bus stop at the end of Ed's street and splintered off, Cassie and Olivia going off towards Olivia's house. That left Tabby and Henry.

'I can wait with you,' Henry offered. 'I don't mind. In fact, I insist.'

She smiled gratefully; it was nice to have someone looking out for her. 'Is this your way of being nice to me because you're feeling guilty about your terrible taste in books?'

He ran his hand through his hair with a chuckle. 'Quite possibly,' he admitted. 'But ask me again tomorrow and I'll definitely say no.'

The bus pulled up and Tabby gave Henry a quick wave before she got on; he watched until she sat down, and the driver drew away from the stop.

As the bus rattled along on the way home, Tabby watched as the streets passed by in a blur of motion.

She couldn't help but think about Henry. There was a thoughtfulness in his every move that she found difficult to understand; he was far quieter than the others, but always seemed present; he was confident in himself, yet there were flickering moments of doubt, hesitation, that fell over his countenance. Tabby finally got it: he wasn't afraid to show his true self, both his strengths and flaws. He was honest. Something that seemed a million miles from her own energy right now.

She debated leaving her phone in her bag, but she knew she had to look at some point and there were at least ten minutes left of the journey. She got it out, and opened the long message trail from Jess.

Even though she knew she shouldn't, she couldn't help but type out quick, anger-induced replies.

Tabby: What do you want from me? I know you didn't send that message accidentally. Why can't you leave me alone?

A chill swept over her body.

Jess: Because I'm not done with my fun yet. Say hi to your new friends for me

Tabby: I told you already: they're NOT my friends.

Jess: Oh yeah? I bet you're loving the fact that they can't see what you're like yet.

Tabby: Leave me alone.

Jess: Bet you don't say that to your new best friends. Tell me, have you got a crush on one of them yet? You look very close in the pictures you've posted. Which one is it?

Ed? Henry? Exchanged friendship bracelets yet? Oh, it's all so COSY

Tabby: No, I don't have a crush. That's ridiculous. Henry is too quiet and has basically no personality. And Ed is the kind of person who finds his own jokes funny. Never in a million years.

Jess: Funny . . . sounds like you're describing yourself

Tabby: Whatever, Jess. You can't get to me any more.

Where did that bravery come from? she thought. *Maybe the Paper & Hearts Society is rubbing off on me.* But it all disappeared as she read the next message.

Jess: can't I? You better not stop talking to me Tabby or I'll just have to tell everyone that you're bullying me. And we can't have that can we? Your mum would be SO disappointed in you

Tabby jumped as the bell rang for someone to get off the bus and the doors hissed open, letting somebody else on.

The girl's blonde hair covered her face as she scanned her bus pass; her suede pink bag, with the tassels hanging down it, seemed to scream out. Tabby already knew what the girl's face would look like. It was a face she'd seen enough times, long ago all toothy grins and crinkled smiles, but more recently only sneers and taunts.

Oh my god, how did she find me?!

But when the girl on the bus turned around, her eyebrows were pencilled on far more than Jess's would ever be, and, on closer look, she was shorter too.

Coincidence, just a coincidence.

Tabby blinked and the ghost disappeared.

If only digital Jess would too.

Ed's Favourite **Harry Potter** *Characters*

Dear person reading this, (most likely Olivia but you never know – one day we might be famous and people five hundred years into the future will be reading this. HELLO FROM THE PAST IF THIS IS THE CASE.)

It was far from easy to come up with a list of my favourite Harry Potter *characters but after two billion seconds mulling it over I have made my mind up:*

1. *Fred and George Weasley. Do they count as one? I'm counting them as one. I aspire to one day be able to pull off pranks equal to theirs.*
2. *Luna Lovegood because she's never afraid to be herself.*
3. *McGonagall. The first true badass.*
4. *Book Ginny and NOT film Ginny. Book Ginny is the best; film Ginny is the worst. You can fight me on this, but you know it's true.*

5. CROOKSHANKS. Because cats rule.

You may have noticed that Harry himself is not featured on this list, and that is for the very good reason that his children should have been named something like Hagrid or Remus or EVEN HEDWIG, AND NOT NAMED AFTER DUMBLEDORE AND SNAPE. I will die on this hill. (Hedwig Hagrid Potter has a fantastic ring to it.)

Olivia: Out of interest and for no particular reason whatsoever, are all of you free for the rest of the summer?! No planned holidays?! No exciting adventures you haven't told me about yet?!

Henry: You know I'm only spending the summer hanging around with you guys and babysitting my sister (and Ed). What are you up to?

Olivia: Me? Up to something? NEVER.

Cassie: you're a total liar and you know it

Olivia: I am not!! Are you free or not?

Cassie: where would i be going?

Ed: I've only got my SUPER AWESOME PARTY (not long to go now, COOL KIDS)

Tabby: I'm free!

Henry: Here would be a good place to insert a scheming face gif

Tabby: Usually when people want to insert a gif, they do it . . . instead of making us strain our imaginations.

Henry: I've got to keep you on your toes somehow

Ed: Insert cry laughing emoji here

Henry: . . .

Cassie: insert a picture of me killing ed with my bare hands here

Chapter Eight

'Are you really going to stay cocooned in your duvet all day?' Tabby stared back as Gran peered down at her on the sofa. She was perfectly fine in her pyjamas, doing nothing and thinking about everything. In the comfort of her own duvet nest, she could feel all the feelings and not have to answer for any of them.

'Probably,' Tabby said, and pulled the duvet tighter. A cereal bowl lay on the coffee table in front of her, with tiny flakes of leftover cornflakes gathered at the bottom, beside a mug of tea that had gone cold from when she'd forgotten to drink it.

'Aren't you going out?' Gran said, picking up the bowl from the table and wandering into the kitchen, straining her voice as she got further away. 'The weather's nice out there. I thought you kids would be making the most of it.'

'Olivia's at church, Henry's babysitting his sister, Cassie's . . . doing whatever Cassie does in her spare time and Ed is most likely sleeping. We still haven't figured out the next meeting.'

It wasn't until she had a day like this that she realised how much she'd come to rely on the Paper & Hearts Society to fill her time.

When they weren't there, Tabby sank in spirits and resorted to bad habits she wished she could shake. Like reading Jess's messages over and over again and feeling generally negative . . .

She couldn't get the image Jess had 'accidentally' sent out of her head. It swam round and round, taunting her, teasing until she wanted to scream.

I wasn't good enough to be friends with her. I wasn't funny enough, wasn't pretty enough, wasn't smart enough. I was always inadequate compared to her.

And then there was her threat . . . *She'll tell Mum I'm bullying her. And who will Mum believe? She can't ignore an accusation like that. I'll never be rid of her.*

Tabby looked back at the messages, her fury mixed with loathing, the words 'I'm not done with my fun yet' cutting her to the bone.

She went on   to Jess's profile and hovered over the block button. With one final look, she hit it.

Block. It's the only way.

She had to say goodbye to the ghosts hanging over her shoulders. She had to say good riddance to the past and her friend who had never been her friend at all. Suddenly, Tabby felt a weight lift.

Now she can't get to me.

Finally managing to extract herself from her duvet to get dressed, Tabby put on some leggings and a baggy T-shirt, and sprayed her armpits with extra-strength deodorant. She lifted her pink and purple running trainers out from one of her suitcases and put them on; the familiar feeling put her in the zone. They'd been a Christmas present last year and were her pride and joy; she thought now of the excitement she'd felt as she'd unwrapped the tissue paper and lifted them out of their box, tugging off her fluffy winter socks and pulling them on. They'd been the perfect fit.

'Oh, love, you look just like your old self,' Gran said when Tabby came out of her room. 'I'm so glad you're getting some fresh air. If you want to wait, I'll put on my Lycra and come for a slow jog with you?'

'No thanks, Gran. I'd hate for you to overtake me,' she teased, grabbing her headphones from where they'd been stuffed down the side of the sofa. 'See you in a bit.'

There was a muggy haze in the air when Tabby got outside, the sun just past its highest point in the sky. In the summer, she usually restricted herself to running early in the morning or late at night to escape the heat, but today she knew she had to forget about that.

The front door shut behind her and she took a moment to open up her favourite running playlist – all the best girl-power songs by people like Beyoncé, Ariana Grande and Demi Lovato – then placed her phone in her armband.

Deep breath, Tabby. She squatted down in a stretch, moving out the parts of her legs she'd be using. *You've got this.* Next, she turned to stretching out her arms and neck, rolling forward and tightening her core as she bent over to touch her toes. *I think you might be stalling now.*

She'd always been so certain when it came to running, had never had to think twice about it. She'd been cross-country champion three years in a row at school and competed all over the county, but this time it felt different.

It was the first time she'd run since the 'Incident', since she'd walked away from the cross-country team for good.

'Come on, Tabby, get going,' she told herself. Out loud. Because then she might actually do it.

She let Gran's garden gate fall closed behind her, taking another deep breath in, feeling the air burn her lungs until she exhaled. Her playlist started and she set off, the impact of her feet against the tarmac reverberating through her body. Before she knew it, she was at the end of Gran's street, then the convenience store two streets over, then the primary school on the edge of the estate until she was winding her way down the main road. She measured the time by the length of the songs playing, felt her heart begin to soar as she kept going and going and going.

You're doing it. You're actually doing it!

She'd just reached the edge of town when she felt something in her head snap.

'You can't seriously think you're good at running when you're as slow as that,' Jess's voice said as she overtook her. 'And you look like you'll trip over your feet any second. Coach won't put you on the team again if you don't step up your game.'

Tabby felt her foot colliding with someone else's, her body giving way beneath her, the tinkle of laughter as the other girls sped past without even a glance behind. The ground was damp under her, her knees scraped and stinging; her cheeks were coated with mud; hot, livid tears welled up in her eyes.

I couldn't do it then.

I can't go on like this now.

Tabby came abruptly to a halt without slowing, holding on to the lamp post to the side of her and leaning her head against the cool metal. She took one hand from the post and turned her music off. *How stupid – you can't just pretend like nothing happened. It all happened to you, because you're a loser.* Her mouth had gone dry and her chest was aching, not from the effort of running but a different kind of ache, the kind she recognised and dreaded.

'I can't believe I won,' Jess said from the other side of the coach on the way back to school, manipulating the golden medal in her hand. 'I'm so proud of myself and how hard I've worked for this. It really is such a fantastic achievement.'

Tabby's knee was red and stinging; her face felt raw and muddy. The more she tried to block out the pain – physical and mental – the more anger rose up within her. She'd deliberately taken herself as far away from Jess as possible, but still her voice reached her.

'And really, I couldn't have worked so hard without Kat and Rach training with me every day. They've been so *amazing.'*

'Awwww,' she heard Rach say, and she could just picture Jess's cat-that-got-the-cream face. 'It was all you, babes. You totally deserve this.'

Tabby had to remember to breathe. The more she focused, the harder it would be for the flashbacks to happen. But it was no use – the more she thought about what she wasn't supposed to be thinking about, the further she slipped.

The image was clear as day in her mind, as if it were happening now and not then. *The coach coming to a halt in the school car park, everyone clambering off, slower than when they'd got on earlier that day. Tabby hung back, watching, with Jess the only one left, taking an age to stuff her headphones into the pocket of her team hoodie.*

As Tabby walked past her down the aisle, Jess stood up straighter, smirking. 'Bit slow today, weren't you?'

Tabby paused and spun around, adrenaline rushing in her ears. Even she didn't recognise the ferocity in her voice as she said, 'You know *why I was slow today. You know* exactly *what you did. I can't believe you'd trip me when you know how much this means to me.'*

'Trip you?' Jess said patronisingly, and raised her perfectly pencilled eyebrows. 'No, Tabby, I think you've got the wrong end of the stick. You fell. Kat and Rach saw it as clearly as I did. I'm sure if you told your lies to anyone, they'd know just how jealous you are of me. So it's best not to say anything, isn't it?'

Tabby gripped her phone in her hand so tight that her fingers began to tingle. 'You haven't heard the end of this, Jess.'

'Oh, I think I have,' Jess said, and pushed past her, waving with her fingers at the last minute before exiting the coach. 'Nice phone, by the way. Got a new case?'

*She looked down at the half-scrubbed out '***Tabby is a loser***' and could no longer hold back the tears as they began to stream down her face.*

She really was beginning to lose her grip on reality now. *Where am I? What am I doing?*

'Tabby? Is that you?' She spun around on high alert, her eyes widening as she took in the person standing close. Too close. Why were they so close? She blinked and the figure was suddenly further away. She must have been imagining it.

She blinked again and Ed came into focus, concern written on his every feature; gone was the cheeky grin she was used to.

'Hi,' she said, but she hadn't realised how weak her voice would be. How weak she was. *So weak*, she thought. *So, so weak.*

'Are you okay?' Ed asked, moving closer.

'No!' she shouted. *Too loud. Too, too loud.*

He took a step backwards. She hadn't realised she was still gripping the lamp post tight and let go, but continued to lean against it to support her weight.

'Sorry,' she said. 'You just startled me, that's all.'

'Are you sure?' Ed asked. 'You look a bit . . . um . . . flustered.'

'Yes, everything's fine.' Said too forcefully. She had no control over herself. 'What are you doing here?'

'I was going to the bookshop,' he said. 'I wasn't following behind you to lure you into a dark alleyway, I promise. I'll leave the stalking to you.'

She tried to crack a smile, but the effort was too much. Even her attempt to stand up straighter, hold herself taller, led to her legs wobbling more than she could cope with.

'Can I do anything?' Ed asked. He'd taken on a hushed tone and she was surprised when focusing on it helped to calm her down.

'I don't know,' she admitted, furrowing her brow. And then, 'Sorry you have to see me like this.'

'Oi, you've got no reason to be sorry and I won't hear it.'

'Please don't tell the others,' she said. She would be mortified if they knew about her panic attacks; they were so put-together and she was so . . . not put-together.

They'll never want to be friends with me then. I'm weak.

'What do you mean?'

'I mean,' she said, determined, 'that you can't tell the others you found me like this. *Please.* I don't want them to know.'

'Sure,' Ed said, and shrugged, 'but there isn't really anything to tell anyway. Now, what do you say to some therapeutic book shopping courtesy of yours truly? That always makes me feel better.'

Tabby had never been more grateful. This time she did manage to smile, but she couldn't hold it for long. 'You do know the way to a girl's heart.'

'That's what friends are for, Tabitha. Next we'll be making each other friendship bracelets and plaiting each other's hair and having *slumber parties*.' He adopted an over-exaggerated American accent for the last part.

Woolf and Wilde, named after Virginia Woolf and Oscar Wilde, was situated on a side street off the main high street, with a whitewashed exterior and a royal purple sign hanging over the door that proudly declared its name in gold lettering.

As Tabby walked in behind Ed, a bell tinkled over the door to signal their arrival and she marvelled at the sight of the floor-to-ceiling bookcases. They took up the entire right side of the building, stretching back until they reached an oval arch at the end; from the other side of the arch came the tinkling of china and a flurry of voices.

She followed Ed through the shop, past the hundreds upon hundreds of brightly coloured books, and under the arch to reach the bookshop cafe.

It was all so mismatched: pink and purple chairs, blue and green tables, people drinking from polka dot mugs and pouring tea from striped teapots. The phrase 'Madhatter's Tea Party' sprang to mind. The counters at the front of the cafe were teeming with beautifully decorated and delicious-looking cakes, which Ed seemed to be staring at without blinking.

'They have the best hot chocolate I've ever tasted,' he said, finally turning away from the display. 'I'm going to get us two extra larges with whipped cream and sprinkles. My treat.' He gave their orders over the counter and rummaged around in the pocket of his jacket for the money.

'Are you sure?'

'Of course,' he said. 'Now go and find us a seat, Tabitha dear, and I'll come over when they're ready.'

Settling behind a table that looked on to the pretty cobbled street outside, Tabby felt suddenly hyperaware of her gym outfit, but she tried not to be self-conscious. *Easier said than done when you probably look as red as a tomato.*

Ed came back with two black and white striped mugs in his hands.

'One large hot chocolate for you,' he said, placing it down in front of her, 'and one for me.'

'Thanks, Ed, you're the best.'

Tabby cradled the warm mug with her hands and took a long gulp of hot chocolate. Ed was right: it *was* amazing. Thick and creamy, just how she liked it.

They lapsed into silence as they drank and when they both looked up at each other they were grinning.

Ed wiped the chocolate moustache from his top lip. 'So, want to share with Ed what's wrong, what's eating away at you?'

Where do I even begin?

'I would but I really can't take you seriously when you're talking about yourself in the third person,' Tabby said. 'Plus, I think this drink has killed me and I've gone to hot chocolate heaven, so I can't possibly find the words.'

He laughed. 'Professor Lupin in *Harry Potter* says chocolate is the best way to ward off Dementor attacks, so I think whenever you're feeling sad or mad or angry, chocolate is always the answer to your problems. Why do you think I spend so much of my time eating it?'

'That's very deep,' Tabby said, but she could hear an underlying sadness in his words that she didn't feel she could press him about or that he wanted her to acknowledge. Not just yet.

There's a belief, Tabby thought, *that when you're friends with a boy you have to fancy him, want to rip his clothes off and giggle whenever you're in his presence.* But all Tabby could think about was how Ed had invited her here today even though he hadn't needed to, how he had made her feel appreciated and welcome from the very first time they had met.

She'd never had a male friend before, and maybe that was where she'd gone wrong, because she could feel herself falling quickly and madly in platonic love with Ed and it felt more warming than the hot chocolate.

'Ed?' she asked.

'Yes, Tabby?'

'Why does Cassie hate me so much?'

'Well, I wouldn't say she hates you. I mean, it's very complicated and I wouldn't exactly call it hate, but . . .'

'Okay, but she seriously doesn't like me. I just want to be able to solve it if I've done something specific.'

'You know, I'm really not sure why we always have to equate things to like and hate and love and all that rubbish.'

'Ed, come on.'

He sighed. 'Things are a bit complicated with Cassie right now. I was hoping she'd tell you herself, but it doesn't look likely. The thing is, last year, at the end of November, Cassie's dad had a heart attack, and they couldn't save him.'

He took a break to take a swig of hot chocolate, his brow furrowed. When he started talking again, there was a scratchiness to his voice.

'She was devastated. Still is. Her mum was diagnosed with depression just afterwards and they had to move out of their house because they couldn't afford to live there any more. Cassie's pretty much her mum's full-time carer now. It's been a tough year for her, for all of them. To be honest, I don't think she can handle any more change; it terrifies her.'

'Oh,' Tabby said. 'I had no idea.'

'Don't say anything, though,' Ed said. 'Cassie doesn't like us to talk about it unless we have to. But I noticed her coldness towards you and I didn't want you to think it was personal.

'I worry about her,' he continued. 'She's got these friends at college in her art class who don't seem to care about her; I try to take her away from them as much as I can, but she still goes back. They're a terrible influence. Rude, ignorant, uncaring. But what can you do?'

So much made sense now. 'Keep trying, I guess. It's still early days; she'll get there. Thanks for telling me. Anyway, you must be excited about your party?' Tabby said, changing the subject. *More excited than I am. Why did I mention it when I was trying not to think about it?*

'Oh, of course. My parties are legendary,' he said, smiling and then looking down into his hot chocolate. 'Cassie's been a great help. She's really good at the party stuff because she knows anyone who is anyone, unlike yours truly.'

Why is he hosting a party if he doesn't even know the guests? Nothing made sense.

She was about to ask Ed more about it when their phones went off.

'Wonder who could be texting both of us at the same time . . .' Ed said.

Olivia: Dear the Paper & Hearts Society members, I am calling an extraordinary emergency meeting on Saturday and failure to attend will result in your untimely death. You've been warned!

They exchanged glances. 'What's that all about?' Tabby laughed.

'Who knows with Olivia? But I don't want to take my chances; death at the hands of Livs does not sound pleasant.'

'How *have* you lasted this long without being killed at the hands of Olivia? Or, for that matter, Cassie and Henry? You're constantly irritating them. Not, I hasten to add, that it's a bad thing.'

Ed tapped the side of his nose slyly. 'That, my dear friend, is my best kept secret. If I told you, I would have to kill *you*.'

'You mean you won't even tell me if I told you *my* best kept secret?'

'I already know it,' Ed said.

'So you know the real reason I'm moving here is because I'm on a covert mission to steal every single one of Olivia's books?'

Ed let out a laugh so loud that a man sitting reading a book turned around to see what the commotion was. 'Now I know you're lying. I once tried to borrow one of Olivia's books and she made me fill in a three-page contract. If you went *anywhere* near her books with even a hint of malevolence, she would detect you from ten miles away and throw her hardback classics at you until you left.'

This time it was Tabby's turn to laugh. 'Death by Thomas Hardy? I can think of worse ways to go.'

'Are we really going to sit here and talk about death all day?' Ed said. 'Come on, we've got book shopping to do.'

They finished the rest of their hot chocolates, Tabby using the spoon to get every last mouthful, and made their way into the main bookshop.

'You can't come to a bookshop and not buy anything,' he said, leading her up to the YA section on the second floor. 'Come on – help me choose something.'

'Well, what are you looking for?' Tabby said, using her perfected technique to scan the shelves. 'Something funny, something sad, something a bit unusual?'

'Surprise me. My reading fate is in your hands.'

She had her work cut out. *What will Ed like? Should I choose something I* know *he'll like or should I go for something that might challenge his tastes? Something long or short? Hardback? Paperback? Fantasy, contemporary, dystopia . . . ? So many choices!*

Aha. As soon as she saw the copy of *The Fallen Children* by David Owen, she knew Ed would love it. She slid it out from its place amongst the books.

'It's based on *The Midwich Cuckoos* by John Wyndham,' she told him, handing over the copy, 'and is about four girls who wake up after a blackout and find that they're pregnant with alien babies. Which sounds horrifying, but the book is great. I devoured it in one go when I read it last year.'

'Seriously? That sounds so weird in the *coolest way possible*,' Ed said, reading the blurb on the back. 'Love it. As Olivia would say, you are the *bestest*.'

Before they headed downstairs to pay, Ed turned to her, the copy of *The Fallen Children* tucked under his arm. His expression came across as shy but friendly. 'You know, I'm so glad you moved here. I can't imagine not having a friend like you now.'

Ed: How are you feeling??

Tabby: Much better, thank you! :)

Ed: Trying to work out what Olivia is plotting . . .

Tabby: I'm praying it's not another Regency dance. I'm not sure my ankle can take another fall!

Ed: Haha I hope you're getting to work on my friendship bracelet IMMEDIATELY

Tabby: It's already finished. I'm expecting mine when I see you, just so you know!

Ed: I am going to make you the best friendship bracelet you've ever seen in your life. JUST YOU WAIT AND SEE

Chapter Nine

Not wanting to risk certain death, Tabby arrived at Olivia's as quickly as she could.

It was only the street over from Ed's, so it didn't take her long to find. She felt a surge of pride when she realised how less anxious she was walking the unfamiliar streets than she had been that first time going to Ed's.

She found Olivia's house number and walked up a small pebbled path leading to a house with a huge bay window and a bright blue door. Ringing the bell, she waited on the doorstep.

Cassie opened the front door, and Tabby felt the familiar dread in the pit of her stomach. Yet this time it was joined by another feeling. *I know now why she's like this with me.*

'Oh, it's you,' Cassie said in a bored voice. 'We're in the kitchen.' And with that, she walked off down the hall, leaving Tabby to come in and shut the door behind her. The only thing willing her to go inside was Ed's words about not taking Cassie's moods to heart.

Olivia's house looked like a proper family home; framed family pictures of holidays and trips hung on the walls, similar to the ones on Olivia's Instagram account, as well as baby pictures of Olivia and her younger sister. There was a pile of shoes by the front door that Tabby recognised as belonging to the Paper & Hearts Society members – Ed's ratty old trainers and Cassie's Dr. Martens, with a squeaky dog toy in the shape of a turkey sitting amongst them.

And the next moment a tiny dog barrelled into her legs. It was a Jack Russell Terrier, wire-haired, its tail flicking back and forth as Tabby knelt down to stroke it behind the ears.

'You found Lizzie!' Olivia said, poking her head around the door frame of the kitchen. The layout of the house was the same as Ed's, the kitchen right at the back. 'Actually, it looks more like she found you. Hey, Lizzie, please stop licking Tabby!'

Tabby squealed at the touch of Lizzie's slobbery tongue over her hand.

'I like her name,' Tabby said.

'I couldn't have a dog and not name her after Elizabeth Bennett from *Pride and Prejudice*, could I? That wouldn't have been on-brand.'

Lizzie pushed at Tabby's heels as she walked into the kitchen, which spanned the entire width of the back of the house. It looked newly decorated, with beautiful French doors leading out on to decking and a long back garden.

Ed was sitting on a bar stool beside the kitchen island, chatting away to a lady Tabby had never seen before and eating a chocolate fairy cake; she noticed he had buttercream stuck to the end of his nose. Judging by the woman's stature and her lovely smile, exactly the same as Olivia's minus the braces, she must be her mum.

She reached out her arm to shake Tabby's hand. 'You must be Tabby. It's so lovely to meet you after I've heard so much about you from Olivia.'

'Hi,' Tabby said, suddenly thinking of her own mum. She missed her so much.

Olivia and Cassie were standing by the kettle, talking as they waited for it to boil; Ed had finished his mouthful of cake. 'Do you know what this is about?' he asked. 'Nobody will tell me what's going on.'

'No clue,' Tabby said, shaking her head.

Olivia overheard and said, 'Stop digging, Ed! It'll be worth the wait, I promise. Have I ever let you down before?'

'Yes,' he said. 'Don't you remember that time we went to the zoo and you told me we couldn't bring a penguin home with us? *That* was extremely upsetting.'

Tabby shook her head at him with a laugh. *Please never change*, she thought.

She looked around, past Olivia and Cassie having a thumb war and Ed wiping up cake crumbs with his index finger, straight to . . . the massive Henry-shaped hole.

'Is Henry not here yet?' she asked.

'He had errands to run, I think. His mum was home and she wouldn't let him come over until he'd finished.' Ed pulled a face. 'Do not get on the wrong side of that woman, I'm telling you.'

'What woman?' Olivia's mum asked and when Ed told her she grimaced too. 'Ah, her. Her next-door neighbour goes to our church and is always passing on horror stories. It's a wonder Henry and Belle have turned out so normal.'

Well, that doesn't sound very good. Ed looked down at his phone, and then perked his head up. 'That's him, now. He just texted to say he's outside.'

When Henry came in, having picked up Lizzie on his way through the hall, he seemed extra cheerful, the dimples never leaving his cheeks as he scratched Lizzie behind the ears.

He pulled out the barstool next to Tabby's and leant his elbows against the marble worktop, Lizzie poking her head through his arms. Compared to Tabby's legs which barely touched the floor, his were almost too long for him to sit happily on the tall chair; he had to bend them at an angle to get comfy.

'Hey,' he said.

'Hi,' she said back, almost forgetting how to speak. *Get with it, Tabby*, she told herself.

He adjusted his glasses to stop them falling down his nose. 'What's this I hear about you and Ed ransacking Woolf and Wilde?'

'Ignore him,' Ed called. 'He's just jealous.'

'You're right, I am. I really wanted to spend time with you, Ed, and then you blew me off for Tabby. I've been in pieces over it.'

'Look, you've been replaced in my affections and you've got to get over it, mate. I've got a new best friend now.'

Tabby knew it was a joke, but she couldn't help but feel a thrill at Ed's words. Not just friend. *Best* friend.

'I'm less sad about you going to the bookshop without us,' Henry said. 'More that Ed isn't giving me his undivided attention. It's all very disturbing.'

'If we're going to fight over Ed,' Tabby said to Henry, 'I think you should know that you *will* lose. I'm more dangerous than I look.'

He grinned. 'Oh, don't worry. I know.'

Henry was about to say something else when Olivia's mum interrupted. 'Are you all staying for dinner? I'm making menudo – I know how much you love it, Ed. And then I really have got to get on with my deadline. It won't finish itself, will it?' She shepherded them out of the kitchen and up the stairs. 'Have a good meeting!'

Tabby was awestruck by Olivia's bedroom. Every inch of wall space was taken up by bookshelves, filled to the brim with hardbacks and paperbacks – mostly double-stacked but with a select few titles face out. Just like a bookshop. She'd never seen so many books in such a small space in her life. There were *almost* too many to take in.

On the far side was the bay window that could be seen from outside, into which Olivia's bed perfectly fitted – a window bed instead of a window seat.

'Do you like it?' Olivia asked Tabby. 'I know it's not much, but . . .'

'Are you *serious*?' Tabby said. 'I love it! It's amazing. I swear you own more books than the library.'

Olivia grinned. 'Thanks! That's the *best* compliment.'

Tabby sat down on the arm of Henry's armchair, leaning against one of the bookshelves. Ed, meanwhile, had spread himself out on Olivia's bed, leaving no room for anyone else, so Cassie was lying on the carpet, staring up at the glow-in-the-dark stars stuck to Olivia's ceiling.

Henry leant in and whispered to Tabby, 'So I may have started reading *Ariel.*'

'And?' she squealed; she was starting to remind herself of Olivia. 'What do you think? Am I right? I'm right, aren't I?'

Henry held his hands up. 'Even though it begrudges me to say so, you're right. Sylvia Plath really was a great poet.'

'I told you so,' she said, lowering her voice. 'You owe me big time. I knew I'd make you eat your words.'

'Stop whispering, you two!' Olivia called, and raised her eyebrows. 'This is very serious business! Can we start the meeting now?'

'The stage is yours.' Henry smiled up encouragingly. Olivia closed her bedroom door to lean against it, reached for the Paper & Hearts Society scrapbook, cleared her throat and declared, 'We are no longer simply members of the Paper & Hearts Society.'

Ed looked at her in confusion. His voice rose as he said, 'We aren't?'

'Let me finish, Edward. That was a pause for dramatic effect, not so that I could be interrupted.

'As I was saying, we are no longer simply the Paper & Hearts Society. We are now . . .' She paused again, then beat her hands against her thighs for a drum roll. 'The Paper & Hearts Society on tour! We must seize the bookish day; look abroad to new shores and exciting ventures!'

'Are we supposed to understand what any of that means?' Cassie said.

Olivia gave up, throwing her hands in the air. 'A road trip!' *Road trips aren't actually a thing, right? Don't they only happen in cheesy American teen movies?*

'You guys, why aren't you saying anything? It's exciting! Why aren't you excited with me?' Olivia dropped down on to her bed with a massive flop. 'Be excited!' She grabbed Ed's arm, shaking it. 'Think about how fun it will be! We have the whole summer ahead of us, we're in the prime of our youth, and we'll have the times of our lives!'

'There's no way I can go,' Cassie said. 'You know I can't, Livs.'

Tabby watched as Olivia's shoulders sank. 'Not even for a few days? Surely your mum would be able to last—' But she shut up when Cassie shot her a look.

'You know I can't leave her.' *End of*, the full stop at the end of her sentence seemed to say.

'How would we even go on tour? It would cost way too much for all of us to get train tickets. I don't think my piggy bank will stretch that far,' Henry said.

'Well,' Olivia said with an enthusiastic smile, 'I was hoping that Ed might volunteer to drive us in the van. Then we'd only have one set of costs, rather than all individually paying.'

'I knew you were exploiting me for my driving licence,'

Ed muttered, but he perked up a second later. 'Hey, this might actually work. You said, Cass, that your aunty is staying with your mum at the moment, so you might be able to leave her. I know it won't be easy, but you can make sure you're in touch all the time.' He looked thoughtful and continued, 'If I beg enough, my mum might just let me take the van.'

Olivia squealed, jumping up from the bed and gathering a stack of papers to hand to the group. 'So Ed and I are in – what about you three?'

Cassie frowned at Olivia. 'I'll check what's happening with my aunty, but I'm not promising anything!'

Tabby and Henry looked at each other, before somehow saying, 'I'm in,' in unison, which made them laugh.

When Cassie looked down at the sheet of paper Olivia had handed her, she raised an eyebrow and said, 'Of *course* you've already planned it. Every single detail.'

'Who do you think I am? I wouldn't be Olivia if I wasn't organised, would I? As you'll see, I've suggested three locations, which I think will give us the maximum amount of bookish fun. It's going to be a very literary road trip!'

Tabby read the three locations: Bath, where Jane Austen had once lived; Stratford-upon-Avon, birthplace of Ed's hero, William Shakespeare; and Haworth, location of the

Brontë Parsonage, where the three Brontë sisters and their siblings had grown up.

She had to admit, it did look fun. More than fun: this would be a chance for her to see more of the country, spend time with her friends and maybe, just maybe, she'd be able to finally move on with her life.

'Does everything have to be themed around Jane Austen?' Cassie groaned as she looked down at the sheet. 'The only reason I put up with her is because of you, Livs, but still you insist on testing me.'

'Jane Austen is my queen. Plus, Bath has lots of bookshops! It will be perfect. Hey, Ed, why don't you take food duties when we're in Bath so you can look up where's best to eat, and Cassie and I will research the best bookish places to visit?'

'Sounds good,' Ed said, 'but *only* if I get to choose the best bookish places in Stratford-upon-Avon. Alas, poor Yorick, you know how much I love Shakespeare. Don't you remember I was supposed to go on a school trip there in Year Seven but I was ill and had to miss it?'

'What about Henry and me?' Tabby asked. 'What should we do?'

'Actually, I've got an idea,' Henry said, 'but, for now, it's a secret.'

'I don't think that's in the spirit of the Paper & Hearts

Society's grand tour,' Tabby teased, earning her a playful poke in the ribs.

'Whose side are you on here?' Henry feigned outrage. 'Just because I want to take my time to think carefully about my decision doesn't mean I'm not entering into the spirit of it.'

'Oh yeah? Sounds to me like you're stalling for time.'

'Just you wait and see,' Henry said, shaking his head with a grin. 'I will prove you wrong and then you'll be sorry.'

'I think we've got lots of ideas for now that we can work with, anyway.' Olivia took in a deep gulp of air. 'I can't believe this might actually happen! You guys are the best.'

'We don't know if we're actually going to be able to get there yet,' Ed said, practical for once.

'Your mum is the coolest, Ed, nearly as cool as my parents are. I'm sure she'll be fine with it.' Olivia started to dance around the room, busting some very strange shapes and making everyone else laugh.

Tabby thought there was something to be said for finding a clan of people who made you feel like you belonged; it made everything seem so much brighter, so much more bearable.

Maybe things were beginning to look up.

They spent the rest of the evening discussing the books they'd been reading recently. Olivia took notes on her laptop, which she promised to write up neatly into the

Paper & Hearts Society scrapbook afterwards.

'So I'm reading this amazing book called *The Loneliest Girl in the Universe*,' she said. 'It's by Lauren James and I honestly cannot put it down. You know when you get a book and you think about it every day? It's like that. And books set in space aren't usually my thing! It was the best surprise ever.'

'The most surprising book I've ever read,' Tabby said, 'was *Of Mice and Men* by John Steinbeck, but it wasn't a good surprise. They made us read it at school and I thought it was going to be amazing because it seemed like something everyone had read, but I hated it. It was torture having to study it.'

'Better than having to study *Romeo and Juliet*,' Olivia said. 'Honestly, how is it the greatest love story ever told? That's not love. You can't just meet someone and fall head over heels for them. Shakespeare was the inventor of instalove.'

'No shaming Shakespeare!' Ed cried. 'As we might be going to Stratford-upon-Avon, I'm going to make you all read his complete works.'

Henry shook his head slightly and looked at Tabby, who bit her lip to stop herself from laughing.

'I'm being serious,' Ed said, to their looks of horror, and put his hands on his hips.

'That would be a first.' Cassie smirked.

'Hey, I almost forgot,' Olivia said, 'the last thing on the agenda is deciding who's going to host our next meeting. Cassie, maybe you'd like to?'

'No thanks, Livs.' *What a surprise!*

'You could come round to mine and we could plan it together,' Olivia suggested.

Cassie paused, her expression glazing over. She shrugged. 'Fine. Deal. I'll do it.'

Really? Tabby thought. *That's all it takes for Cassie, the world's greatest criticiser of the Paper & Hearts Society, to host a meeting?*

Once it was decided, Cassie lay back down on the floor and got out her phone; it made Tabby feel better about her own phone addiction.

'Have any of you heard of oakavenue52 on Instagram?' Cassie said. 'They haven't got any pictures, or even any followers, but they just sent me a private message.'

'I don't think I've heard of them. Who do they follow?' Ed asked.

'Only us. Me, you, Tabby, Livs. That's it.'

'What did the message say?'

'All it says is: "One of you is a backstabbing bitch." Dramatic, much? If I wanted a fortune cookie, I'd have got a takeaway.'

An uncomfortable sensation had started coursing

through Tabby's bloodstream, making her twitchy and unsettled. Her heart thudded in her chest. She got out her own phone, typing in the username and clicking on the profile. There was no profile picture, no bio. No photos. She refreshed the page again, again, again. Nothing.

There's got to be something, she thought, *anything.*

The others had got out their phones too – minus Henry, who'd stood up and was looking over Olivia's shoulder at her screen.

'I got the same,' Ed said, his forehead creasing. 'Isn't that weird?'

'And me,' Olivia said. 'Did you, Tabby?'

Tabby jumped. 'Hmm?' she said, clicking her phone closed as quickly as she could, hiding the fact that no message had appeared. 'Yeah, I did. Weird, right? I bet it's some stupid spam thing and they've just found a picture we're all tagged in. It's probably a fake account – there are loads of them out there these days.' She was surprised at how convincing she sounded.

Cassie rolled her eyes. 'The internet is full of creeps.'

'Yeah, it is,' Tabby said. In trying not to look cagey, she knew she only looked extra shifty. 'We should just ignore it, I think. There's no point worrying over something like this.'

You guys don't need to worry anyway.

Because 52 Oak Avenue was Tabby's old address back in Cheltenham, the place she'd lived all her life until now. And there was only one person who knew that, who would use it against her, making her paranoid.

How stupid to have thought she could move on.

Chapter Ten

'A road trip? I'm just not sure, Tabby.' Mum's voice crackled through the speaker; her face in the FaceTime screen frowned. 'You've only known these kids a few weeks; now you want to go to the other side of the country with them in a van driven by a teenager. And I know what you said before, but I'm not sure you should be going with boys.'

Tabby's heart sank. She'd expected her mum to have something to say about the road trip, but she hadn't thought she'd be so against it. She didn't say anything back, just sat looking at her in disbelief. What was she going to do now? She didn't want to be the only one to miss out. *I've got to go.*

'Look, I'm sorry, but I don't think this is a good idea. Not right now.'

'Dad?' Tabby whispered; he was sitting next to Mum, keeping quiet. Tabby could just make out his tall, thin frame beside Mum, his thick-rimmed glasses giving him away as he leant in closer to the screen and pursed his lips.

He sighed. 'I'm not sure either, love. It does seem very sudden. We haven't even met these new friends of yours. How do we know they're good people?'

Just like you knew my old friends were good people? she thought bitterly.

'If you were older, we might consider it,' Mum said, 'but you're only fifteen. You've got plenty of time yet to explore the big wide world.'

That's it then. I'll just sit here and watch as they go off without me and make new memories and inside jokes. I'll never fit in – they'll pretend to my face that they had an 'all right' trip, but they'll have had the best time of their lives, and they'll be happy I was never there. Who am I kidding? They'll forget all about me.

Tabby felt a hand fall on her shoulder, and Gran leant over so that she half-appeared on screen. 'Now, now,' she said, her voice firm, 'if I remember rightly, Sarah, when you were fifteen you begged me to let you go to that music festival all your friends were going to. And when I said no, you snuck out of the back window with your backpack and our tent and went anyway, leaving a note saying you'd be back in a few days. So let's not mention Tabby's age. She is a responsible young adult, and I would place my life in her hands. These kids are book lovers, not drug addicts or sex maniacs. And if Tabby wants to go, I say she *should*. It will be good for her.'

Mum kept quiet on the other line and said, 'We'll think about it and I'll call you later, Mum. But this is between parents and daughter, so don't think you can go meddling.'

Gran rolled her eyes before turning back and winking at Tabby.

'It won't be long before we see you, anyway,' Dad said. 'Are you coming back up here for moving weekend to say one last goodbye to the house?'

Tabby shrugged. She felt too despondent to put any effort into the conversation now. *I wish they'd trust me.* 'Maybe.'

'Cheer up,' he said. 'I know this seems like the end of the world, but it isn't.'

Not to you, she thought. Tabby picked at the hangnail on one of her fingers, not looking into the screen. 'You haven't heard from Jess again, have you?'

'No, why?'

'No reason.' *So she hasn't told Mum I'm bullying her. But it won't be long, I'm sure . . .*

Dad's face lit up. 'Oh, that's given me an idea! Why don't you speak to Jess and invite her to stay with us once we've moved in? That's why you asked: you must be missing her, right?' He nudged Mum in the side, making her smile. 'We may not be good parents saying no to our little girl travelling around the country, but we can do one thing right.'

They can't know what's going on; I have to deal with it myself. Tabby's eyes widened and her heart started racing. 'You know what? I'm going to have a think about that, but I just remembered I've got to go out and get something for Gran. Okay, love you, speak soon, bye.'

And she hung up the FaceTime call, her parents' faces fading away into the home screen.

Gran cleared her throat. 'Got to go out and get something for me? Funny, I may be getting old, but I don't seem to remember that.'

Tabby spun slowly around; Gran had her arms crossed and her pencilled-in eyebrows raised. 'I, uh . . . Did I say "Gran"? I meant . . . garden. Got to go out and get something for the garden.'

Great lie, Tabby. You could win an award for that one.

Gran drew closer, so close that Tabby could smell her sweet perfume. She pointed to just below her hairline. 'Look here, Tabby. Look very closely. Do you think I've got "fool" written on my forehead?'

Tabby closed her eyes and hugged a sofa cushion to her chest in defence. 'No,' she said. 'You don't.'

'I know you're disappointed they won't let you go on your road trip, but there's no need to be rude. And spinning them lies to get off the phone won't earn you any points. Just leave them up to me; I'll work on them.'

Tabby grasped at her lifeline. 'You're right, I shouldn't have pretended to be helpful just to get rid of them. Sorry for using you as my out, Gran.'

'Well, if you're going to use me as your out, you can come out to the garden with me and do all the deadheading. My hanging baskets have got plenty of life in them yet.'

It's what I deserve, Tabby told herself.

@cassie.artx *the paper & hearts society planning with @bookswithlivs + rewatching season 1 of the good place which is basically my fave. perfect way to spend the day with my perfect person*

@bookswithlivs *I am SO EXCITED! It's going to be the best yet! Thank you for an excellent day!!*

Cassie: listen up folks: next tp&hs (as i'm now shortening it to) is planned out so you better be ready on monday at 11 so ed can pick you up

Olivia: What Cassie meant to say is that Ed has very kindly offered to take us to the meeting stop and will pick each of us up at approximately 11am.

Cassie: yep, that.

Ed: I'm going to need the practice if I'm going to DRIVE HALFWAY ACROSS THE COUNTRY

Cassie: you overestimate your driving skills. one tiny practice isn't going to help.

Ed: Thanks for your faith!!!!

Tabby: So 11am on Monday. Got it. Are you sure you're okay to pick up, Ed?

Ed: Anything for you! But Cassie is pushing her luck. I might just leave her behind

Cassie: i'd like to see you dare

Chapter Eleven

Ed was a force to be reckoned with behind the wheel.

Tabby clutched hold of the fabric car seat; it was either that or Cassie's thigh and she didn't think Cassie would appreciate that. She was sandwiched in between Cassie and Henry in the back, and Olivia was sitting shotgun.

Ed had a bad habit of braking quickly before he turned the corner, throwing them all forward, only to press on the accelerator once he had carefully manoeuvred it, throwing them backwards again. Olivia hadn't stopped complaining of car sickness the entire way.

They'd picked Tabby up at Gran's house, which had set Tabby into a panic. *What will they think of it? Will they judge me? Will* Gran *judge* them*?* There were so many unknown factors, and she didn't like that.

As soon as Tabby had heard the doorbell go, she'd raced to get it, but Gran had got there first. She'd squeezed herself into a pair of jeans – 'I've got to look hip for you kids!' – and had swapped her old slippers for a pair of suave new ones that had been sitting at the bottom of her wardrobe. It wouldn't have been too bad, but she'd also dug out her best pearl earrings.

When Tabby had mentioned her extra attention to her wardrobe, Gran had simply preened her hair with her hand and said, 'If I'm going to be standing on the doorstep saying hello to your friends, there's the chance of bumping into Mr Helstone, isn't there? You never know, he might walk past. I've got to be looking my best, Tabby. You just don't understand these things.'

Ed had stood on the threshold, grinning from ear to ear. 'Hi!' he'd said, reaching his hand out towards Gran. 'You must be Tabby's sister.'

Gran had giggled, a sound Tabby hadn't thought would ever come out of her elderly grandmother's throat. 'I wish. The anti-ageing cream must be working! I'm Tabby's gran, Nancy.'

Tabby squeezed past Gran to greet the others.

They made their way up the front garden path – Cassie staring down at her phone, Olivia grinning so widely the metal of her braces was showing, and Henry, his hands in his trouser pockets.

'Oh my!' Gran said. 'Aren't you a lovely bunch? Now I understand why Tabby's been spending all of her time with you.'

Cassie put her phone away. 'I like your earrings,' she said to Gran, surprising all of them, by the looks on their faces.

'Oh, thank you, dear.' Gran smiled. 'And aren't you fashionable! I'm rather envious.'

She surveyed Cassie's get-up of a pale blue denim pinafore over the top of a plain white T-shirt, her legs bare, topped off with a pair of grey high-tops.

'So what are you kids up to today?' Gran asked. 'Anything exciting?'

'Olivia and Cassie won't tell us,' Henry said. 'As per usual.'

'It's a secret!' Olivia grinned. 'Speaking of, have you told your gran about our road trip, Tabby?'

Tabby's heart sank. 'About that—'

But Gran cut in. 'Of course. She's told me all about it. I just wish I was . . . oh, ten years younger! I'd be coming with you. Are you sure I can't be an honorary member of the Paper & Hearts Society?'

'Sure you can,' Ed said enthusiastically. 'There's room in the van for one more!'

Tabby laughed in appreciation before turning back to Gran in disbelief. 'But Mum said . . .'

'What your mum doesn't know won't hurt her,' Gran said, and patted Tabby's shoulder. 'It'll be our little secret.'

'Does that mean . . .?'

Gran smiled. 'You, Tabby, shall go on your literary road trip after all. Now, don't you have somewhere to be?'

Olivia squealed. Henry and Cassie rolled their eyes but laughed. In that moment, it took all of Tabby's strength not to hug Gran in an embarrassingly over-the-top way in front of her new friends.

Half an hour later, the Paper & Hearts Society arrived at a car park in the middle of nowhere.

Tabby slid the van door open and jumped out, straightening her legs to get the blood back into them. Olivia and Cassie were already bounding away. Ed, Tabby and Henry followed as best as they could, although Tabby found that both of them outpaced her, forcing her to speed up.

They joined Cassie and Olivia by the edge of a colossal lake, a footpath snaking its way round the circumference and bordered by a wood. The water gleamed in the summer sun, tiny ripples dancing on the surface like kaleidoscopes of light.

'Welcome to the lake, Tabby!' Olivia said, a big grin on her face. 'And welcome, victims.'

Henry shook his head. 'Seriously, Livs, come on. Why have you two dragged us out here?'

Cassie cleared her throat. 'We're re-enacting *The Hunger Games*. Or *Lord of the Flies*. Or one of those other books where everybody dies. Basically: don't expect to make it out of here breathing.'

Ed's mouth hung open. 'So you've dragged us out here to kill us?' he squeaked.

'I didn't drag you out here for fun, did I?'

Olivia whacked Cassie's arm. 'Enough with the morbid stuff. Let me explain.' She cracked her knuckles. 'We thought the perfect bonding exercise for the Paper & Hearts Society would be to do a team game! So we're playing Sardines but I had to give it a bookish twist or we'd be the most pathetic book club ever. So pretend we're in *The Hunger Games* or *Lord of the Flies* or whatever. Please?'

Sardines, Olivia explained, was the opposite of hide-and-seek. One person had to start by hiding, and it was everybody else's job to find them. Once another person had found the first person to hide, they would join them in hiding until only one person was left. They would be the loser. Or, in Cassie's words, 'They're the one to die. Simple.' She folded her arms across her chest. 'Now can we start? I'm getting bored of watching Ed process his life flashing before his eyes.'

They discussed who would be 'it' first and Henry volunteered. 'I don't have any energy left to run about like a fool for ages. I've already been doing that this morning.' Tabby gave him a questioning look. 'A hyperactive little sister,' he explained. 'She didn't want me to leave the house and kept clinging to me.'

'At least it's not a cat peeing on your legs this time,' she joked.

'Stop nattering, you two,' Olivia said. 'Henry's got to go and hide. Everyone shut your eyes. Seriously, when did you two become the ones who won't shut up when you're supposed to? Go hide, Henry.' And with that, she shooed him off and set the timer on her phone to give him a chance to find somewhere.

They all shut their eyes and waited.

Tabby sensed Olivia rocking back and forth on the balls of her feet beside her, impatient or excited, or both.

The buzzer on Olivia's phone went wild.

'Go, go, go!' she shouted, waving the phone in everyone's faces. 'Run for your lives!'

'But I have no clue where I'm going!' Tabby admitted.

'Don't worry about it,' Olivia comforted, already beginning to walk off. 'If you get lost, just scream and I'm sure we'll track you down.'

'Thanks, I guess?'

They split up, each going in a separate direction to try to be the first to find Henry. Tabby, however, hung back, taking a moment to collect her thoughts. She felt anxious and hated herself for it.

When she turned, though, she found that Cassie was right there. 'Uh, Tabby?'

'Yeah?'

Cassie scuffed the toe of one shoe against the ground, watching her movement intently. She scratched her neck. 'Your gran's really nice.'

'Thanks?' *Is that all she wants to say?*

Silence. But then Cassie continued with, 'She just got me thinking, that's all. And I realised that maybe I've been unfair on you. You know, all that talk about not trusting you . . . Seeing how much your gran loves you made me think about someone who loved me once too, and how they would have felt about me treating you like that. So that's all. I'm sorry.'

Tabby was speechless. 'It's okay,' she eventually settled on. *Did that really just happen?*

'And now I have to go and win this thing.' And, as if she were never there at all, Cassie loped off, leaving Tabby to stare at her retreating back.

Instead of running , Tabby walked the perimeter of the lake, gazing out at the Canada geese gobbling up birdseed that kids in prams threw down for them, and seagulls screeched overhead like mothers angry with their children. She didn't think she could run anywhere; she was too gobsmacked.

Cassie apologised. To me. And I thought she'd always hate me.

She sheltered under the shade of the trees, entering the wooded area that bordered the lake.

Maybe I'm not so bad after all.

She looked up in wonder, taking her time to walk forward and savour every second. *In fact . . .* She pulled out her phone and opened up the camera, positioning herself so that the lake could be seen behind her. Dappled light hit her face, painted marks on her cheeks and swam in front of her eyes. She took a quick selfie, the shutter interrupting the dominant sound of the birdsong.

No, that one's not right.

She snapped away until she got one she didn't despise, where the spots breaking out on her chin couldn't be seen and she looked vaguely happy. The perfect selfie was an art form to Tabby.

'Psst! Tabby!'

What was that? She looked around, darting glances over her shoulders and turning in every direction. She must have imagined it.

No. There it was again. 'Tabby! Tabitha!'

She stepped off the path, scrambling up a small bank to get a better vantage point. She took a step back, surveying further, and jumped as something grabbed hold of her arm.

Resisting the urge to scream, she stopped dead. *It's a snake. It's got to be a snake and they bite and I'll have to suck the venom out or I'll die and I'll never be found out here. I saw it in a film once and oh GOD.*

Or it was some pervy bush-lurker and . . .

'Tabby,' the voice came again, accompanied by a laugh. Scratchy leaves brushed against her bare arms; she shut her eyes to brace for the impact. This was it. Her death. She was sure of it.

'Ohmigod, Henry!' she squealed as she opened her eyes. 'I thought you were a serial killer!'

'Shh . . .' Henry whispered, unable to contain how funny he found the situation. 'You'll give away our location!'

Tabby crossed her arms across her chest. 'You could have thought about that before you dragged me into a hedge. If I drop dead from fright, my murder will be on your hands.'

There was barely enough room for them to stand up – they were in a hole in the hedge, just about big enough for both of them to fit, but Henry had to curve himself into a strange position because he was too tall for the height of the hedge itself.

'Did your selfie come out okay?'

Oh noooooo. I can't believe he saw that! Tabby felt her cheeks go bright red. She decided to go confident with her reply. 'It did, thank you very much, and I didn't need a filter in the end,' she said. 'How did you choose this place anyway?'

'When we used to come here as kids, this was my favourite hiding spot. It was an exciting den that we could play in – pirate ships and hide-and-seek and castles. Make believe. I'd forgotten how much I'd grown, to be fair.'

'You're terrible at this game, you know. You're not supposed to give away your location.'

Henry sat down on the ground, pulling his legs into his body. 'It was getting boring, just sitting here waiting to be found. And it's good to spend more time with you.'

She felt a thrill go through her. *It's good to spend more time with you.* His words were like music to her ears; could it really be that she was truly one of them now? She couldn't imagine what life would be like without the Paper & Hearts Society.

She loved the way that whenever Henry laughed at something she said, his glasses would slip down his nose and his hair would fall into his eyes; she loved the way Olivia injected passion into everything she did. And then there were Ed's (often awful) jokes . . . And the new side to Cassie that she was beginning to see.

'What if I don't want to talk to you?' Tabby teased. 'Maybe I'll just sit here and ignore you until we're found.'

'I doubt it,' Henry said, and he reached into his pocket and drew something out. It was a book, so battered that it looked like someone had run over it with a car, submerged it in a gallon of water and then dried it by chucking it into a fire. It was the worst-kept book Tabby had ever seen.

It was only when Henry opened it up – cracking the spine so far back that it made her cringe – that she peeked inside and could see the words of Sylvia Plath staring back up at her.

'That is very unfair,' Tabby said. 'Trying to win me around with Sylvia Plath. Underhand tactics!'

He slowly peered up from the book to look at her. 'Oh, you want to talk to me now?'

She batted his shoulder with her hand. 'Maybe I have changed my mind just slightly.'

'Okay then,' he said, and placed the book on the ground between them. 'What is it you like about Sylvia Plath so much?'

Where to even begin?

'I suppose I love how dark she is. Not just in her poetry, but in *The Bell Jar* too. It helped me a lot, to feel like I was less alone. I think so many of us feel sad or angry, but we never talk about it. And she made me feel like I was okay to feel the way I did. She helped me when I found it hard to help myself. I left my copy of *The Bell Jar* at home but I keep renewing my library loan here so that I've got it with me. My copy's falling apart too, though, because I've read it so much now.'

'Helped you? In what way?'

It would be so easy to tell him about Jess. Tell him about how stranded I felt. How I still feel like I'm rebuilding the broken pieces of my personality that were crushed. How much I hate myself for not being stronger, not being the person who could have stood up to her.

'Oh, no way in particular. Just in general.'

He nodded, as if he really did get it. 'You're mysterious, you know that?'

She scoffed. 'Are you serious? You're the mysterious one!'

'Me?' He pointed a finger to his chest. 'How am I mysterious?'

'It's obvious. Olivia is clearly the natural leader of this group; Ed is the funny one; Cassie is, well, Cassie. I'm the newbie. *You* are the mysterious one.'

'I am most definitely not mysterious,' Henry spluttered, his face turning red from laughter. '*You're* the mysterious one.'

'Tell me something about you then that will make you less mysterious.'

He thought about it for a minute, grazing his lips with his teeth and gazing at the ground. 'Okay . . . Well, I once tripped holding scissors and had to have stitches in my hand because I was close to being impaled. You can still see the scar faintly here.' He held out the palm of his hand for her to look at the constellation of lines on his skin. 'When I was younger, I read a book and then believed that everyone was actually hamsters rather than humans and refused to sleep for a week. And, finally, I love writing short stories.'

Tabby rolled her eyes. 'Such a mysterious hipster.'

He feigned offence. 'What's that supposed to mean?'

'Mysterious writers are all hipsters.'

'I am not a hipster,' he insisted, tweaking his glasses, but Tabby could tell he wasn't truly offended because the grin hadn't slipped from his face.

'That's what a true hipster would say. You're a walking cliché.'

'Says the one who spent half an hour taking selfies.'

'It wasn't half an hour!' Tabby spluttered. 'And I bet you've never taken a selfie in your life. You don't even have Instagram!'

'I'll have you know, I'm the selfie king,' Henry said. 'Dog filters, flower crowns, fake lipstick . . . You name it, I bet I'll look amazing in it.'

'Not vain at all,' she said, and shook her phone in front of his face. 'In that case, prove it.'

Henry leant in close, tapping the screen to find the perfect filter as Tabby held the phone out in front of them. She could feel his shoulder brushing hers, their heads touching as he came closer to fit into the frame. Virtual glasses covered their real glasses on-screen, and Tabby pulled the phone back in as soon as the picture had been taken.

Waiting for @TheIncredibleEd, @bookswithlivs and @cassie.artx . . . Where are you?! :D

She framed the words in a pink textbox before sending it out to the world. Or as much of the world that followed her on Instagram.

They sat in comfortable silence for a few minutes, the only sounds their breaths and the squawking of geese from the lake.

'Do you know how predictable you are, Henry Gillingham?' They jumped at the approaching voice. A few seconds later, Cassie's head poked through the hedge. 'Seriously?' she said, holding up her phone.

'It wasn't that predictable if you had to look at Tabby's post to guess where I was.'

'Budge up,' she said, forcing Tabby to scoot closer to Henry. 'How did you find him first?' Cassie asked, looking at Tabby. 'There's no way you knew he was here.'

'Magic.' Henry winked. 'You obviously weren't good enough, Cass.'

'Yeah, right. You two should have kept it on the low-down if you didn't want to be discovered. The whole point of this game is to not give your location away.'

But Tabby had mostly forgotten about the game. And she couldn't believe that Cassie was acting as if nothing had happened. She was an enigma.

'What were you talking about anyway?' Cassie said.

'Nothing much,' Henry said, and smiled at Tabby as if to say, 'Our conversation was between us.' Or maybe it was more of a *I'm smiling but our conversation didn't really mean that much to me* smile. She tried not to overthink it.

They sat back in comfortable silence, watching through the gaps in the hedge as dog walkers passed by on the path and a swan glided over the surface of the lake. It stretched its wings out and craned its long neck.

'I'm scared of swans,' Cassie said casually. 'I feel like if you were chased by one, it would scar you for life. You know what else will scar me for life? Waiting on this dirty ground for Ed and Olivia. Where've they got to?'

It wasn't long before Olivia found them, exclaiming that she couldn't believe Henry had hidden in such an obvious place. 'I thought it was too obvious!' she wailed. 'I could have found you ages ago!'

Tabby was relieved when ten minutes later Ed caught up with them too and she could get out of the hedge. After the car squish and now this, for a change she actually *wanted* to go for a run.

'Does this mean I'm the dead one?' Ed said.

He ran away screaming as Olivia chased after him, crying, 'Surrender!'

'They're such dorks,' Henry said, pulling stray twigs from his hair. 'I'm sure I'm the only sensible one here.'

'You can't say that when you have leaves all over your head,' Tabby said, and reached up to remove one he hadn't found. He caught her hand and surveyed the leaf she'd captured.

'I've got no clue how that got there,' he said, and flicked it back at her. 'You'd think I'd been stuck in a bush or something.'

'You were too distracted to notice,' she quipped. *What's got into me?*

'It's not my fault you dragged me in to take selfies,' he said, and Tabby pushed his shoulder away, laughing.

They walked back to the van. Well, Tabby and Henry walked. Ed had put Olivia on his shoulders and was laughing hysterically as he tried to run with her, crying out all the way that she was too heavy. Cassie followed them, recording the entire spectacle on her phone for an Instagram story.

'Time for our shelfie for the scrapbook!' Olivia called as they got closer to the van. Ed leant down and Olivia slipped off his shoulders. 'Gather in, gather in!'

Tabby stood in between Olivia and Henry, who was crouched down slightly so he could fit into the frame; Cassie stood in front but behind Ed, pretending (at least, Tabby thought she was pretending) to strangle him with her bare hands.

'This time we've all got to say . . . "I survived *The Hunger Games*!"' Olivia declared, and snapped the picture.

Inside the van, Olivia pulled a plastic wallet filled with paper from the footwell. She handed some paper sheets around yet again. Tabby couldn't help but love her organisation. Someone needed to keep them in check.

'Here we have it: more details about the road trip! I've been losing sleep trying to plan it. Take a look and see what you think.'

According to Olivia's careful schedule, the ideal time to leave for the road trip would be the Monday morning after Ed's party on the Friday, which would give them a week and a half to finalise all details, pack and recover from the party.

'We'll travel to Bath on the Monday and have all day there,' she said, twiddling her hair round her finger as she recalled the information, 'then the next morning we'll set off for Stratford-upon-Avon, spend the day listening to Ed go on and on about Shakespeare, and then travel up to Yorkshire that night so we can spend the following day at the Brontë Parsonage.'

Just imagine if Gran wasn't on my side. I wouldn't have been part of any of this.

'I'm gonna get so many good art opportunities while we're away,' Cassie said. 'My Instagram's been looking bare of artwork over the last few weeks; I've spent too much time doing Paper & Hearts stuff.'

'Cassie, you haven't heard from that weird Instagram account again, have you?' Tabby asked.

Act casual. Hopefully she won't have thought any more about it.

'I don't think so,' she said. 'Let me check.'

She fiddled about with her phone for a minute. 'Oh.' For once, Cassie looked shocked. 'Oh, wow.'

'Show me,' Olivia said, trying to look over her shoulder.

'No, I don't know if you should see this,' Cassie replied, turning the phone away. At this angle, though, Ed was able to duck down and look. He snatched the phone from Cassie before she could stop him and zoomed into the picture . . .

'What the . . .? That's so creepy!' Ed exclaimed.

He showed Tabby, and she was sure she felt the ground shake beneath her.

On the screen was a drawing of four stick figures, their bodies roughly sketched. Instead of drawn faces, though, each figure had the face of one of the members of the Paper & Hearts Society, apart from Tabby. But that wasn't all – their eyes were hollowed out, their lips scribbled over so that they looked scratched.

Across the top, hastily written, was 'WATCH YOUR BACKS'.

'Who would do such a thing? I don't understand.' Olivia looked like she was on the verge of tears, her lips quivering, her eyes shining.

Cassie put her arm around her shoulders. 'I'm not going to let this drop. I must have watched every episode of *Catfish* and I've been taking notes. I'll find out who it is, and then they're going down. If the profile had a profile picture then I could do a reverse image search, but there isn't one, which makes it tricky. I'll set up a notification so I can see as soon as anything else is added on the account.'

'I'm sure it's just spam.' Tabby pretended to shrug it off, feeling sick to her stomach.

Cassie shook her head. 'It's too targeted; it must be someone at least one of us knows. I'm going to keep tabs. Nothing will get past me.'

'Thank goodness for that!' Tabby said, lying once more. That was the very thing she was worried about most of all.

Record of Today's Meeting by Cassie

So Olivia is making me write this in the scrapbook ***(I AM NOT MAKING YOU!!!)*** *even though I told her I have better things to do with my time but she's giving me the evil eye right now so I suppose I should write something to make her happy.* ***(I'm not giving you the evil eye!! Stop making me look bad!)***

In today's meeting we re-enacted The Hunger Games *but it was pretty boring because there was a distinct lack of murder.*

Olivia is now reading over my shoulder and would like me to give my predictions on the fate of the Paper & Hearts Society members and who would be the winner/last to survive, so here goes:

Ed: There is no way Ed would make it out alive. He would be the first to be killed because he'd spend too much time complaining about how hungry he was and somebody would come up behind him and kill him.

Tabby: Would probably make it halfway through the competition through sheer luck but would be too worried about upsetting someone if she killed them so would keep putting it off until she was killed herself.

Me aka Cassie: The winner, obviously. But don't expect me to tell you the tactics I would use to win because I don't give away my secrets.

Henry: Definitely one to watch. He looks all innocent but really he's quietly working out ways to murder you in your sleep. (Not that I think Henry is capable of murder. But if he was, then I wouldn't underestimate him.)

Olivia: Would be the first to be killed because she'd either get too excited about the whole situation or try to make friends with everyone and forget the aim of the game.
(ARE YOU SAYING YOU WOULDN'T CREATE A KATNISS AND PEETA SITUATION WITH ME AND GET US BOTH OUT OF THERE ALIVE?!?!)

Olivia, I love you, but the only way you will end up as the Girl on Fire is if you set yourself on fire. And I don't trust you with matches.

~ Cassie

Now this is Olivia here and I would very much like to state that Cassie is WRONG and I would be the victorious winner. Just saying.

Olivia: Ed, have you been looking into places we can eat when we're in Bath? And Cassie, have you finalised our schedule for the Brontë Parsonage yet? Details please!! I need to put it all into our itinerary

Henry: Are you really going to plan out every minute of our days?

Olivia: Who do you think I am? Of course I am!!!

Ed: I think I'm all sorted. I'll private message you because I DON'T WANT TO RUIN THE SURPRISE

Tabby: Is your caps lock stuck again?

Ed: YES IT IS LEAVE ME ALONE

Olivia: Love you Ed!!! And what's the van situation looking like??

Ed: My mum is offering to pay for our fuel while we're away and she sent me and my brother out there earlier to tidy it up. Daniel was NOT impressed but he didn't have a choice

Tabby: Do you need me to do anything? I don't want to be the one not taking on any workload! I'm happy to help. :)

Olivia: Don't you worry about a thing! We have it covered!

Henry: Are you trying to get me to reveal my surprise? Don't worry, I've got it sorted, Tabby :)

Olivia: Hi Tabby! I know this may seem like a suuupeerrrr weird question, but (hypothetically speaking, OF COURSE!) what would you say if you wanted to message someone to tell them you'd like to talk to them, something personal about maybe liking them in a way that's more than friends, but you're too scared they'll say no or ignore you?

Olivia: I've got a friend who was wondering this and I just have a feeling you're good at these things, haha!!

Tabby: I suppose that would depend on what you wanted to talk about. Is it something you could type in a message or is it something that's serious enough that you'd need to do it in person?

Olivia: It's not something you could say easily face to face or over a message. But I guess in person would be better

Olivia: That's what my friend thinks anyway

Tabby: Well, is this person going to Ed's party tomorrow night? Because that might be a good place to suggest talking. It'll be less intense if you're around loads of other people. If you need to talk to someone in person, then it's good to say exactly when and where so that there's no confusion. Just message them now and say something like 'Hi, do you think we can find some time to talk alone at Ed's party? There's something I've been meaning to say that I can't over a message.'

Olivia: You're the beeessttt! Thank you! <3

Tabby: You're welcome! :D

Olivia: OMG, I DID IT. SENT.

Tabby: You mean your friend sent it?

Olivia: Oh yes, yes, that's what I meant!

Ed: I HAVE A QUESTION FOR YOU

Tabby: Does the question involve your caps lock being stuck?

Ed: NO BUT NOW I'M DELIBERATELY GOING TO TYPE IN ALL CAPS

Tabby: In that case, I can't promise I'll respond

Ed: OH FINE

Ed: I'll stop

Ed: The question is, will you come and help me tomorrow morning to set up for my party? I NEED YOU, BEST FRIEND (and everyone else, because we may be brilliant, but I doubt we're *that* brilliant)

Tabby: Only if your cat doesn't try to attack me again ;)

Ed: Mrs Simpkins will be on her best behaviour, I PROMISE, but also she'll prefer you if you start referring to her as Mrs Simpkins . . .

Tabby: I'm in! :D

Things I need to pack for the road trip:

- *Sleeping bag*
- *Make-up bag*
- *Make-up remover*
- *Sunglasses*
- *Toothbrush*
- *Toothpaste*
- *Hoodie*
- *Pyjamas*
- *Three sets of clothes*
- *Converse*
- *Phone (of course!)*
- *Headphones*
- *Phone charging packs*
- *Purse*
- *Books!*

Chapter Twelve

'I still can't believe your mum is okay with this,' Tabby said to Ed, who was standing in the middle of the kitchen with his hands clamped to the sides of his head.

'I can't either,' he said. There was a glossy sheen to his forehead and a panicked look in his eyes. 'Did you remember to put Mrs Simpkins's food bowl upstairs in my room? I really don't want her to get scared if she finds lots of people in the kitchen.'

'Yes, and that's about the fifth time you've asked. It really will be okay, Ed. We've got it under control.'

'Have we? Did you clear my mum's ornaments from the mantelpiece in the living room? Because last year someone broke a misshapen dolphin that my brother made when he was six and I didn't hear the end of it for months. I can't have a repeat of that.'

'Can you please chill?' Cassie said. 'You're putting me on edge.'

She was sitting at the kitchen table, painting her

fingernails an electric blue colour that apparently matched the dress she was going to wear that night.

'I'm going to go and see what Henry and Olivia are doing in the living room,' Tabby said, patting Ed on the back. She needed a break from the worrying, although it was kind of nice looking out for someone else for a change. 'Just shout if you need anything.'

Henry and Olivia were hanging homemade paper chains from one corner of the living room ceiling to the other, joining them in the middle by the overhead lampshade.

'So then she told me that if I'm going on the road trip, I have to babysit Belle for the entire week afterwards because she doesn't want to fork out on a childminder when nursery is closed for the summer,' Henry was saying, standing on a stool to reach the ceiling. Because he was so tall, though, he had to duck. 'I can't wait to get back to school now. I love Belle, but spending all day with her is a nightmare.'

Olivia was standing below him, handing him the paper chains. 'What does your dad think about it? Surely he's more understanding.'

'What do you think?' he said. 'As usual, he won't go against Mum. So my fate is decided.'

Tabby didn't want to push in, but she also didn't want them to think she was eavesdropping on their conversation. It reminded her of the first time she'd met them.

'Hey, guys, is there anything I can do to help?'

'I think we're almost done,' Henry said, stepping down from the stool. 'I don't know why Ed's so insistent on putting this stuff up anyway. Nobody will notice.'

'He does seem a tad stressed,' Tabby said.

'I haven't seen him like this since . . .' Olivia said, 'well, since his party last year. He keeps putting himself through it, though. Don't ask me why; it would have been much nicer if we'd continued our *Harry Potter* movie marathon, just the five of us.'

'Yes, but we'd have to go back and start it again,' Henry said, winking at Tabby, 'because somebody fell asleep.'

'That wouldn't be the only problem,' Tabby said, and grinned up at Henry. 'We would have to stop before *Deathly Hallows* because Henry would cry too much. We'd never get to the end.'

'Ha, ha,' he said. 'Just because I'm in touch with my emotions, no need to make fun of me.'

'Would I ever?' Tabby said, pretending to be outraged.

He responded by dumping the remaining paper chains over her shoulders and darting out of the way before she could throw them back at him.

'Seriously, Henry,' Olivia said, 'I have never in my entire life seen you mess about so much. What's got into you?'

'Tabby's a terrible influence,' he said. 'I'm going to have to stop talking to her because she's leading me astray.'

'More like you're leading *me* astray,' she protested. 'I was never like this before I came here.'

'I bet you'll be dancing the night away tonight.' Olivia joined in the teasing. 'If we need to find you, we'll just say, "Has anyone seen the girl who's the life and soul of the party?" and everyone will know we mean you.'

How had Tabby forgotten about the actual party part of the party? *Will they really expect me to be dancing the entire night? Will they want me to drink alcohol and talk to everyone and be full of energy?*

She tried to quell the rising panic. 'Ha ha, that will be me all right!' She gulped. 'I think I'm just going to go to the toilet. Be right back.'

Tabby headed to the door under the stairs next to 'Harry's cupboard'. After she was done, she stood looking into the mirror above the sink. Her cheeks were flushed and there were sparkles in her eyes.

I'm happy, she thought. *I'm really happy. I don't remember the last time I felt like this. But can it really last tonight, when I hate parties so much? They're my worst nightmare.*

Voices drifted through the locked door. 'Hey, what did you want to talk to me about?'

'Oh!' That was Olivia's squeak of surprise. 'Um, actually, can we speak later when nobody else is about?'

'Sure,' Cassie said. 'Come find me if I arrive before you? It's nothing serious, is it?'

'No, no!' Olivia continued to squeak. 'It's nothing bad, I promise. I just . . . there's something I've been meaning to tell you. Hey, is that the kettle I can hear boiling?'

Tabby heard them move away and she waited before opening the door, not wanting them to think she'd been listening in on them.

What can Olivia want to talk to Cassie about that sounds so serious? Wait. She remembered the message Olivia had sent her. Of course – *Olivia's nervous to admit her feelings to Cassie!*

She thought back to all the times Olivia and Cassie would find reasons to be closer to each other, thought of Cassie's protectiveness and how uncomfortable Olivia had been at the Harry Potter movie marathon, when she'd left the room. *It has to be Cassie.*

She would have to quiz Olivia on it when they got ready together later; Olivia had offered for Tabby to go over to her house so she wouldn't have to go all the way home and back again before the party started.

She dried her hands, took one last look in the mirror and headed to the kitchen, where Ed was laying out plastic cups with a force that threatened to shatter the kitchen work surface.

'Everything okay?' Tabby asked, coming up behind him. He nearly jumped out of his skin.

'Excellent!' he said. 'I couldn't be better! I'm having the time of my life here!'

Tabby moved over to take a seat at the table. 'Maybe it would be best if you didn't have another party next year, Ed.'

He didn't reply.

'Cassie, can you *please* stop texting?' he practically screamed. 'All I can hear is your fingernails tapping against the screen. You're driving me up the wall!'

Cassie slowly lowered her phone. 'Chill, dude. I can't stop texting; I've got to see what time Sara, Yaz and Scarlett are arriving tonight so we can coordinate.'

Tabby had somehow forgotten they would all have other friends. It seemed like her perfect bubble might burst. *What if those girls are like Jess and the others?* She felt sick.

Ed groaned. 'I can't believe you invited them *again*. You'll go off and I'll lose you for the entire evening. I can't face getting more stressed than I already am. Please put your phone down and help prepare!'

'Fine,' Cassie said, but she leant in closer to the phone screen, frown lines appearing between her eyebrows.

Olivia had drifted away, as if she was going to leave the room, but now she got closer and looked over Cassie's shoulder. 'What is it?'

Cassie turned the screen to show her properly. 'An update from that creepy account.'

Tabby's breath caught in her throat. *No. It can't be. Why won't she stop?*

'Oh, I *love* conspiracies,' Ed said. 'What's the update?'

Cassie clicked around, her nails still tapping; she seemed extra conscious of them now she was wearing nail varnish.

'Woah.'

The anticipation was killing Tabby. *That can't be good.*

Cassie passed around her phone for them to look at; she didn't need to say anything. None of them did.

Tabby was the last to receive it, Olivia reluctantly handing it over. She was looking for any sign in their faces that they knew she was aware who the account belonged to.

Looking back at her from the screen was her own face, the same picture she'd taken with Henry at the last meeting. But instead of Henry by her side, there was only her, a speech bubble coming out of her mouth. 'Hi I'm Tabby and I'm the biggest loser in the world. I have no friends and I never will do because I'm pathetic. Somebody love me! I'm desperate!'

One by one, as if in slow motion, they turned to look at her. Olivia was straight by her side, arms around her shoulders, squeezing her as tight as she could.

Tabby was in shock; it hadn't hit her. *How am I still being bullied when I moved away from the bully? In a minute I'll pinch myself and will wake up. None of this is real. This isn't happening.*

'I'm fine,' she said, when really she wanted to scream, 'This will never be okay! I will never be fine!' Instead she added, 'It's just someone playing a prank. No big deal.'

'No big deal?!' Olivia cried. 'This isn't just someone having a laugh; this is personal! Look how they addressed you, Tabby – someone's taken time to make this. It's not just random.'

'Can you think of *anyone* who might have it in for you?' Cassie pressed. 'Have you upset anyone? Has anyone ever hinted that they don't like you, that they might want to get revenge or something? *Think.* Even a tiny thing might lead us closer to catching who this is.'

I can't tell them. I can't. *If I do, they'll realise how pathetic I really am. They'll know I'm weak enough to be bullied and then they won't be friends with me. Who would be? I can't let myself be vulnerable like that.*

She wasn't sure how she did it, but she managed to play it cool. 'I don't know anyone who would do this,' she said, trying to laugh it off. 'There are so many trolls out there. It's definitely not personal.'

'I *will* get to the bottom of it,' Cassie said, taking her phone back. 'Whoever this is, won't get away with it. Not when I'm on the case.'

But she will. She always does.

'Ooh, I'm so scared,' Ed joked, but then sat up straighter. 'More importantly, has anyone remembered to go through the party playlist? I won't have anyone complaining about my song choices again, even if I do regret putting Justin Bieber on the last one. Oh god! Why is this so *hard*?'

It's going to be a long day . . .

Chapter Thirteen

***@bookswithlivs** Getting ready for @TheIncredibleEd's party with @WhatTabbyDid!! :D*

Tabby tugged her black and white body-con dress down in the mirror glued to Olivia's wardrobe door, biting her lip as she tried to get it lower on her thighs.

'Oh god, I haven't worn this in a year. It's way too short now.'

'You look fine, Tabby!' Olivia tutted, rushing around to find her bag and shoes. She'd opted for a floral skirt ('It's vintage, you know!'), with a white crop top, and added big flicks to her eyeliner. It had taken tipping practically her entire wardrobe on the floor to find the perfect outfit, and the contents of her make-up bag were strewn over her bed. She turned coy. 'A certain someone will think so, at least.'

'What's that supposed to mean?' *Don't blush, Tabby.*

'You think I haven't noticed you and Henry making

lovey-dovey eyes at each other? Because I have! You're so obvious about it.'

I think my whole body has just imploded. 'Obvious about what?' *Okay, that sounded way too defensive.* 'There's nothing going on between Henry and me.'

'Yet.'

'Never!' Tabby exclaimed. 'He doesn't see me in that way, no matter what you think.'

'But you feel that way about him?'

'I didn't say that,' she said, but then changed her mind. *I have to be honest about something.* 'Maybe a little bit. I can't really work out how I feel. But hey, how about this person you want to talk to tonight? Are *they* a special someone?'

Olivia looked away, and when she turned back round again the excitement had gone from the air. She was biting her lip. 'Tabby, have you ever heard of being "demisexual" before?'

'"Demisexual"?' She played the word around in her mouth, the latter syllables rolling about on her tongue.

'It means that I only feel attracted to someone if I have a connection with them,' Olivia explained. 'I don't have crushes on celebrities and I've always felt uncomfortable around people if they're discussing who they fancy because I just don't *get it*. I'm happy for them, like I would be if anything happened between you and Henry, but just don't get crushes. I have to get to know someone first, feel comfortable around them, and even then it doesn't mean I'll necessarily like them . . . like that.'

'So it's like asexual?'

Olivia half nodded, half shook her head. 'Kind of. It's on the asexual spectrum. And it will be different for everyone – my experience being demisexual would be different to someone else who identifies in that way, just as there's not one way to be straight.'

Tabby had never known people her age to be so open before – in her old life, everyone had wanted to be the same and if they weren't, even if they hid it, there'd been the fear of being made fun of, picked on. Everyone had to be identical.

'When I first heard the term "demisexual", it was like a light bulb came on in my head. I felt like I knew who I was, even if it was only just *slightly* better than before. And it was difficult – I didn't accept that this was who I was right away, but now I'm comfortable being me and that's the most important thing.' Her shoulders drooped, as if all her energy had been spent. She let out a breathy laugh. 'Wow, nothing like baring your soul to get into the party spirit, am I right? But, back to your original question . . . Yes, it is a *special someone* I want to speak to tonight. And that special someone is Cassie.' Olivia sank on to her bed, burying her face in her hands. 'I'm so nervous. I don't know what to tell her, but I know I can't keep how I feel to myself any more. But where do I even start? I wish it didn't have to be this difficult.'

'Well,' Tabby said, 'what is it about Cassie that you love? When you look at her, what do you think?'

Softly, she said, 'When I look at Cassie, I don't want to rip her clothes off or . . . or snog her face off. It's not like that. When I'm with her, I feel safe and warm, full of love. We've been best friends for so long; we know each other better than anyone else. I can't imagine wanting to be with anyone but her, and when we're not together I wish she were there so we could talk or joke around or even just be in the same room, not talking. When she's there, I'm at my happiest.'

Tabby felt her heart melt. 'I think you've found your place to start.'

Olivia threw her arms around Tabby's shoulders. 'You know you're fabulous, don't you? Thank you, Tabby.'

'Anytime,' Tabby said, and awkwardly patted her back. She still wasn't used to all this affection. 'One last question, though. What's with Cassie and those girls she mentioned today?'

Olivia muttered, 'They're Cassie's friends from college. The less said about them, the better. She's a completely different person when she's around them. She invited them to Ed's party last year and ended up going to another party with them. I just hope she doesn't leave Ed like that again. He was really upset.'

Tabby looked down one last time at her outfit. She'd paired the too-short dress with a pair of wedges and a gold clutch bag, aka the Keeper of the Mobile Phone. She didn't want to admit it to Olivia, but she wanted to make an impression. Just a little bit. Dressing up was the perfect distraction – you could become someone else, forget who you were.

'Ready to go?' Olivia buckled up a pair of enormous heels and was finally done.

'Have a fab time, girls,' Olivia's mum called after them down the street. 'Don't be too late getting back; we would like some sleep tonight.'

'I don't really know what to expect,' Tabby admitted as they walked down the street. She was glad she'd worn somewhat sensible shoes once she saw Olivia teetering along in her heels. She stood nearly as tall as Tabby in them, and every now and again she had to clutch hold of Tabby's arm in a death-like grip in order to keep upright. 'I know it's a party, but I don't really like drinking.'

'You'll be fine, honestly. I promise I won't leave your sight and I'll introduce you to everyone too. Let your hair down! Enjoy yourself!'

Easier said than done. I've never enjoyed myself at a party.

Olivia stumbled, grabbing Tabby's arm at the last minute to stop from toppling over completely. 'These stupid heels . . . I knew they were a bad decision!'

As they approached Ed's house, Tabby noticed a small group of people loitering outside, cans in their hands. She shrank back behind Olivia. *Finally, some good to come out of her wearing those massive heels!*

'Hi!' Olivia was saying, stopping by each person to grin and grab hold of their shoulders as she swayed back and forth on her heels. 'How are you? I'm so excited! Have you been inside yet?'

Tabby's vision was beginning to blur and she felt as dizzy as Olivia looked on her heels. *Breathe in, breathe out. Breathe in, breathe out. No, not that fast. And again . . . Breathe in, breathe out. Breathe in, breathe . . .*

It was no good. The more she tried to concentrate, the more she was losing her concentration.

'Tabby, meet Carrie. We're in the same English class! Miss Forster on a Monday morning. Not the best of fun, I can tell you. Carrie, this is Tabby! She's just moved here. Oh, and this is Sofia! And this is Ife!'

She felt bombarded with information; Olivia was saying something else, the girls were smiling back at her, but she couldn't even relax enough to see what they looked like. They could literally be anyone.

'You weren't even invited.' No, not now, not here. She couldn't risk thinking back to then. But the voice of past-Jess wouldn't let her go. *'What the hell are you doing here, Tabby?'*

She tried to look defiant, raising her head and looking Jess straight in the eyes. 'I'm doing what everyone else is doing. Why can't I be here?'

Jess grabbed her forearm tight, her nails digging in. 'Because I don't want you here. Nobody wants you here. So get out now before I drag you myself.'

Tabby had switched to autopilot, splashing a tight smile over her face, and was relieved when Olivia moved on and they went inside.

What's got into you? she scolded herself, trying to shake her head out of its nonsense.

She pulled herself away from Jess's grasp, trying not to wince or look down at the crescent-shaped nail marks in her skin. 'Or trip me up like you did at the cross-country competition?' The loud noises of the party were starting to make her dizzy and she stumbled back. 'Don't worry, I didn't really want to be here anyway. I've got better things to be doing.'

She took herself up to the bathroom upstairs, which seemed to take an age to become free. She splashed water on her face, touched the side of her arm with soft fingertips.

When she finally came out, after many angry fists had banged against the door, she felt more composed.

Until . . . The girl thundered towards Tabby at a rate that could definitely not herald good things. Elizabeth Dickens, with reddish-brown dyed hair flying around her face, was someone she'd never had a lot to do with. She was part of a different group, and they'd never had any of the same classes, but Tabby vaguely knew of her because their year group was only small and everyone knew at least something about everyone else.

'Why would you call me a slut?' Elizabeth spat, venomous. 'You must have known how upset I was about my boyfriend breaking up with me, and now I hear you're spreading lies and slagging me off behind my back?'

'But I never . . .' spluttered Tabby, backing away. 'I would never—'

'Don't deny it,' she said, advancing forward. 'I know you did because Jess just told me. She didn't understand either how you could say something so awful about me.'

Cold, hard realisation dawned on Tabby and she ran outside as quickly as she could, out into the cool air of the night.

She had wanted to ring her parents and get them to pick her up. Just like she wanted now. But they were miles and miles away, and Mum would be sure to say, 'I told you so.'

'Olivia! Tabby! I could not be happier to see you right now.' Tabby blinked furiously up at Ed, who seemed a frantic kind of jolly, – a little flustered and most likely under the influence. His gaze darted back and forth, as if he couldn't decide what he had to do next.

'Hi, Ed,' Tabby said weakly, arranging her face into a smile that disappeared within seconds. Ed didn't seem to notice, though – he'd gone into host mode, ushering Olivia and Tabby in and turning back to the next people who'd arrived.

There weren't that many people – about twenty-five – but they clustered in groups in the hallway, in the kitchen, crowded the sofas in the living room with drinks cans in hand, listening to the music blasting from a speaker somewhere. Tabby was distracted by all the unfamiliar faces, their images clouding as they passed over her to speak to Olivia.

'I'm going to see if I can find Cassie. Do you want to go and get us a drink?'

Tabby didn't have time to respond before Olivia was asking a group, 'Have you seen Cassie anywhere? She should be here by now.'

'Upstairs,' one girl pointed out, messing with the strap of her black denim dungarees with one hand and composing a tweet with the other.

Tabby watched Olivia bound off, leaving her gawping at her retreating back.

How could this be so awkward? Tabby didn't do awkward any more; she hated the prickles that swept over her skin, the fuzzy feeling in her head.

She brushed against bodies on her way out to the kitchen; she sucked her breath in as she squeezed through the gaps, as if that would help in any way. Her gaze dropped to the floor, concentrating on her feet wending past other peoples' shoes. *Why do they want to stand in the hallway, for god's sake? There are far comfier places than the wall.*

Just as Tabby went to look up, her body collided with another, the impact knocking her into someone who grunted as she crushed their toes under her wedges.

'Sorry, sorry!' she said, arms waving frenziedly, but they'd already brushed past. *Just find the door, Tabby, and get the hell out of here.*

She turned back to the doorway, looking into the eyes of her injurer. *Henry*. His face was a picture of concern: eyebrows knitted, lips tight together, glasses sliding down his nose.

Tabby's shoulders slumped and her eyes closed for a few seconds. 'It's you,' she said, relief dripping in her voice.

'It's me,' Henry replied, leaning down closer to her face so that she could hear what he was saying. 'Are you okay? It's pretty overwhelming in here!'

Tabby nodded, which eventually transformed into a loose shaking. 'I don't know, really. I'm sorry I stood on you.'

He touched her elbow, jerking his head in the direction of the kitchen. 'Don't be silly. Come with me.'

The kitchen seemed much bigger than everywhere else, despite the clusters of people hanging about, and it was quieter too. Henry kept close to Tabby as he led her out to the back garden.

The door stuck slightly and Henry had to push his shoulder against it to make it budge. Even the stuffy summer breeze that rushed against Tabby's face was a welcome relief from the stifling, unmoving air of the house and the loud bass of the speakers. They sat down against the brick wall to the side of the door, feet stretched out in front of them.

'Better?' Henry asked, turning his head from where it rested against the wall to look at Tabby.

'Much,' she replied, eyes closed. She kicked off her wedges so that her bare feet touched the patio slabs.

They sat in comfortable silence, Tabby counting the beats of her heart with one hand pressed against the pressure point under her right ear.

Henry was the first to talk. 'Do you want to talk about it?'

'It's just so busy in there,' she said, her words coming out slowly as she tested them in the space between them.

'With people I don't know and loud music and drinking. It's not my life.'

She popped an eye open to judge his reaction; Henry nodded carefully. 'I get it,' he said. 'I know we joked earlier, but I don't think you're supposed to go rushing in there and dance on the tables.'

'I hate it. I hate being new. I hate feeling as if I should be acting like everyone else. It terrifies me. It's like I forget how to breathe. As soon as Olivia went off, I didn't know what to do.'

'Olivia gets caught up in the atmosphere,' Henry explained. 'She doesn't mean it nastily. It's just how she is: she thrives off noise and big groups.'

'Not really my scene,' Tabby said wryly.

'Me neither.'

'And here was me thinking you were the party king!'

Henry spluttered, showing his teeth in the grin that spread over his face. 'Don't tell anyone about this. It will ruin my reputation.'

A nervous buzz filled the air between them, humming electricity that made Tabby close her eyes and part her lips. Anticipatory. It would be so easy to lean in and close the gap and . . .

Something distinctly like the sound of Taylor Swift's 'Shake It Off' jumped between them: the ringtone of Henry's phone, loud and insistent.

'Shake It Off'? Really?

'Ed chose it, not me.' The grin on Henry's face soon faded as he answered the call.

Were we going to . . . ? No. Don't think about it. You're desperate.

'Hello? Yes, Ed, we're outside. Calm down, mate. I'll come now. Where are you? I'll be right there, I promise.'

Henry jumped up without another word, gripping the phone tightly in his hand, and pulled Tabby up from the ground.

'What's going on?'

'Olivia and Cassie are upstairs apparently having the biggest argument of their life and Ed is freaking out big time and I have no clue where he is now. I couldn't understand half of what he was saying.'

She tried to keep up with Henry as they passed quickly through the house. 'Why are they arguing?' Tabby asked.

'I don't know,' Henry said. 'But whatever it is, it can't be good.'

They got to the bottom of the stairs, looking up to see Cassie standing at the top opposite Olivia. Their arms were flying, their faces aflame with animation, their cries easily heard over the sound of the music and the people.

'I can't believe I said all of that to you and you threw it back in my face! Is that all I am to you? A joke?!'

'Now you're being ridiculous!'

'No, Cassie, *you* were being ridiculous. How would you like it if you bared your entire soul to me and then you came to find me and I was laughing about you behind your back? What was it you said again? "I wish she'd get the message." Can't you see how much that kills me?!'

Cassie shook her head and stomped down the stairs. 'I'm done, Livs. I'm not arguing any more.'

'What's going on?' Henry said, catching Cassie before she disappeared.

'Stay out of it,' Cassie said.

'But where's Ed gone?'

'I don't know! Do you think Ed is really my priority right now?'

Henry looked around, peering over the bannisters, then turned back to Cassie. 'I've got to go and find him. Are you all right here?'

'I'm fine!' Cassie said. 'It's everyone else that's not!' She paused, and then lowered her voice. 'Has Ed . . . been drinking?'

Henry groaned. 'I thought someone was watching him! We have to find him.'

Cassie threw her head back to the ceiling and groaned, but as soon as she took one look towards the stairs, her eyes widened and she shot off in the opposite direction.

Tabby and Henry turned at the same time to find Olivia coming towards them, sniffing, kohl black smudged around her eyes and running down her cheeks to pool at her jaw. Her hand crept up to wipe the snot from underneath her nose, but she eventually gave up and left it to run, bursting into a fresh round of tears when she took in Henry and Tabby.

Henry gathered Olivia into his arms, shielding her from the rest of the party, as everyone strained their eyes to see what was going on. 'Hey, Livs. Do you know where Ed is?' His voice was soft, guiding.

She burst into another sob, her shoulders shaking. 'H-he went out-outside the front.' She tucked her head into Henry's armpit, her eye make-up working its way on to his shirt.

'I'll go,' Tabby offered. Henry mouthed, 'Thanks,' over the top of Olivia's head, and led her off in the direction of the bathroom.

Tabby went out the front, cursing the fact that she had to push past everyone again. *Isn't it time for them to go home already? Can't they see something's going on?*

'Ed?' she asked, spotting him sitting alone on the pavement a little way down the road. His head was bent over the rest of his body, and he clawed his face with his fingers, red welts trailing from his cheeks to his chin.

'Oh god, Ed, are you okay?'

He didn't look up, not even when she sat down next to him. She could instantly smell alcohol clinging to him. He let out a huge sigh, morphing into a groan. His voice was raw, a low rumble from his chest. 'I don't want you to see me cry.'

'There's nothing wrong with crying, Ed.' Tabby felt the urge to reach out and rub his back, but she didn't. She didn't know what to do, really. *All I can do is be there for him*, she told herself. *That's what friends are for.*

'I didn't think it would upset me this much.' He wiped his nose on his bare arm, grimacing. 'But then . . .'

'I'm listening,' Tabby said softly, trying to draw his attention away from the thoughts that were clearly swirling around his mind. Tabby got it; she'd felt exactly the same so many times recently.

'I don't want to be a bad friend,' he whispered, wiping his nose on his sleeve. 'I saw Olivia and I just . . . froze.'

'That's okay. You can't be expected to know what to do all the time.' She touched his shoulder lightly.

'But I need to be there for them,' he sniffled. 'They're always there for me and when it comes to it, I can never do the same. I just want to be enough for them.'

Someone walked past, hollering and patting Ed on the back, laughing heartily and swigging from a can. Clearly not noticing he was upset. Ed buried his head further in his hands.

'You probably think I'm a freak for crying like this,' he muttered. '*Pull it together, Ed.*'

'You are *not* a freak, Ed. You are allowed to cry and you're allowed to feel emotion. You wouldn't be human otherwise.'

'Never let me near alcohol again, Tabby, please,' he groaned, finally lifting his head up. He still wouldn't look her in the eye, though, choosing to stare at his feet instead.

'You need to get that emotion out somehow, Ed,' she replied tenderly. 'Maybe it's the only way you know how at the moment – drinking.'

He nodded, gulping in air and swallowing it down. 'My parents divorced two years ago. They said they were happier apart than they were together, and everything was fine. My brother was okay with it too. Nobody seemed to mind . . . but me. The others supported me through it all: let me stay at their houses when I didn't want to be at mine, distracted me with cute animal GIFs and tried to cheer me up.'

'What happened?' she asked. She remembered Henry mentioning it, but it was different hearing it in Ed's own words. 'Only if you feel comfortable talking about it, of course.'

'They just fell out of love. One day, it all seemed to be going well, and the next . . . my dad moved out. I still don't understand how it happened so quickly. I'd thought the arguments were normal, like every other family. But they obviously weren't.' His voice broke again. 'This whole party has been a total failure, and I knew it would be. I never even wanted to do it, but I felt like I had to. I just want to make people happy, you know? But the opposite always happens. I can't win. Olivia and Cassie are in there fighting and I'm out here; I should be with them, sorting it out.'

'But you need to take time for yourself, Ed, and that doesn't make you a bad friend, I promise. Speaking about your problems and sharing how you feel is only going to make you a better friend because it means that you can sort through it all and then we know not to worry.'

He sniffed some more and chewed on a fingernail absent-mindedly, his eyes unfocused and clustered with unshed tears.

'Sorry to burden you with all of this.'

'Don't be silly. It's not a burden. It's what friends are for.'

'Thank you,' he said, pulling her in for a light hug. 'Thanks for being there for me.'

Tabby's phone pinged. ***Going to take Olivia home. Are you okay with Ed?*** It was Henry. She leant back on her hands, looking down the street to see the retreating figures of Olivia and Henry as they made their way back to Olivia's house in the opposite direction.

We're all good, she typed back. ***Speak to you tomorrow when everything's cooled down?***

Sounds good x, he responded.

She put her phone away and gave her full concentration to Ed. 'What happened in there, with Cassie and Livs?'

Ed shook his head. 'It's all a blur. I went upstairs because I was wondering where Olivia had got to and someone told me she was up there with Cassie. I found them tucked into a corner of the landing. I could hardly hear what they were saying, but Olivia was talking for a while and then Cassie said, 'I can't talk about this,' and she got up and went back to her college friends. I could see the look on Olivia's face, hurt and confusion, and she followed Cassie. Everything went so quickly after that: Cassie leant down and said something to Georgie, and that's when it kicked off. I rang Henry right away and bolted.'

'This is such a mess,' Tabby said. 'How are we ever going to get this solved before the road trip? It's in three days!'

Ed threw his hands up in the air. 'God knows. It's going to be a disaster. Nothing is ever straightforward with us.' He stretched his legs out, followed by his torso. 'I should probably wrap everything up in there. Could you maybe . . . stay and help?'

'Sure, what are besties for?' Tabby said, and they both got up at the same time, walking back to the house, where people were starting to make their own way out.

'Great party, mate!' somebody shouted, but Ed kept his head down and tried to herd them out. Tabby attempted to get people to move too, but they acted as if they couldn't see or hear her, so she gave up and headed to the kitchen.

'Tabby!' She spun around at the sound of her name being called. It was Cassie, a frown on her face as she looked down at her phone. 'Have you seen this?'

She handed Tabby the phone, open to the Messenger app where their group chat was on-screen. Tabby blinked down at the latest message.

Olivia has left the group chat

'I've messed up big time.'

Chapter Fourteen

Henry: I'm at home alone with Belle all day today because my parents are at a work function. Want to come over and see if we can sort this out?

Tabby: Sure, I'll be half an hour!

It was two days after the catastrophe at Ed's party, and none of them had heard anything from Olivia. Dead silence. She had completely shut herself off and wouldn't answer her phone or messages, or let anyone in to see her at home. When Tabby had gone round, her mum had said that she was in the bath, although she did look uncomfortable.

Henry's house was closer to Gran's bungalow than she expected, only a fifteen-minute walk away. *No buses this time, thank god.*

It was a three-storey monstrosity, a new build that had young trees planted outside and a big drive leading up to the front door. The doorbell buzzed under her fingertips, and she took a step back, looking through the frosted window to check for movement. Nothing.

'Sorry!' The front door swung open a few seconds later, revealing a flustered Henry with his fringe hanging over his glasses. 'Have you been out here long? Come in.'

He moved out of the way to let Tabby in, and she kicked off her shoes, leaving them by the front door. *Is this awkward? I can't tell if this is awkward!*

'Is anyone else here?' she asked, but before Henry could answer, she heard an almighty scream. In fact, she didn't so much hear it as *feel* it.

What have I just walked into?

A tiny girl with curly hair in pigtails hurtled towards her and wrapped her arms around Tabby's knees, burying her head between them.

'Belle!' Henry said, grabbing the girl's hand and extricating her from Tabby before she could do any more damage. 'What have I told you about doing that to people you've never met?'

The young girl took a step back and looked up at Tabby, her bottom lip quivering and her eyes wide. 'My snail died,' she said. 'Henry ate him.'

Henry shook his head and picked Belle up, wrapping her legs around his sides. Tabby could see the resemblance – the dimples in Belle's cheeks, her inquisitive eyes. But it was still strange seeing Henry holding a small child in his arms.

'I didn't eat the snail,' he explained to Tabby. 'Did I, Belle? You know it was only an empty shell that we found.'

'Bad brother!' Belle cried, hitting Henry on the arm with a tiny fist.

He rolled his eyes. 'Now you're just showing off.'

'I don't think anyone else is coming,' he said as they walked into a large conservatory at the back of the house, overlooking the garden, where there was a swing set and a plastic climbing frame. 'Cassie and Ed have gone off the grid too.'

Henry put Belle down, and she scrambled away to pick up a toy car that was lying on the wooden floor, rolling it around so that the scratching sound of plastic against floor could be heard.

'I'm four, you know,' Belle explained, and chucked the car back on the floor before hopping over to Tabby, who had sat down on one of the big sofas.

'That's super old,' Tabby said, bending down slightly so that their heads were a similar level. 'You're very grown up.'

'Henry said I was naughty.'

'Can you stop painting me in such a bad light?' Henry cried at his sister, although Tabby knew there was no seriousness to his words.

'Shall I tell you a secret?' Tabby said to Belle, and the younger girl pulled herself on to the sofa and drew her ear closer to Tabby's mouth. Tabby leant in, whispering, 'Henry's really the naughty one. He's only telling you that you are to make himself seem better.'

Belle's eyes lit up and Tabby couldn't help but pull her in even closer so that she was almost positioned on her lap. She poked Tabby in the side and giggled. 'Are you Henry's girlfriend?'

'Belle!' Henry scolded. 'You can't go around asking people that. Say sorry to Tabby, please.'

Tabby deliberately looked into Belle's eyes, trying to ignore the warmth creeping into her cheeks.

Instead of the apology, Belle burst out with, 'I have a boyfriend. His name is Max and he's a cat.'

Tabby spluttered with amusement. 'A cat? What kind of cat?'

'We saw him on a walk one day,' Henry said, getting up from the sofa opposite. 'She keeps telling everyone they're going to get married.'

'We are!' Belle screamed. 'And then I'm going to marry Felicity. She's also a cat.'

'Great,' Henry said, exasperated. 'Now, do you want anything to eat, Belle? It's time for your snack.'

'I want Tabby to get it. Not you.'

'Please remind me never to let you two in the same room again,' Henry directed at Tabby. 'I'm beginning to think you could take over the world.'

After offering Tabby tea ('Lots of milk, right?'), Henry left her alone with Belle, who had decided to tip everything out of her doll's house and was watching it all crash to the floor.

When he got back, Henry handed Tabby the kind of mug you got with Easter eggs, a big chocolate logo plastered on the side. She immediately took a sip, savouring the feeling of the hot liquid sliding down her throat.

For Belle, the novelty of Tabby had clearly worn off, and she seemed content with bashing a plastic digger against the wall of the now empty doll's house.

'Where do we even start?' Tabby said, sighing. She took another sip of tea to gather her thoughts. 'Have you heard anything at all from Livs?'

He shook his head. 'I've rung, I've messaged, I've been to her house, but it's always the same: no response. Her sister answered the door one time, but she wouldn't let me in. It seems she's given strict orders to turn us away.'

'Yep, I had that with her mum,' Tabby said.

Henry tugged at his hair. 'I don't know how we're going to contact her if she won't answer any of our messages and won't let us see her.' Frustration blazed in his every feature, in the way he held his body tight. 'We're supposed to be going on a road trip tomorrow. I just want to know if she's okay.'

‘It’s not your fault, you know,’ Tabby said, reaching a hand out to touch his back gently. ‘You shouldn’t beat yourself up about it.’

I’ll be extremely disappointed if they don’t make me an Agony Aunt badge after this.

‘We’ve been friends for so long that it’s weird if we fall out. Cassie’s the worst: she hates stuff like this. She puts up a front, but it will be eating her up inside.’

‘Right. Her dad . . . That’s understandable. If I were in that position, my worst nightmare would be losing someone else I was close to.’

‘You’re a great friend, Tabby,’ he said, turning his head so he could offer a smile loaded with gratitude. ‘It wouldn’t be the same without you now.’

She sat back into the sofa. *Friends. Friends, friends, friends.* She’d got it all wrong, misread the signs. And here she was, trying to make something happen that was never, ever going to happen. Never mind Henry’s ‘Shake It Off’ ringtone. She should change hers to ‘Wildest Dreams’.

In the harsh daylight, without the high of the party and with the low of Olivia’s disappearance, she knew in her heart that it would never happen.

You shouldn’t even be thinking about this when you’ve got far more serious things to worry about.

She thought about the picture Jess had posted of her. *‘I’m Tabby . . . I’m desperate!’*

Was she desperate? Did Henry think she was? *He must do. It was spelled out for him in the picture; he'll know exactly what I'm like and will run a mile.*

'Where do we go from here?' For a moment, she had to remember what they were talking about. Right. *Olivia.*

'We've just got to get on with it, haven't we? I promise you, she's not going to miss this road trip for the world. We have to trust that she'll talk to us in her own time. As long as the four of us are ready tomorrow morning, just as if none of this happened, then we have to believe Olivia will come.'

Henry sighed. 'I wish I had your confidence.'

Oh, if only you knew . . .

Henry: Can you please come back?? Belle won't go down for her nap and is dancing around the house, screaming about how much she loves you

Tabby: What can I say? I have that effect on people ;)

Henry: In all seriousness, thanks for today. This is all such a mess

Tabby: Life would be boring if there weren't any messes. It's the mess that makes the good bits even better.

Henry: Great wisdom! See, you're not the newbie any more: you're the wise one.

Tabby: I'll take that! But only if you refer to me as 'O wise one' every time you see me and bow down

Henry: I've changed my mind! You can still be newbie Tabby

Tabby: GREAT.

Tabby: Olivia may not be here to make a plan of action, but I AM. Listen up, society members. The road trip is going ahead tomorrow morning, exactly as already arranged. Ed, you turn up in the van at Olivia's as if nothing is the matter – if she's up for it, GREAT. If not, come and pick the rest of us up and we can try together to get her to come.

Ed: YES, BOSS.

Cassie: and if she still doesn't want to come? i'll stay behind and work on my art project if she's not coming.

Tabby: We're not going to entertain that possibility. Positive mental attitude! Your art project isn't as important as us!

Ed: Wow, you FORCE OF NATURE. It's a PLAN.

Chapter Fifteen

Monday morning. Heavy rain hammered tirelessly against Tabby's bedroom window, the wind howling like a wolf from a David Attenborough documentary. Her piercing phone alarm cut through the sound of the outside, carefully set the night before. Any other day, she would have hit the snooze button or waited until her gran came in to wake her up, but this morning she forced her eyes open.

Tabby looked over to her door to check her weekend bag was still there, packed with so much stuff that the zip wouldn't close. She'd tried to pack lightly, but it was impossible. She had reasoned that under normal circumstances, she would have asked Olivia for packing advice, but that hadn't been possible of course, so in it'd all gone. She changed into the clothes she had laid out the night before – a pair of harem pants matched with a tank top and a grey zip-up hoodie. Just comfy enough for the long journey.

'I'll be up in a minute, love,' Gran muffled from behind her bedroom door as Tabby made her way to the bathroom. 'Let me get these old bones out of bed.'

Splashing cold water on her face, Tabby studied herself in the mirror. She hadn't really had reason to think about how she looked first thing in the morning until now, but she'd be waking up with her new friends for the next four days and she suddenly felt self-conscious. There were black and purple shadows under her eyes and her eyelashes were pale, almost invisible, so that her eyes sank back into her face. There was a smattering of tiny freckles over her nose that was usually covered by a thick layer of foundation, which also aided in covering the red spots that had sprung up on her chin and forehead. She'd never had so many spots before, but they'd popped up one after the other, harsh red against the pale of her skin, and hadn't budged for months – just when one went away, another would take its place. They were bad enough, but then there was the scarring afterwards too.

Oh well. If they want me at my best, they have to have me at my worst too.

Gran had got up and was waiting for Tabby in the kitchen, standing by the whistling kettle and spreading jam on a piece of toast.

'This weather isn't nice to be going out in. Especially not for driving. I hope you kids will be all right.' Gran looked concerned, and Tabby couldn't help but notice how tired she looked.

'We'll be okay. You can go back to bed if you want; I know it's early.'

'No, I'm fine,' Gran said, chivvying herself up and passing Tabby a slice of buttered toast. 'I've got to see you off, haven't I?'

'Thank you. You know I love you, don't you? Thank you for letting me stay with you this summer. And thanks for being the coolest gran in the world.'

Gran kissed her forehead. 'I love you too, Tabby dear. I only wish I were your age and could experience all the exciting things you've got ahead of you. You're a very special girl.'

'Don't go overdoing it at Zumba when I'm away,' Tabby said, scoffing down her breakfast. 'I don't want to come back to find you've tangled yourself in a knot.' She wrapped her arms around her grandmother.

'I can make no promises,' Gran said. 'I'm training for OAP Zumba Champion of the Year. It keeps me young!'

Tabby spent the last few minutes before Ed was due to arrive double-checking she had everything she needed. She ran through the list on her phone, and looked around her room to make sure she hadn't left anything she would need.

Before she could check again – *Now you're being silly, Tabby* – she heard a horn beeping outside. *This is it*, she thought. She wasn't sure if she was more excited or nervous.

She grabbed her weekend bag, backpack and sleeping bag and took them into the hallway. 'They're here!' she called to Gran, who came out from the kitchen to stand at the front door.

'What if Mum asks where I am?' Tabby asked. *She'll freak if she finds out.*

'I told you,' Gran said. 'Leave your mother to me. I gave birth to her, didn't I? I know how to sort her out. Now go! Stop stalling! You've got memories to make.'

Tabby gave Gran the biggest hug she thought she'd ever given in her life, breathing in her lavender scent, then picked up her bag and tried to shield it from the rain as she ran to the van.

I'm really going to spend the next few days living out of this thing? It doesn't feel real!

Ed held the door open for Tabby and she climbed into the passenger seat, feeling damp already. She passed her bags back to Henry and Cassie to stow in the back. 'Is Olivia not here?'

Cassie and Henry looked tense.

'She wouldn't come out when I went to pick her up,' Ed said. 'I called her and waited and waited, but there wasn't so much as a curtain twitch. She's not coming.'

But without Olivia, there is no road trip. It would never be the same. This was all her idea.

'We need to go and get her,' Tabby said, and Henry nodded. 'Stick to the plan. Not take no for an answer. We have to believe that, deep down, she does want to come really.'

'If it means Olivia going and me staying, then I won't come. If that's what it takes, I'll do it,' Cassie said, doodling in her sketchbook to avoid looking anyone in the eye. Tabby noticed how exhausted she suddenly appeared, wearing far less make-up than usual.

'Either all of us are going, or none of us at all,' Tabby said. 'We're the Paper & Hearts Society. We're a team.'

With a beep of his horn, and a 'Let's do this,' Ed started the engine and they set off. Tabby turned to wave to Gran, but it was so rainy, she couldn't make her out.

Tabby was worried, of course, but she also couldn't stop thinking, *I'm going on a road trip! Me, Tabby, who's never stayed away for more than a sleepover without her family before. That's if Olivia comes . . .*

Ed turned the heating on as soon as they'd set off. He seemed in his element, in driver mode as they turned on to the main street and he concentrated on the road ahead, not saying anything for once. The only sound was the windscreen wipers squeaking as they moved back and forth.

'What are we going to do once we get to Olivia's?' Henry interrupted the silence.

'I'll go,' Tabby offered. 'I won't take no for an answer.'

'Fingers crossed it works,' Henry said, and smiled weakly.

Ed pulled into Olivia's street and found a parking spot to manoeuvre into.

'I'll be right back,' Tabby said, wincing as she opened the van door and the damp hit her. 'With Olivia in tow.'

She walked up to Olivia's house and knocked on the door. She tried to shelter as best as she could under the slight overhang of the door frame, but she still felt cold and damp. *Come on, Olivia. Answer!*

Nothing.

She knocked again. *I don't want to wake anyone.*

The door swung open. 'What do you want?' Olivia stood in the open doorway, glaring. When she saw it was Tabby, her expression softened. 'Oh, it's you. I thought it was . . . Never mind. What are you doing here, Tabby?'

'The question,' Tabby said, 'is what are *you* doing here? You should be in the van right now, on your way to Bath with us. What happened to the Three Musketeers but five of us with books and not swords? What happened to having the best bookish time of our lives? We need you!'

Olivia shook her head, her mouth a tight line. 'You don't.'

'Oh yeah? Who's going to give Ed directions if you're not there? We'll end up in Scotland if we're not careful.'

She grimaced. 'Cassie doesn't need me. She made that clear.'

Tabby tried to reach out for her, but Olivia skirted her touch. 'Cassie needs you more than she needs anyone else.'

'She's got a funny way of showing it.'

Tabby snorted. 'Now you're just being stubborn. Look, I'll give you ten minutes to get your stuff packed. If you're not in the van by then, we're leaving without you. Your choice.' *This has got to work; it's the only plan we have.*

There was a shuffling behind Olivia that revealed itself to be Olivia's mum. She placed her hand on Olivia's shoulder. 'Livvy, why haven't you got your bags yet? We agreed you'd go. Hello, Tabby! Are you excited for the road trip?'

Tabby raised her eyebrows at Olivia, who looked particularly sheepish. 'I'm just going to go and grab my stuff now,' she said. 'I'll be right there, Tabby.'

And with that, Olivia disappeared into the house, leaving Tabby with Olivia's mum.

'She's been looking forward to this for weeks,' she said, and leant past Tabby to wave to Ed in the van; Cassie and Henry couldn't be seen. 'It's so sad the weather isn't nice for you.'

But Tabby couldn't pay as much attention to her as she would have liked because all she could think was, *Does this mean it's actually worked? How did I just manage that?*

Olivia came back with five tote bags draped across her shoulders. *What has she got in there, the kitchen sink? There's no way one person can need that much stuff.*

She wouldn't meet Tabby's eye as she gave her mum a hug and pulled on her shoes and jacket.

'Have an amazing time! Don't forget the camping chairs,' Olivia's mum said, handing the fold-up chairs to them in one hand while sheltering herself from the rain with the other.

'Do you want to sit up front with Ed?' Tabby asked Olivia.

'Okay.'

'Shall I take your bags from you and pop them in the back?'

'No, thanks. I'm fine.'

I'm not the enemy here!

Olivia strode off, getting into the front without another word. Tabby found her new seat in the back, between Cassie and Henry, just like when they'd gone to the lake, and buckled up.

Henry tapped her on the shoulder. 'What's going on?' he mouthed.

She shrugged, as if to say, 'I'm as clueless as you are.'

'I'm only here,' Olivia said, not even turning around, 'because I shouldn't have to miss out and I thought of this whole thing, including the Paper & Hearts Society group. That's all.'

Henry cleared his throat. 'Can we please agree to enjoy ourselves? How many people have best friends they can travel with like this? We don't need to spoil it by constantly arguing. I'm here to have a good time whether you like it or not.'

'Exactly,' Tabby agreed, trying to inject far more cheer into her voice than she actually felt. 'We're here now. We have to make the most of it!'

'Maybe you should tell that to some other people,' Olivia muttered. Cassie shifted awkwardly in her seat next to Tabby.

It was a long journey to Bath. Not because of the distance – it only took an hour and a half from Dorset – but because you could cut the tension with a knife.

'Have you got any music, Ed?' Tabby asked as they left their town behind, and he turned on the CD player.

Take That's 'A Million Love Songs' began to play. 'Ugh, my mum was the last one to use the van,' he said, but let it continue anyway, drumming his fingers to the rhythm on the steering wheel.

Awkwaarrrddddd.

Henry coughed. 'Have you not got anything else?'

'There should be a purple tote bag in the back,' Ed said. 'Rummage around in there. See what our options are.'

Tabby picked it up from the floor in front of her. 'Umm . . . Looks like it's either Dolly Parton, Elvis Presley or old-school Justin Bieber? What's up with your mum's taste in music?'

Ed bit his lip but didn't take his eyes off the road. 'Actually, that last one is mine.'

'I *knew* you were a secret Justin Bieber fan.'

'Secret?' he said. 'It was never a secret, baby!'

Tabby passed the Dolly Parton CD forward to Ed.

'You know, Tabby,' Olivia said from the front, still not turning around, 'I think it's so lovely how close you and Ed have become lately. You're such *true* friends.'

'What's that supposed to mean?' Cassie cut in, hurt on her face.

'Nothing.' Olivia sat further back in her seat, crossing her arms.

'It didn't sound like nothing,' Cassie pushed. Tabby could tell she was getting fed up of treading on eggshells.

'Here we go . . .' Henry shook his head, wincing at the evil look Olivia shot Cassie as she spun round.

'Oh, sorry, did you say something?' Olivia spat. 'I didn't quite hear you.'

Cassie shook her head and closed her eyes.

'I love this song!' Ed practically screamed, turning it up. 'Come on, everyone. Sing along!'

It was '9 to 5', but no one else sang. It seemed everyone was happy to let Ed, who knew all the lyrics, take the limelight.

Tabby felt her phone vibrate in her pocket.

Henry: I am so fed up of this. It can't go on. It'll make the entire road trip torture

She lifted her head up to find Henry looking at her.

Tabby: I know, but what can we do? We've just got to put up with it. We'll have to resort to chatting over Messenger if we have to. I am fluent in emoji

By the time they'd crossed over the Dorset border and skirted their way around Wiltshire, heading straight for Bath in North Somerset, the rain had ceased, and the sun was beginning to poke through the clouds.

Olivia was finally speaking again, but only to give Ed directions; he couldn't bear the satnav's voice and claimed he'd throw Olivia's phone out of the window if she turned it on again.

The buildings began to change as they got into Bath – tall, sandy-stoned houses grew out of the streets, imposing and magnificent. Each had its own character and charm, its own story. It made Tabby feel homesick – the Regency architecture reminded her so much of her hometown of Cheltenham.

Ed found the car park they'd planned to stop at, carefully reversing into a space and switching the ignition off. 'Holy Jane Austen, am I glad to be here.'

'Out of the van, you two,' Henry said, ushering to Tabby and Ed. 'Cassie, Olivia, you stay exactly where you are. You're going to sort this out now, or I'll make Ed turn around and go home.'

'I'm not doing this now,' Olivia said, opening the door and stepping one foot out. 'No way.'

'Just sit down,' Henry said, with more force than Tabby had ever heard him use, as he got out of the van. 'Talk. Now.'

Tabby and Ed darted a glance at one another before quickly grabbing their backpacks, stepping out of the van and shutting the doors.

'If this works, I want a knighthood,' Henry said.

'If it works,' Tabby said, 'I will find a sword and knight you myself.'

'Shh . . .' Ed said. 'If we strain our ears enough, we'll be able to hear.'

They all leant against the van behind the passenger windows so they couldn't be seen.

'Livs . . . You're my best friend, my number one. I hate fighting with you. It feels so wrong. It's not us.'

'You should have thought about that. I've been nothing but supportive of you. I've held your hand through the past year, wiped your tears away, spoken to you at all times of the day and night when you needed me, and just once I wanted something in return. I wanted you to listen to what I had to say, but you couldn't even do that.'

'I was in shock,' Cassie was saying. Tabby imagined her with her hands in her perfectly put together hair, pulling at it in frustration. 'Never in a million years did I expect you to say what you said. I didn't think you felt that way about me.'

'It doesn't matter now. I said it. It's done. But I take it back. Just forget it.'

'You take it back?' Tabby imagined Cassie freezing, her mouth gaping open. She repeated herself. 'You take it back? All of it?'

'Yeah, that's what I said. It clearly meant nothing to you.'

There was a sob. 'Nothing? It *didn't* mean nothing to me! That's the problem. Don't you see? It means *too much* to me, Olivia. It means too much to me and it terrifies me.' There was a pause and Cassie's voice turned softer. 'I panicked, Livs. And I messed up, big time. I *can't* lose you too.'

And there it was. The truth. The heart of Cassie.

'I've already lost my dad. Do you know what it would be like if you were gone too? Even thinking about it tears me in two. I know that if we were in a relationship, I'd hurt you. I'd upset you or things would end messily, and I wouldn't be able to live with myself. I can barely keep myself together.'

Olivia's voice was soft too. 'So you were so scared you'd mess things up that you messed them up anyway?'

Another pause. And then a strangled laugh. 'Hey, I didn't say it made any sense.' Pause. 'What do you want, Livs? I'm listening now.'

'I just want everything to go back to normal,' Olivia said. 'Even if you don't feel that way about me, I don't want things to change. We're best friends first. "One word from you will silence me on this subject for ever."'

'Are you seriously quoting Mr Darcy? At a time like this?'

There was a sob and then silence and then a giggle and then silence again.

She didn't know why she did it, but in that moment Tabby looked across at Ed, expecting to find him concentrating on being able to hear. Instead, his face was contorting, his mouth opening wide, and his nostrils flared.

'*Ah-CHOO!*' he sneezed, banging his head against the van.

'What are you doing?' The van door slid open, revealing Cassie, with Olivia behind her. Their faces were flushed, their eyes bright. They both looked like they'd been crying. Cassie had her make-up bag out and was holding a deep red lipstick in one hand, her compact mirror in the other.

'Tabby lost a contact lens,' Ed blurted out, looking down at the ground and rubbing his head in pain.

Cassie put a hand on her hip, drawing out the movement so that it seemed to last a century. 'Tabby doesn't wear contact lenses, do you, Tabby?'

Tabby froze to the spot, looking desperately round at Henry and Ed, her eyes so wide they began to sting. She was suddenly very conscious of the glasses on her face. 'Someti—'

'She thought she saw one,' Ed interrupted. 'On the floor. Under the van. We were looking for it.'

'Right . . .' Cassie raised one eyebrow. 'Did you find it?'

Ed shook his head over-dramatically. 'No. I think it was a bit of dirt. Stupid Tabby!' He gently smacked her on the arm, starting up an awkward chorus of laughter.

'Stupid me,' Tabby said, throwing her hands in the air. 'Maybe I should get my eyes checked after all.'

'Guys?' Olivia said, following Cassie out of the van. 'Forget what I said before. I will never, ever turn my back on the Paper & Hearts Society. I love you too much for that.'

I think I may be in a dream, Tabby thought. Judging by Henry's and Ed's reactions, they obviously felt the same way too.

We've just got to embrace this for what it is. Explanations can come later. 'And we love you too, Livs. Now can we go and see Bath already? I'm way too excited.'

JANE AUSTEN

Born: 16 December 1775

Notable Works: *Pride and Prejudice*, *Persuasion*, *Sense and Sensibility*, *Northanger Abbey*.

About: Jane Austen was born in Steventon, Hampshire. She lived in Bath between 1801 and 1806 and is best known for her books about comedy of manners and the society of Georgian England.

Died: 18 July 1817

Chapter Sixteen

Olivia dug around in her bag, balancing it on one knee as she held a leg in the air, grinning to herself. 'Stop it!' she said, hearing the others' groans as she pulled her hand out. 'They're fun!'

Revealing five pastel-pink flower crowns, like something you saw on a Snapchat filter, she handed one to each of the road-trippers.

'I like it,' Tabby said, fixing hers around her hair so that it wouldn't fall off. The plastic petals were surprisingly soft, the band moulding around her head so that she could hardly feel it. It transported her back to being six years old again and running around the garden of a friend whose birthday party had been fairy-themed.

Cassie took hers from Olivia, placed it on her head and used her compact mirror to check that every single hair was in the correct place. 'Your turn, Ed.'

Ed took a crown in a reluctant move. 'Nobody look!'

he called out, tucking his head down into his shirt. 'You'll all laugh at me!'

'We won't laugh,' Tabby said. 'Come on, show us!'

He ducked around the side of the van, and when he peeped his head over the top the flower crown sat in the middle of his head. Tabby's face heated up as she tried to hold in the laugh, but she couldn't – it was like trying to keep all the air in a balloon when you'd already let go and it was speeding around the room. She spluttered along with everyone else.

'See!' Ed said, his face bright red. 'I knew you'd laugh!'

Cassie leant over and flicked him on the head with her fingers. 'You look like you've walked out of a meme.'

'I do not,' he said, looking in the wing mirror closely. 'Okay, maybe I do . . .'

'How about you, Henry? Or are you too hipster for a flower crown?' Tabby raised her eyebrows, challenging him. She stole the crown out of his hands and placed it on his head, making the others burst into laughter again.

'Not a hipster,' Henry griped, though he couldn't help but laugh too when Olivia snapped a photo on her phone to show him.

'Okay, peasants! We are ready to go! Follow me!' Olivia called.

They walked down the hill out of the car park, playing follow-my-leader behind Olivia. If Tabby looked up high enough, past the tarmac on the roads, and blocked out the sound of car engines, she could almost see it as it once was in Jane Austen's day – the architecture and the skyline had hardly changed at all.

'Where are we going?' Ed asked, trying to keep up. Olivia was on a mission, and nothing was going to stop her from reaching it. Her flower crown sat atop her head, her yellow rain mac unzipped with the edges flying about, as she pushed her way through the crowds.

Then she spun around, walking backwards so she was facing them, without caring if she bumped into anything. 'We, my lovely friends, are here to soak up the atmosphere and relax. I have it all planned out, don't worry! But first: ice cream.'

Henry reached out an arm to stop her from crashing into a tourist; Ed clapped his hands, rubbing his palms together. 'Lead the way, mighty Olivia!'

They walked further down the streets, past the various shops and the abbey, snaking round to the River Avon. Tabby lagged purposefully behind, trying to take in everything she could see – the people crowding the pavements chattering in different languages, the windows of independent shops containing little trinkets and gifts. It reminded her of a game she used to play when she was younger, imagining the lives of the people she passed in the street: who they were, what their jobs could be, and the big life event that had changed them for ever. She wondered if other people did the same and what they'd think of her, whether they'd think up something exciting or mundane. Everyone had a story. If only she could be honest about hers to the people she loved the most.

They came to a stand-still by stone railings, overlooking the weir and Pulteney Bridge. Gulls floated on the surface, flexing their wings and squawking over the rush of water. The bridge was an incredible structure – shops crossed the full span on both sides, and where it adjoined the building to the right, people sat around on a terrace, lifting cups up to drink. It was clear that this wasn't just any bridge; it demanded attention.

'There's a shop over there that sells ice cream, I think.' Olivia stood in front of the other four, phone open to her notes app. 'My parents gave me the cash and told me to treat you all, so you can put your money away and, Ed, you come with me. I'm sure your muscles need a workout so carrying ice cream will do.'

Ed raised his arm, tensing the muscle. His skin was covered with small constellations of beauty spots, dark against his pale flesh. It barely moved as he strained to flex it.

'Weakling,' Cassie called. 'I have more strength in my little toe than you have in your whole body.'

'Just because I don't spend all day lifting weights in the gym, doesn't mean I'm weak. I have a strong personality.'

'That's all that matters, Ed,' Tabby consoled.

'Flavour preferences?' Olivia asked.

'Mint choc chip, obviously.' Cassie leant an elbow against the balustrade effortlessly, her brown bob brushing against the collar of her denim jacket. She'd emblazoned fabric badges and enamel pins on the front and the arms.

One read, 'Feminist AF', while another displayed the iconic *Jane Eyre* quote, 'I'm no bird; and no net ensnares me.'

'Strawberry, please,' Henry said, and blanched at the funny looks he got in return. 'What? What's wrong with that?'

Tabby tried to look blasé. 'Oh, nothing. I just had you pinned down as a more adventurous ice cream lover, that's all.' She kept her face dead straight and attempted to keep eye contact.

'You're right; I should have chosen something masculine instead, like the tears of cute puppies or . . . or sweat. Very macho.' His subsequent grin made Tabby's stomach flip.

'Tabby?' Olivia asked.

'Uhh . . .' Her voice stuck in her throat at the thought of deciding. 'Just vanilla for me, thanks.'

Henry leant in deliberately close. 'Not something more exotic? I didn't have you pegged down as the boring type, Tabby.'

She pushed his arm. 'Shut it, Gillingham.'

'Or . . .?' His breath tickled against her ear. Her breath caught in her throat.

'Or . . . Well, I don't know. But it will be something very horrible.'

The others were staring at them. Cassie had her eyebrow raised; Olivia exchanged a look with Ed.

'What is it?' Tabby asked, scratching her neck.

'We said we were going,' Olivia said. 'Will you be okay here while we're gone?'

'I think it's me you should be asking that to,' Cassie said, her dry tone more prominent than ever.

Tabby pretended she hadn't heard and fixed her gaze on an abandoned piece of chewing gum on the pavement.

'Well, we're going . . .' Olivia said.

'Be good, kids!' Ed called as they retreated.

Cassie had taken her phone out of her jacket pocket. Tabby was watching, mostly to avoid accidentally flirting with Henry. Or maybe it wasn't an accident.

'Are you looking forward to your stop on the trip, Cass?' Henry asked.

'Yeah,' she replied, and went back to her phone. End of conversation.

‘Are you?’ Tabby asked him. ‘You still haven’t revealed what you’re up to.’

‘It’s a secret,’ he said, tapping the side of his nose. ‘Just wait and see.’

‘Mysterious,’ Tabby sang under her breath, which earnt her a dig in the ribs.

Tabby and Henry looked down at the weir, watching the gulls bobbing on the water, cawing for attention.

Something had shifted, something Tabby felt afraid to acknowledge or admit. *We’re friends*, she scolded herself. *He’s not interested.*

Her body refused to listen to her, though.

When she’d been younger, she’d thought that when you touched someone, they would be able to read your thoughts. That Gran would know that it was her who had stolen the last chocolate biscuit from the tin, and that Mum would discover it was her who had spilt glitter paint all over the carpet rather than the friend she had over to play. Tabby wished more than anything she could reach across now, touch Henry’s arm and find out how he really felt about her.

‘Ladies and gentlemen, boys and girls, we bring you ice cream!’ Olivia and Ed appeared, carrying mini tubs of ice cream. ‘Vanilla for you, Tabby . . . Here’s yours, Henry . . . Cassie, mint choc chip!’

They moved over to sit on a grassy area on the other side of the road, which they then discovered was actually a roundabout, albeit one of the most scenic roundabouts Tabby had ever seen.

Ed lay on the grass, his limbs splayed out in front of him. 'To friends!' he cried, toasting his ice cream in the air.

'Who said we're your friends? I thought you knew we're just using you because you can drive.' Cassie stuck her tongue out at him, twisting round and leaning against Olivia's knees.

Ed clutched a hand to his heart, rubbing at an imaginary tear from the corner of his eye. 'You pain me.'

'What's the plan next?' Tabby asked, finishing her final mouthful of ice cream and craning her head around Ed's body to look at Olivia.

'A tour! I have it all planned out. Trust me.'

'Let me guess,' Ed grumbled. 'More walking?'

But he followed along anyway. He always did.

They'd been walking for at least half an hour and Tabby was beginning to feel short of breath. Olivia had led them to the Royal Crescent, a grand Georgian structure renowned for appearing on Bath postcards, and had proudly exclaimed, 'Jane Austen mentioned it in *Northanger Abbey* and *Persuasion*. It's like we're really in the books!'

Then she'd *persuaded* them to walk past a house Jane Austen had stayed at on Gay Street, walking down one of the many Bath hills from the Royal Crescent to get there, before wandering through the high street.

It was the worst way she could have organised her tour; it meant they'd had to walk down hills away from the car park, only to retrace their steps to go higher again.

'If we don't stop soon, I'm going to collapse in a heap on the ground,' Cassie complained. 'I need to rest. We've been walking round and round in circles.'

Olivia stopped. 'Well, I do have one more idea up my sleeve . . .' They were standing at the bottom of Milsom Street and, with a 'I think this is the way,' they gave into following Olivia once more.

It's like a wild goose chase, Tabby thought, *except we're not even chasing anything.*

They didn't need to go far; what Olivia was looking for was only around the corner. They may have been walking for what felt like hours, but their energy returned as soon as they spotted it: Topping & Company Booksellers. *A bookshop!*

It had a warm, inviting shopfront, just as any good bookshop should, and it had the same feeling on the inside too.

Walking in, Tabby entered a book lover's haven. Running down the middle of the shop were tables laden with carefully chosen books, and all of the wall space was taken up with bookshelves. She was sure she was walking with her mouth gawping open.

Woah. 'This is *seriously impressive*,' she said. This was the dream. If she lived in Bath, she'd be in here every day and would have no money left because she'd buy so many books.

Cassie was taking so many pictures, spinning around to get new angles, that Tabby thought she must be dizzy. 'I've got to draw this as soon as I can,' Cassie said in awe. 'It's like a book cave in here! So awesome.'

Henry had loped off to one of the recesses, moving back and forth as he looked for a book. Tabby thought it was cute how he was biting his lip as he searched, but she left him to it, and joined Olivia in the children's section at the back of the shop.

'I just *can't*,' Olivia said to her. 'Isn't this perfect? I've always wanted to visit.' Like Henry, she also searched back and forth over the bookcases, but she put more energy into it, humming as she went.

'Got it!' she said, and pulled out a copy of *Nevermoor* by Jessica Townsend. 'I've been wanting to read this for ages. My sister and her friends have all been reading it, but she won't let me borrow her copy. It's about a girl who's supposed to die on her eleventh birthday but gets whisked away instead to compete to join a society. Hey, like us!'

Ed came around the corner, then. 'Do you think they'll let me live here?'

'I highly doubt it,' Tabby said. 'You'd want to bring Mrs Simpkins and I don't know if she'd be good for business.'

She moved away to explore the rest of the shop. Henry was still in the corner he'd taken himself off to, but when she came up behind him, he nearly jumped out of his skin.

'You scared me,' he said, laughing. 'What are you doing?' He turned his back to the shelves, keeping his hands – and whatever was in them – behind him.

'What am *I* doing?' Tabby said. 'You're the one acting so weird.'

His shoulders visibly relaxed, but he still didn't move his hands. 'Okay, maybe that was the wrong question to ask.'

'You think?' she said, raising her eyebrows. 'You're up to something, I can tell.'

'Me?' She imagined he would have pointed to his chest if he had his hands free. 'Never.'

'I'm going to turn around now and leave you to be secretive on your own, but I fully expect you to reveal what you're scheming when you're done.'

He smiled and let her walk away, and out the corner of her eye she caught him finally move his hands from behind him and tuck a book between his arm and the side of his body.

Cassie was still playing with her phone when Tabby

found her near the front of the shop, but she stopped when she saw Tabby coming.

'Are you going to buy anything?' Tabby asked.

Cassie shrugged. 'Nope, don't think so, but I got some good drawing inspiration so it's not too bad. You?'

'Me neither. I think Olivia's got enough for both of us.'

Olivia, Ed and Henry were queued up at the till with the books they'd picked out, so Tabby and Cassie waited outside for them.

'Hey, Cassie,' Tabby said. 'How did you get into drawing? You're so good at it.'

Cassie smiled. 'The first time I can really remember thinking, *I'd love to do that for the rest of my life* was at a cousin's wedding when I was little. Before the wedding, I was watching a mehndi artist working on my mum's hand, and it was the most beautiful thing I'd ever seen. Have you ever seen henna tattoos? They're incredible. Even at that young age, I could recognise the skill that goes into art. And ever since, I've worked hard so that one day I can live my dream.'

Tabby smiled back. 'That's such a nice story.'

'I hadn't thought of that for ages,' she said. 'Huh.'

Henry was the last to come out of the shop, after Olivia and Ed, carrying a paper bag.

He looked shy as he held it out to Tabby. 'Don't freak out, but I bought you something. It's only little, but it reminded me of a conversation we had before. I thought you might like it.'

She gave him a questioning look, but he pushed her to open it, excited. As slowly as she could, drawing out every motion, she reached her hand inside the bag and pulled it out. It felt like a hardback without a dust jacket, and anticipation prickled over her skin as she waited to see what it was.

Oh my. 'Henry . . .' she gasped, running her hands over the cover. 'This isn't little! This is . . . it's incredible. *Thank you.*'

She'd never received a gift like it before. Not something unprompted, unexpected.

Because there, held between her hands, was the most exquisite copy of *The Bell Jar* by Sylvia Plath Tabby had ever seen. It was different to her second-hand paperback and the library copy she'd been borrowing; it was black with a gold spiral adorning the cover and – she opened it up and put her nose inside – it smelled good too. *Was that weird?* She always liked to smell new books.

There was only one thing for it. She reached up and hugged him. Only for a second, but it was enough.

She couldn't stop grinning as the five of them went in search of food, heading back down yet another hill.

Tabby ended up walking next to Cassie. 'I'm trying to look into this oakavenue52 account,' she said. 'They've liked every single one of my pictures this morning. It gets creepier and creepier.'

'Maybe you could just block them?' *Yes, why hadn't she told them all to block the account? That would stop Jess.* 'They won't be able to see your pictures then, if you're worried about it.'

Cassie screwed up her face. 'I'm not worried,' she said. 'I'm *determined.* Aren't *you* worried? That was some pretty mean stuff they said about you.'

She tried to inject lightness into her reply. 'Oh, I'm sure it's just someone messing about. Nothing serious.'

But the little voice in her head said, *You should be worried. About Jess, and about what will happen if they ever find out.*

Ed led them into a traditional cafe selling cream teas. Huge scones with jam and cream were just what they needed.

I have to stop Jess and the oakavenue52 account before Cassie gets there first. My two worlds can't collide right now. Tabby tucked herself away in the corner of the table they'd chosen and got her phone out.

Henry went up to order for all of them, which left Tabby with Olivia and Cassie opposite, giggling, and Ed, who had taken the seat next to Tabby. He was trying to ignore them but failing. He kept nudging Tabby under the table with his leg.

@WhatTabbyDid *@oakavenue52 I know what you're doing and it won't work.*

'I'll just talk to myself,' Ed said. 'No problems here. Nobody worry about me.'

'Hmm?' Tabby snapped up, locking her phone. 'Oh, sorry. Just checking Facebook. More cat videos, as usual.'

'Ooh, let me see!' Ed said, but she angled her phone away from him.

Leave my friends out of it. They've got nothing to do with you.

Tabby clicked send before she could take it back. The read notification popped up within seconds. Then the dots appeared as Jess typed back, miles away, wherever she was – in her bedroom, in the supermarket, at the park. It didn't matter where; she was always online, in her messages and statuses and pictures. She was always haunting Tabby.

'Antisocial,' Ed coughed. 'I'll just sit here by myself, talking to myself, driving myself insane by listening to the continuous sound of my own voice.'

'Do you have to be so irritating?' Tabby snapped before she could help it. She looked up from her screen to find Ed gaping at her.

'Sorry,' she said, pinching the bridge of her nose. 'I didn't mean that.'

Henry came back then, carrying a tray with big pots of tea and scones. He placed it down in the middle of the table.

'What's going on?' he asked.

The typing bubbles disappeared from Tabby's phone screen.

'I think Tabby's hangry,' Ed said. 'I've never seen her like this before but I'm very concerned. Here, Tabby, you can have my extra scone if you like.'

'Thanks,' she said, 'but I'll be fine.'

Chapter Seventeen

The square outside Bath Abbey was packed with people: tourists like them, someone busking with a guitar, young children chasing their shadows as the afternoon sun rotated in the sky. And pigeons. Lots of pigeons.

They'd only just arrived outside the abbey when Cassie declared she had some important shopping to do, dragging Olivia off with her after promising they could find a bookshop on the way. Tabby knew it was just an excuse for them to spend time together, especially after everything that had happened, but that didn't stop it from being any less boring as they waited for them to return. So much for Olivia's tour guide plans . . . The carefully timed itinerary had gone out the window.

Tabby was staring down at her phone. *Again*. 'I can't believe they'd abandon us like this. They said they'd be back by now, didn't they?' The screen was blank, her notifications empty.

Henry, standing next to her, rolled his eyes. 'For the five hundred billionth time, yes. But don't worry about it. You know what Cassie and Olivia are like.'

'That's the thing,' Ed moaned. 'We don't know what they're like any more.'

'Have you got signal on your phone?' Tabby asked Ed.

'Chill!' Henry said, pulling on the strap of her rucksack. 'We'll find them, okay? They've probably lost track of time and will come running back soon.'

Ed snorted. 'That's if they want to come back and hang out with us . . .' He'd been making similar comments ever since they'd gone off, scuffing his shoes on the ground and making a bad attempt at trying to act as if he didn't care. 'It's not that I'm unhappy . . .' he continued. 'It's just none of us have ever been in relationships. I don't want it to change anything – make us split off and divide or something.'

'That's understandable. At least you're talking to us about it,' Henry said.

'I'm getting in touch with my emotions,' Ed grumbled, looking at Tabby. 'I'm trying to be a better man.'

Tabby felt odd around Ed, guilty about her earlier outburst. She'd apologised again, but he'd told her to forget about it and concentrate on getting her blood sugar levels back up. Plus she was now feeling extra guilt building about knowing who was stalking them all on Instagram and not telling them.

Suddenly Ed's expression changed. He looked like a child at Christmas, filled with excitable energy. 'Wait here! I've just had the perfect idea.'

Before Henry or Tabby could protest, he ran away, blending in with the crowds. Tabby looked concerned.

'Maybe you should check your phone to see if he's messaged you about where he's going,' Henry teased.

She narrowed her eyes. 'Are you mocking me?' She folded her arms across her chest but couldn't maintain her serious pose for long. 'Okay, maybe I should chill a little bit.'

'See? I'm always right.'

'Not always, He—' But she was cut off by Henry grabbing her hand and leading her across to a recently vacated bench. *Oh god, is this another moment or is he just being friendly? Why can't I read the signs?*

They sat side by side, watching the pigeons waddle along the ground looking for tiny scraps of food. 'So, it's just us,' she said, feeling betrayed by the slight wobble in her voice. 'We obviously smell or something, seeing as the others couldn't wait to get away from us.'

Henry leant back into the bench, stretching his legs in front of his body. 'It does seem that way.'

'Well, it must be you. It's definitely not me.'

He twisted around so that he was grinning right at her. 'Are you sure about that?'

She poked him in the side and laughed. 'Definitely.'

The sun shone through his hair, highlighting the ends golden as he smiled down at her. They really were sat very closely – far too close really, if she thought about it enough. Friends didn't sit this near, their body heat radiating to each other's skin, enough that it made Tabby's heart hammer in her chest, enough that her lips parted in anticipation. Maybe, just maybe, this time would be . . .

'I'm back!'

Tabby shot up, the jolt sending a ripple of pain up her neck as she turned to find Ed behind them, his hands resting on the back of the bench.

'What did I miss?' He had a lazy grin on his face, a box in his hands.

Tabby cleared her throat. 'Um, nothing. There was a pigeon on the floor and . . .' She trailed off. *Shut up, Tabby. He saw, you idiot! Pigeon . . . Where did that even come from?*

There was still a spring in his step as Ed came to sit down on the bench, opting to squeeze in between them. He looked back and forth between Tabby and Henry. 'Nice pigeon, was it?'

'What have you got in the box?' Henry asked, Tabby cursing his ability to change the subject so easily. *How is he always so composed?*

'Wait until you see this! I've always wanted one.' He picked at the Sellotape on the box with a fingernail, ripping it open and pulling out a metal contraption.

'What is it?' Tabby furrowed her brow.

Ed shook his head in disbelief. '"What is it?"' he repeated in an imitation of Tabby's voice. 'This, Tabitha, is a selfie stick! How do you not know that? I can't believe I didn't think to get one before.'

'A selfie stick.' Henry's expression was blank. 'But why?'

'Why not?' Ed got his phone out of his rucksack and started fitting it to the stick, checking it was on properly and setting the timer on his camera before holding it up in the air, the metal stretching out to get them all in the frame.

'Say cheese!' he called. 'Or should that be "pigeons"?' The camera clicked, the photo appearing in the tiny box in the left-hand corner. He brought the selfie stick in, pressing on the photo to see it properly on the screen.

'Not good enough,' Ed said. 'My hair looks awful. New one, please!' Tabby also noticed that her hair needed brushing, but her Tangle Teezer was still in the van.

Tabby and Henry reached up to touch their heads at the same time, the flower crowns still stuck on top like tiny floral birds' nests. Until they'd seen the photo, they'd both forgotten they were there, even as they'd been looking at each other.

'Smile, you two!' Ed said, perfecting the art of ventriloquism as he kept his mouth straight for the picture. Just as the timer counted down, his phone buzzed with a message, and Tabby rushed forward to read it.

'Hey!' Ed said. 'We'll have to do another one! That's just a close-up of your mane of hair.'

'It's Olivia! Read it, Ed. Quick!'

He unfastened his phone from the stick, tapping on the message with one finger and shoving the selfie stick into Henry's chest. 'They want us to meet them somewhere . . . Livs has sent a screenshot of Google Maps.'

The location was on the other side of the river, over Pulteney Bridge, the same bridge they'd stood looking at earlier. 'Sydney Place,' Tabby read out. 'I suppose we'd better set off, then?'

Ed shook his head, fiddling around with his phone. 'First I've got to upload one of these selfies to Instagram. Got to keep my fans happy. Which do you think shows my best side?'

He turned the screen to show Henry, who looked almost disgusted. 'Ed, apart from us, it's only your mum who follows you.'

'And? At least she'll be able to show Mrs Simpkins.'

'Ready now?' Henry repeated when Ed was done, and they set off.

Ed navigated, claiming he'd once been in the Cubs and was very good at it, but Henry and Tabby ended up taking over. It turned out that Ed had only lasted a week and hadn't got to the map-reading part.

They walked down a long avenue of grand Georgian houses, their tall Bath stone exteriors catching the light of the afternoon. Tabby felt as though they'd just walked on to the set of a period drama. It wasn't hard to picture horse and carts and fancy carriages driving along here with rich passengers on their way to take the waters in the Roman baths.

They rounded the corner of Great Pulteney Street to Sydney Place and saw Olivia and Cassie standing a way down it. They hadn't seen Henry, Ed and Tabby coming towards them, or Tabby assumed Cassie would have removed her hand from around Olivia's waist.

Ed whistled, low and long. From down the street, Olivia's head snapped to attention, her eyes resting on the three of them coming towards her.

'Hi!' she called, extricating herself from Cassie's touch. 'You found us!'

'You were a bit elusive for a while,' Tabby said, 'but we amused ourselves, don't you worry.'

Ed nudged Tabby's arm. 'Someone over here made friends with the pigeons. She's quite the Doctor Dolittle, you know!'

Tabby blushed, betraying her emotions for all to see. For once, she just wanted a moment with Henry where something didn't interrupt them.

'Why here?' Henry asked, looking up at the row of buildings. Houses once, now presumably flats. A black bin bag hung on one of the rungs of the building in front of them; a bike leant against the railing. Number four, Sydney Place.

'This, my friends,' Olivia said, spreading her hands out, 'is the place that Jane Austen resided when she was in Bath. I thought we should come and pay homage.'

They craned their heads to see to the top, chimneys piled high on the roof. 'Can you believe that Jane Austen probably stood in this exact spot?' Olivia said, reverence in her voice. 'The greatest author of all time. Right here. Alive. Here.'

'Here?' Henry asked. 'Be quite clear now: was it here?'

'Shush, you,' she scolded. Olivia took a step backwards with an intake of breath and looked over to Cassie, raising her eyebrows. Cassie nodded, one sharp movement of her head. That was all it took.

'Um, guys?' Cassie said, shuffling from one foot to the

other, her hand wrapped around her neck. 'Can we tell you something?'

Their bodies moved closer together of their own accord, so that they were almost leaning on each other. Their shoulders brushed – once, twice – a reassurance: *I'm here.*

Tabby knew what Olivia was going to say before she said it.

'So . . . uh . . . Me and Cassie . . . Cassie and I . . . We . . .' She cleared her throat, eyes darting frantically around as they tried to find the best place to fix on to. 'We are, well . . . I suppose we have a thing going on.'

Ed raised an eyebrow; Henry scratched his head.

'Oh, come on, Livs.' Cassie took over, grinning. 'What Olivia means to tell you is that we have finally sorted ourselves out and would like to announce to you that we are now an item. Although not in a literal sense; don't objectify women, kids. Wedding invitations to follow soon.'

A splutter erupted from Olivia's throat. It looked to Tabby like she was overheating, going into overload. 'Uh . . . Well . . . Um . . .'

'It was a joke, Livs,' Cassie said, beaming from ear to ear. 'Now, can we all go back to normal? I want to enjoy this road trip without all the confusion and drama.'

'Oh my dear, sweet GOD.' Ed clamped his hands to his face, dragging his eyelids down with force as he looked at his phone.

What now?! I thought he'd at least pretend to be happy for them! Oh god, it's Jess again, isn't it . . .

Olivia bit her lip, fiddling with the sleeve of her cardigan.

'The parking ticket runs out in five minutes! We'll never get back in time. My mum will kill me if I get the van clamped!' He ran his fingers through his hair, kicked at an invisible stone on the pavement.

'We'll have to try,' Tabby said. 'We can run for it, can't we?'

'Across town? We'll never make it!'

'Come on,' she said. 'Where's your sense of adventure? We just need one of us to get there on time.' She patted Ed on the shoulder. 'We've got this.'

'If I trip,' Cassie said with a steely glare, 'I am suing you, Edward.'

'No time for that,' Ed said, drawing in a big breath. 'We need to go!'

The sight of five teenagers running for their lives through the streets of Bath, rucksacks on their backs, probably should have seemed out of place, but nobody paid any attention to them. They ran back the way they'd come, over Pulteney Bridge and through the streets, their breath sounding in their ears and stitches in their sides.

Olivia suddenly stopped and bent down, clutching herself just below her ribs. 'You go ahead,' she said to Tabby, who had just passed her. 'I'll catch up at some point.'

Tabby was properly running, letting the moment sweep her up; she felt alive as she kicked her feet against the pavement and let her body go. *This is what it should feel like.* The escape, the release. The total freedom.

She was getting closer to Ed now, out in front, propelled by the urgency to get back. Tabby pulled up alongside him, watching the look on his face as he noticed her, and then she was overtaking, reaching her hand out to take the keys from him like they were in a relay race.

Tabby used the rest of her reserve when she could see the car park in sight, only slowing down once she was over the hill. She gulped in air like she hadn't been breathing. It almost did feel like that – she'd used parts of her body she'd forgotten could be used, had cleared her mind as she thought about nothing but her feet on the floor, the swing of arms as they propelled her forward.

Her first priority was getting a new ticket. She went over to the machine and pulled her purse from her bag, slotting the coins in and pushing the button. Every second felt like an hour passing as she waited for the ticket to come out, but eventually it did, and she half-jogged over to the van.

She unlocked it and hopped up into the driver's seat, touching the steering wheel with the palm of her hand. She reached forward to retrieve the old ticket and replace it with the new one.

That's weird. She got out her phone, checked the clock, looked back down at the ticket. It didn't run out for another hour. She checked again, just in case. No, it definitely hadn't run out. She popped it back on the dashboard, jumped out of the van and shut the door behind her. She leant up against it, stretching the muscles in her legs out slowly, feeling the soft aches in them.

It was another four minutes before Ed turned up, dragging his legs behind him. His face was tomato red, his breathing heavy in his chest.

'What happened to you?' she said, folding her arms over her body.

Ed collapsed on the tarmac, shaking his head. 'I don't think that was a good idea.'

'You're right,' Tabby said, figuring the best way was just to tell him straight. 'Because the ticket doesn't run out for another hour. At least we got in the exercise, though, hey?'

'What?' Ed looked up at her as if she'd sprouted another head.

She said it slower this time. 'The ticket doesn't run out for another hour. We just ran across the city for no reason.'

‘Ha ha, very funny. I thought I was the comedian of the group.’

‘Ed, I’m serious. We didn’t need to run back. It hasn’t run out.’

Ed heaved himself off the ground, opening the van door and checking the ticket himself. He quickly pocketed it, looking over his shoulder as he did. ‘We can’t tell the others about this.’

‘Don’t be silly,’ Tabby said. ‘You only made a mistake.’

‘Not just a mistake! They’ll kill me. You know how much Cassie hates exercise. Anyway, where did that insane running talent come from? You’ve been hiding it from us!’

Tabby smiled. ‘Not hiding, just not showing. It isn’t that important.’

Ed held out his hand for Tabby to high-five. ‘Girl, you are seriously talented! You’ve got moves!’

‘Oh, stop it. I just enjoy it, that’s all.’

She shuffled from foot to foot, scrunching up her face. ‘I’m, uh . . . I really am sorry, about before. I shouldn’t have snapped at you like I did.’

Ed put his arm around her shoulders and ruffled her hair. ‘You think that’s the worst I’ve heard? I am friends with Cassie, you know. Anyway, we had to have our first argument at some point. At least we’ve got it out of the way now.’

'It is a relief.' She snuggled into his side. 'You're the best.'

'I know. I'm your fairy godmother and you're my bestie.'

Tabby raised her eyebrows. 'Bestie?'

'You, Tabitha Brown – wait, do you have a middle name?' She shook her head. 'Okay, you, Tabitha Brown, are my best friend. My confidante. My whole life.'

'Now you're being dramatic.' She thanked him by poking him in the cheek.

When Henry, Cassie and Olivia finally came down the hill towards them, walking beside each other like a pop band line-up, Tabby had begun to notice the sun shifting in the sky, casting the kind of shadows on the ground that could only mean evening was approaching.

'Did you get the parking sorted?' Olivia asked, surveying the van's wheels to check for clamps. She seemed satisfied once she saw Ed's and Tabby's relaxed faces.

'Yep, we sorted it, just in time.' Tabby noted the way Ed's body relaxed.

'We should grab some food to take back with us tonight. I think we passed a supermarket on our way in, didn't we?' Olivia said.

They'd booked a space on a campsite just outside of Bath, paid for by Ed's mum who liked to know they were all safe somewhere, not camped up on a roadside in the wilds of Somerset where anything could happen to them, or the van.

Tabby felt her tummy growl in response to Olivia's question.

'We'll head there then. It's a plan!' Ed said, jumping up into the driver's seat and adjusting the rear-view mirror. Olivia hopped up next to him in the passenger seat.

Tabby slid the main door open, clambering on to one of the seats at the back and yawning as she did up her seat belt. It seemed like they had covered so much ground already, and it was only the first day.

'When were you going to mention your marathon-level running skills, Tabby?' Henry said, grinning.

She shook her head. 'Very funny. There's nothing to mention.'

Ed scoffed. 'Yeah, right! You were like a whirlwind out there!'

'It's true,' Cassie said. 'If I ever need a superhero to model for one of my art projects, I know who to use now.'

Olivia grabbed Cassie's arm. 'A Paper & Hearts Society comic. Genius! Can you imagine it?'

'I'd rock the tight leggings and cape,' Ed said.

Although Tabby didn't want to admit it, she was proud of her running speed today. Maybe one day she would get back to cross country after all.

Ed started the engine, reversed back hesitantly, drove out of the car park and back on to the road.

Sitting beside Henry, Tabby felt awkward rather than happy. She also really hoped she didn't smell after her run. She hadn't forgotten their earlier moment, replaying itself in her mind, over and over, each time adding a new layer of embarrassment as she thought about her behaviour, about what might have been.

Chapter Eighteen

The van nestled in a corner of the campsite, the grass cut short, hedgerows alive with life. Tiny sparrows flitted about, making the most of the remaining light; a blackbird chirped in a nearby tree, the first awake, the last to bed.

Dusk was fast approaching, red and orange lines streaking across the sky. The atmosphere had cooled down a few degrees so that everything seemed calmer, as if the landscape were relaxing its shoulders and breathing for the first time all afternoon.

The Paper & Hearts Society lounged around outside the van in camping chairs, their legs out in front of them, arms hanging limply by their sides.

Tabby was the first to speak. 'I like it here,' she said. 'It's as if we're the only ones in the world.' The others nodded their agreement.

'That's if you can ignore the sound of the road behind us.' This from Henry, ever the practical one.

'Well, there is that I suppose.' Tabby leant her head back against the side of the van and closed her eyes, letting the last of the sun dash over her eyelids.

The events of the day seemed to collect in their limbs, putting them into a slumber that made their voices quieter than usual so that Tabby had to strain her ears to hear everyone properly. Well, everyone except for Olivia. She'd come alive again, seemingly able to revitalise herself within minutes of sitting down and eating. 'I have an idea,' she said, bolting upright.

'I've had enough of your ideas,' Ed said, slowly shifting up with a groan. 'Your idea left me, Henry and Tabby stranded for an hour and we had to run across the city.'

'Oh shush, Ed.' Olivia shooed him away with her hands as if to brush away his words. 'This is a *good* idea.'

'What is it?' Tabby asked, the excitement in Olivia's voice waking her up just a little.

Olivia grabbed Cassie's and Henry's hands next to her, put on a deep voice like a voiceover on a TV talent show, and said, 'We're going to play the bookish version of Never Have I Ever.'

'There's no such thing as a bookish version of Never Have I Ever,' Henry said, looking at her as if it was the worst thing he'd ever heard in his life.

'You're such a killjoy.' Olivia got up and opened the door of the van, rustling around in the bottom of her bag. 'One: I just invented this game, and two: we have chocolate!'

They all perked up at that.

'Chocolate is way better than alcohol,' Ed said. 'I think I like the bookish version of Never Have I Ever a lot better than the normal one.'

'Cassie?'

'I won't say no to chocolate.' Cassie pulled a face, her message clear: anyone who turned down chocolate was a fool.

'I'm in,' Tabby said and nudged Henry beside her with an arm.

'All right, I suppose I'm in too,' he said, tipping his head back in defeat. 'So how does it work?'

'I'll start,' Olivia said. 'Okay . . . Never Have I Ever . . . read multiple books at once.' Everyone else reached for the bag of chocolates, each picking one out and unwrapping it, discarding the wrappers in the middle of the circle they'd formed without realising.

'If all of the rounds are going to be like this,' Ed said through a mouthful of chocolate, 'I'm going to be really happy.'

'Shut up and eat your chocolate,' Olivia retorted, Cassie's speech patterns rubbing off on her. 'I was only going easy for the first round.'

Ed went to take another chocolate from the packet, but Olivia smacked his hand away, giving him a warning look. 'No more chocolate, Ed! You'll have eaten it all by the time we've finished!'

'It's my turn anyway,' Ed said, his mouth so full of chocolate that when he smiled his teeth were coated in brown gloop. 'If I want chocolate, I shall eat it.' He took another chocolate just to prove his point, grinning extra widely. 'Never Have I Ever . . . been told off by Olivia for eating chocolate.'

Olivia smacked her hands down on the ground. 'I knew you wouldn't take my awesome idea seriously!'

Ed grabbed the packet, taking out a handful of the chocolates, unwrapping them, and making a point to pop them in his mouth one after the other so that his cheeks soon resembled those of a hamster. 'Sorry, I can't hear you over the sound of eating this chocolate.'

'I give up,' Olivia huffed, emptying the bag to reveal only three chocolates were left. 'Why do none of you appreciate my talents?'

'We appreciate you,' Henry said. 'We just have a funny way of showing it.' He yawned, covering his open mouth with the back of his hand and dragging the other hand through his hair. 'We should call it a night if we're going to get up early enough to make it to Stratford in the morning.'

'Woo!' Ed jumped up, pulling the door of the van open wildly. He flung one leg inside while swinging his body around and throwing the other leg into the air. 'Go, Shakespeare!'

'You do know there are other people staying here? You don't have to be the centre of attention all the time,' Cassie said, sliding the door open and hopping up in the back. She grabbed her sleeping bag from the back where she'd stashed it. 'Be serious for a second; how are we organising sleeping arrangements?'

I completely forgot the sleeping part of the road trip. What if I snore?! What if I talk in my sleep?!

'I've got it arranged,' Ed said, pulling something out of the back of the van. It was a tent. An unbuilt tent, which Ed had conveniently lost the instructions to. 'Henry and I will sleep in the tent, and you girls can stay in the van.'

'But why didn't you say this earlier?' Olivia exclaimed. 'It will take us ages to build it!'

And take them ages it did. It turned out that none of them were any good at putting up a tent, especially not when it was getting dark and Ed kept tripping over the poles.

'I can't believe I have to put up with Ed's snoring,' Henry complained, sticking the final tent hook in the ground after forty-five minutes.

'I don't snore.'

'You so do,' Cassie said. 'And you know it.'

'I feel very attacked right now,' Ed said, wiping away an imaginary tear. 'I'll forgive you, though. You're all starting to grow on me.'

Olivia opened the rear door and passed them their sleeping bags. Tabby took hers and started to unroll it in the back of the van. Gran had sworn it was last used on a camping trip back in the 1980s. Which explained the smell of mothballs.

She laid it out on the back seat, tucking the seat belt holders in so that they wouldn't dig into her body during the night. She pulled out the hoodie she'd brought to sleep in from her weekend bag. It had taken her ages to choose what to wear at night, not least because she didn't want to be embarrassed by her old, tatty pyjamas. The ones with the sausage-dog print wouldn't have been flattering.

'Uh . . . Ed? Shall we go and . . .?' Tabby looked out of the window to see Henry jutting his head towards the campsite shower block.

Ed got his meaning right away, picking up his bag and leaving the girls to it. Tabby breathed a sigh of relief.

'Are you finding it awkward?' Cassie asked.

'Just a bit,' she admitted.

'Don't worry, I found it weird the first time we went away, but you get used to it. You can trust all of us one hundred per cent.'

'Cassie's right. And it's okay to feel awkward, especially if you're not used to being away from home,' Olivia said.

Tabby felt her nervousness loosen. 'It's not about you guys,' she said. 'I just . . . I can't explain it. I suppose I'm not used to sharing so little space in totally new surroundings.'

She tried not to watch as Cassie and Olivia got undressed in front of her, completely comfortable with their bodies and not ashamed to show skin that was usually covered up.

'A neat trick I learnt is to get in your sleeping bag and change under there,' Cassie said to Tabby. 'It's completely flesh-free.'

She smiled gratefully. She did as Cassie suggested, wriggling into her sleeping bag and pulling the hoodie and a pair of old jogging bottoms in with her. She wrestled with swapping her jeans for the bottoms, with trying to squeeze into her hoodie within the constraints of the tight bag. Eventually, she victoriously unzipped the sleeping bag, a grin on her face as she put her clothes in her weekend bag.

The next minute, Ed and Henry were calling goodnight from inside the tent, pitched just outside the van.

Night had well and truly fallen; even the birds had gone off to roost. As they all got comfy in their sleeping positions, Tabby settled down, her eyes adjusting to the dark.

'Night,' Olivia whispered, and before Tabby knew it, she was asleep.

Chapter Nineteen

Light poked through the windows of the van as Tabby found herself waking up, a dull ache in the bottom of her stomach making her feel nauseous. It took her a few minutes to get her bearings, listening to the soft breathing and occasional snore around her, trying to concentrate on anything but the cramps.

Her legs were zipped up in her sleeping bag, a mermaid tail out in front of her, just as she'd always wished for when she was younger. Now, though, all she wanted to do was get the hell out as quickly as she could.

She was crammed in beside Olivia, who was next to the door. Tabby bit her bottom lip, trying to decide what to do, fiddling with the zip of her sleeping bag. She took a deep breath in through her nose, out through her mouth, and then touched Olivia's shoulder gently.

'Mmmm?' Olivia mumbled, eyes still closed but knitting her eyebrows together.

Tabby tried to keep her voice down as much as she could. 'Are you awake?'

'Mmmm . . . No, it's your turn to host a meeting.'

'What is it?' Cassie's voice came from the front.

'I need to get out and I need my bag.' Tabby thought her voice was far too loud, as if the part of her brain controlling volume hadn't yet woken up, was still snoozing like she wished the rest of her body was. 'Do you mind if I scramble over you?'

'Are you okay?' *Cassie sounds like a little kid when she's half-asleep*, Tabby thought.

'I don't know. I need to go to the loo.'

'Give me two seconds and I'll be properly awake.'

Tabby grabbed her bag, chucked on her Converse and glasses, and the two of them snuck out. They padded over the grass to the campsite's communal toilets, with their tiled floors that looked like a haven for bacteria and hidden fungus, the slight smell of nappies in the air that you eventually got used to.

Tabby went into a cubicle, crouching and pulling down her jogging bottoms, revealing a bright red stain in her pants. Luckily it hadn't gone through to her jogging bottoms. Her tummy cramps stabbed her in the gut, as if to say, 'Ha ha! Surprise!' and she groaned, leaning her head back against the wall, attempting to control her breathing.

'Are you all right in there?'

Tabby fished around in the bottom of her backpack, emptying all of the compartments, pulling out empty packets of paracetamol and forgotten wrappers. *No tampons, no sanitary towels. How could I be so unprepared?* At least she'd remembered a clean pair of pants. She could praise herself for that much at least.

'Cassie?' she said. Her voice still seemed so much louder than normal. 'Can you do me a favour?' She hated asking, felt ashamed for some reason, even though she knew she shouldn't. There was nothing wrong with period blood – this wasn't *Carrie*.

'Sure. What is it?'

Tabby looked back down at her underwear. 'Do you have a sanitary towel I could pinch?'

She could hear Cassie rustling around in her own bag, and then a second later her hand appeared under the cubicle door. Tabby took the wrapper from her and shrugged off her pants, pulling on the clean pair and tucking the sanitary towel into place.

'Thanks,' she said as she emerged from the cubicle and washed her hands. 'I should have remembered . . . I'm so stupid.'

'It happens to the best of us,' Cassie said. 'No big deal. We'll pick up some more when we get to Stratford to tide you over for the next few days.'

I don't know if I've ever been alone with Cassie like this before.

'Thanks again for helping me,' she said, trying to find something to say. *I don't want this to be awkward.*

'Let's go and sit outside until the others wake up. The weather's too good to go back to sleep.'

Cassie led the way over to a wooden bench that looked out over the rest of the campsite. They sat watching the silent van in the distance, taking in the calm of the early morning.

Cassie shuffled about, picking at her nails. *She feels awkward too.* 'Look, Tabby,' she said, gazing down at her hands, 'I know I already apologised to you, but I still feel guilty for how I acted when you first joined our friendship group. It was out of order and I shouldn't have mixed you up in all my issues.'

'It's okay,' Tabby said, but Cassie pushed on.

'I need to explain myself. It doesn't excuse it, but it's a start. I hate talking about it, but I have to.' She took a breath. 'At the end of last year, my dad died. It was a shock, a major shock. It shook the entire foundation of my world. One minute he was here, the next I was having to face life without him. I miss him every single day. I hear someone whistling as they walk past my house and think it could be him, walking through the gate. My mum and dad were so in love – I've never seen anything like it. They were inseparable. His death may have hit me hard, but it hit Mum harder. She couldn't function any more – our lives got flipped upside down. And that means I have to be there for her more than lots of other teenagers have to be there for their parents.'

'I'm so sorry,' Tabby said. 'I can't even begin to imagine how hard it is for you.'

Cassie shook her head. 'My mum isn't a burden, if that's what you're wondering. That's what lots of people assume. But she's my mum. I'd do anything for her, just like I would have done anything for my dad. And that's why I acted like I did; because so much in my life had changed, I couldn't cope with anything else being different. I really am sorry. I should have trusted you more.'

'It's understandable; I don't blame you. I'm just glad we're cool now.' *Maybe now that we're sharing, I should tell her everything I know about the oakavenue52 account and Jess.*

Cassie put out her fist and bumped it against Tabby's. 'We're cool. Period buddies now, right?'

'Aha, yep.'

They were interrupted by Ed's head emerging from the tent, floating between the zip so that he looked like he'd been decapitated.

'Morning, sleepyhead!' Cassie called. 'Rise and shine!'

'Ungghh,' Ed grunted, giving Cassie the finger. 'Too. Early.'

It wasn't long before Olivia and Henry were awake too, and they all gathered round to eat breakfast; Ed had brought a box of cornflakes with him and was eating them dry out of the box with a spoon. Everyone else was content with supermarket pain au chocolat.

'That is so disgusting, Ed,' Cassie said. '*How* are you doing that?'

Through a mouthful he said, 'It does taste a little bit like cardboard, but you get used to it after a while. Want some?'

'I'd rather not,' she said.

Ping. Tabby took her phone out from her hoodie pocket.

***@oakavenue52** sent you a photo*

It was a screenshot of a map, Tabby's icon floating over the campsite they were staying at.

No. She felt her hand shake and clamped her phone down underneath her leg. She looked around to see if any of the others had noticed, but they were still discussing Ed's cereal.

***@oakavenue52** did you know Keeley from the sixth form cross-country team can drive? We've been training together and thought we might take a little drive today*
***@oakavenue52** this spot looks particularly good*

Tabby opened the Find My Friends app, deleting Jess from her contacts as quickly as she could, as if her phone was on fire and she'd be burned if she wasn't quick enough.

'I'm trying to work out the caption for my next Instagram photo. How does this sound?' Ed asked. '"Moving on to Stratford-upon-Avon today. Time to shut up and Shakespeare!"?'

Cassie pretended to throw up.

'Actually, I don't need your opinion. I'll post it ... Done!'

'No!' Tabby cried, frowning. *He can't post where we're going! No, no, no. She'll know where I am! She'll know!*

'Oh, should I have added something else?' Ed asked, confused. They all seemed to turn to Tabby in slow motion to gawp at her reaction.

'I meant ... No way! That's amazing!'

It took everything for Tabby not to pass out on the spot. *She's going to find me. She'll come here and she'll ruin everything for me. Any hope I had of a future friendship with the Paper & Hearts Society will be over.*

WILLIAM SHAKESPEARE

Born: 23 April 1564

Notable Works: *Romeo and Juliet*, *The Tempest*, *Macbeth*, *Hamlet*, *Othello*, *Richard III*, amongst others.

About: William Shakespeare is perhaps best known now as the playwright who has ruined the lives of many students who find his language testing, but he has enriched the lives of many others. He was born in Stratford-upon-Avon and wrote 37 plays and 154 sonnets during his lifetime. He married Anne Hathaway (not the actress) and died on his birthday.

Died: 23 April 1616

Chapter Twenty

'Right,' Ed said, not taking his hands off the wheel. 'We're all very quiet in here this morning, so I'd like to offer you some light entertainment, something I am sure Shakespeare would have highly approved of.'

He flicked one of the buttons on the dashboard and the speakers came to life. Olivia and Cassie jumped out of their seats; Henry dropped his book to his lap.

'Behold! My most favourite audiobook in the world – a true masterpiece, an experience that everyone should . . . well, experience. Are you ready, Tabitha?'

Is it possible she'll be able to find me in the whole of Stratford-upon-Avon?

'I said, are you ready, Tabitha?'

'Sorry, yes!' Tabby exclaimed, in her best fake enthusiastic voice.

'This is . . . *Angus, Thongs and Full-Frontal Snogging.*'

'Seriously, Ed?' Henry groaned. 'You made us listen to

all ten books four months ago. Can't you give it a rest for this trip?'

Ed tutted. 'You are not a true fan. You can like something traditionally girly and not have your heterosexuality questioned, Henry.'

'This is not about my sexuality or how I'm jealous that I haven't got a sex god as a boyfriend, as you have mentioned before. Louise Rennison may have been a fantastic author, but I can appreciate her writing without you making us listen to the audiobooks five billion times.'

'The film was better,' Cassie chipped in.

'Sacrilege!' Ed screamed. It was amazing that he'd managed all of this without averting his gaze from the road. 'Who are you horrible people? That's it. I'm turning around and dumping you all back home. No Shakespeare celebrations for you!'

'One problem.' Olivia was trying not to giggle. 'We're on the motorway.'

'Good point,' Ed replied. 'Now shut up and listen to *Angus, Thongs and Full-Frontal Snogging* and channel your inner Georgia Nicolson, please.'

It didn't evade Tabby's notice that Henry had sneakily put on his earphones without plugging them into anything.

The group stood outside Shakespeare's Birthplace, a commanding building in the middle of the Stratford-upon-

Avon high street. To their right was the house itself – with its instantly recognisable wattle and daub exterior and tourists snapping pictures left, right and centre.

'I'm feeling emotional just looking at it,' Ed said dramatically. 'The site of the birth of the greatest writer to ever walk this planet! Wipe the tear from my cheek, please, Tabitha. No, don't poke me!'

Tabby's stomach ached, a gnawing sensation that made her want to double over. The paracetamol she'd taken earlier had worn off and now she just felt grumpy and sore. To top it all off, the boiling hot sun had decided to make an appearance, making her sticky and irritable.

They walked into the foyer, paid for their tickets and made their way through to the main exhibition.

'Are you okay?' Henry asked, turning round so Tabby could catch him up. 'You seem a bit out of it today.'

Don't mind me, she wanted to say. *I'm just non-stop bleeding, dizzy as I always am on my first day of my period. Plus, I'm also worrying about being stalked by the girl who has it in for me. Y'know, the one behind the creepy fake account? Everything's going GREAT.*

'I'm fine,' she said, pretending to take an interest in one of the objects in a display cabinet.

'Good. Hey, I spoke to Ed and Olivia earlier and mentioned this place called Hall's Croft to them, where Shakespeare's daughter lived. It's only around the corner, and it's supposed to be really beautiful, but both of them said they'd rather go somewhere else. Do you maybe want to come with me while they go off?'

'Have you asked Cassie?' she said, looking round to where she was standing next to Olivia; they were both pointing at one of the displays. 'She might want to come too.'

'Er . . . I already asked her and she said no.'

Oh. 'So just us two?' she said. *Why is my voice so squeaky?! Do NOT blush.*

He nodded. 'Yeah. You up for it?'

'Sure,' she said. 'Sounds like fun. It's a date.'

OH NO. OH NO. I DID NOT MEAN THAT. TAKE IT BACK, TABBY. 'Not, um, like that . . . I just meant . . . Well, you got what I meant. Yeah . . . Shall we, maybe – ' she pointed over her shoulder to the door – 'Go outside and find the others?'

Together, they walked into the main house, skirting round large clusters of people and soaking up the Shakespearean vibes. As they walked up the tiny stairs, they came to a landing, which looked up to a hayloft, a wool fleece visible high up above them on top of a wooden table. It was impossible, really, to imagine Shakespeare here with so many people crowded into one small space. Children made their way up the stairs, a sea of brightly coloured shirts and loud voices. Tabby watched as one picked her nose and wiped her findings on her trousers. *Lovely*.

Tabby and Henry crammed themselves up against a display panel. Looking closely, Tabby could see it was a windowpane scribbled with hundreds and hundreds of names. *The people who visited here, leaving remnants of themselves behind.*

Ed came up behind her, whispering, 'Charles Dickens and John Keats are apparently on there, you know. Can you imagine? They stood in this very room too! I wonder if they were on a literary road trip as well.'

'Probably not in a van like yours,' Tabby said. 'Road trips would have taken a lot longer in their day.'

'I can't believe we're actually here,' he said, gazing around in awe. 'Dreams *do* come true.'

He only grew more enthusiastic as they got further around – when they stepped through to the room where Shakespeare had supposedly been born, Ed gasped, 'Little baby Shakespeare! Born in this room!' Tabby thought he might cry with joy. 'Hold me, Tabby. I think I might die.'

He kept reciting facts. 'Shakespeare was born in 1564 . . . his father was a glove maker and then the mayor of the town . . . he'd lived there for the first five years of his marriage to Anne Hathaway . . . but not the actress!' he exclaimed. 'Just saying.'

Having looked around upstairs, they made their way down to the ground floor. Eager to get away from Ed's facts, Tabby went on ahead. She'd just reached the bottom when she heard the familiar *ping* that signalled a message. There it went again. And again.

Jess is going to find me. That's her, telling me she's here. She could be in this room right now, watching me.

Another tourist behind her got their phone out, laughing as they showed something to their companion, and the notification sounds stopped. Tabby could already feel herself heating up, could feel bile rising in her throat and tears clouding her eyes and she couldn't breathe, she couldn't get any air in and she was going to die and she couldn't do it, she couldn't do it, she couldn't do it . . .

I've got to get out of here. I've got to get out of here. I've got to get out of here.

She didn't know where she was, couldn't see anything, couldn't think straight. Her body had shut down, was trying desperately to get air in, to fight, to disappear.

Her chest had seized up; she could feel herself wheezing. She fought the urge to scream. She shut her eyes tight, could see spots forming behind her eyelids. *I'm being watched. There's nowhere I can go.*

'Oh my, what's going on? Is she okay? Cass, go and get Ed and Henry. Quick!'

She felt a light touch on her shoulder, squealed and recoiled. 'Don't touch me,' she wanted to say. 'Don't touch me, don't touch me.' But nothing would come out of her mouth.

'Tabby, you're safe. It's me, Olivia. I'm here now.'

Tabby dared to open her eyes, her lids sticking together through a gloop of hot tears and runny mascara. She was outside, had somehow wandered through the rest of the building in a blur, and was now in the garden. 'Olivia?' she whispered, her voice barely there.

'It's me. I'm here.' Olivia shielded Tabby from the crowd, her body close but not touching. She turned to take off her bag and get out a packet of tissues and a bottle of water. Slowly, she handed them to Tabby.

With shaky fingers, Tabby unscrewed the cap from the water bottle and took a little sip, just enough to wet her lips. Her mouth felt like sandpaper, as if she'd eaten something revolting and couldn't get the taste out. She felt hollow inside, like somebody had scooped her out and chucked away the bits that made her *her*. An empty shell. That was what she was.

Olivia bent down so that they were on an equal level. 'Can I get you anything? Is there anything you need us to do?'

Tabby swallowed hard, trying to get her body to work again. 'I think I need to clean my face,' she said. 'And I should probably get up.' She looked around at the kids playing, the adults taking pictures of the gorgeous flowers and an actor in the centre of a patioed area reciting a soliloquy.

'I need to get up,' she repeated, not making any attempt to move. The ground was so much easier, so comfy. If she just stayed here now . . . No. She had to try to get up. Squeezing her eyes together, she used her hands to push herself from the ground, wobbling once she was standing upright. Everything seemed so bright, so loud and close. She took another sip of water.

'We'll find a toilet and get you cleaned up,' Olivia said, taking Tabby's arm. 'Can you walk?'

Henry came rushing out. 'Tabby, are you okay?' he asked, reaching for her other arm. 'What's going on?'

She concentrated on leaning against them both. The next time she looked up, they were back on the high street and Olivia was scouting up and down for the best location.

'Over there,' she said, pointing out a small cafe. 'You buy something, Henry, while we go and get sorted out. Can you text Ed and Cassie and let them know where we are?' *But what if she's in there? She could be anywhere.*

Tabby meekly followed, grateful to have someone telling her what to do, but still feeling paranoid. She looked around the cafe, scanning the faces for Jess. While

Henry went up to the counter, Olivia cajoled Tabby into the disabled toilet and shut the door behind them.

'Right,' she said. 'Let's get you cleared up.'

Tabby sat down on the closed toilet seat, taking a deep breath in. She didn't even care about the toilet smell; she just had to get the air back into her lungs as quickly as possible.

'I'm sorry,' she said, letting more tears fall.

Olivia stopped what she was doing, put her hands on her hips. 'You don't have to be sorry, Tabby. These things happen. I should know better than most; I very nearly didn't make it on this road trip. We have our moments!'

Tabby gave a weak attempt at a smile. Olivia had taken a packet of make-up wipes from her bag and held them out for Tabby to take one. She did so, feeling the cool moisture on her face. She scrubbed away, watching as the white material turned black from her spoilt make-up.

There was a knock at the door. Tabby's heart rate rocketed. *That could be her. That could be Jess, right now. She's found me.* 'Are you in there?' It was Henry. She let her shoulders slump in relief.

Olivia bent down so that they were on eye level. 'You don't happen to have any concealer hidden in your bag, do you? That'll freshen you up; we've got to have you looking your best.' She raised a knowing eyebrow. To the closed door she said, 'Give us a minute, Henry.'

'I think there's one in the inside pocket of my rucksack, and mascara too. Are my eyes red?'

'A little bit, I won't lie. But they'll be okay. Right, now close your lids halfway and look up. I don't want to poke you with the mascara wand.'

Tabby did as she was told, afterwards looking in the toilet mirror. The finished look was an improvement from the blotchy redness of before, but she could still tell she'd been crying.

She didn't want to check her phone, but she felt she had to. Her hands were still shaking as she lifted it out of her bag and turned on the screen.

No notifications. No messages. Nothing.

Not the *I'm standing behind you* messages she'd expected to see, or an update on where Jess was.

There wasn't anything logical in a panic attack – they didn't need to make sense. They just happened, whether she liked it or not.

Olivia opened the door to find Henry standing close by. With a tentative smile, he handed her a packet of shortbread. 'Thought these might come in handy. Just don't let Ed go anywhere near them or they'll be all gone.'

'We'd better get going,' Tabby said. 'Ed and Cassie will be bored by now.'

'All sorted and no need to worry,' Henry said. 'They're waiting for us outside. Ed said something about book shopping and then a visit to the church next.'

As they left the cafe, Olivia held Tabby back. 'When you're ready to talk about what that was all about, then we're here. But take the time you need, okay?'

Jess was right; she had got to Tabby. There was no way she could escape this now. At some point, she'd have to confess.

Chapter Twenty-one

'We don't have to go,' Henry said. 'We can just tag along with everyone else to the bookshop.'

His eyes, full of warmth and care, seemed more hazel than usual in the summer light. *No, I need this*, Tabby thought. *Some normality. A distraction. Something to remind me of who I am without Jess in my life.*

She shook her head. 'No, it's fine. It will be good to go somewhere quieter.'

She and Henry walked with Olivia, Ed and Cassie to the local Waterstones. Before Olivia had even walked through the door, she'd spotted a beautiful edition of *Pride and Prejudice* in the window and was off, dragging Ed and Cassie by the arms.

'Book shopping!' she exclaimed. 'Somebody restrain me before I spend all my money. Ed, can you keep hold of my purse please?'

And then it was just the two of them. *Very, very alone.*

They wandered past the black and white grammar school – where it was said Shakespeare had attended when he was young – and down the road to Hall's Croft. The street leading to it was lined with striking red-brick houses, and heat crept up from the pavement. It was the perfect summer's day.

'We're here,' Henry said gently as they rounded the corner to the entrance. He was being ever so gentle with her, more cautious than usual.

Tabby was immediately struck by its grandeur, with its multiple chimneys and Jacobean exterior, just the type of thing you saw pictures of in history books. It was similar in style to Shakespeare's Birthplace, but she liked it more right away; there was a peace here that you couldn't quite replicate in the middle of the high street.

They entered and handed over their tickets, watching as they were scanned by the machine, and walked through to the main building. A large stone fireplace greeted them to their left, and portraits of people wearing huge ruffs hung on the walls. Henry took the lead, walking up the wooden staircase to the upstairs rooms.

She could only imagine what it would have been like to live here. Even in more recent times, it had been used as a school before being bought by the Shakespeare Birthplace Trust. Tabby thought that she would get so much more schoolwork done if she got to work here, thinking back to the stuffy halls of her old school, graffiti over the walls and years old chewing gum under the seats. In comparison, this was heaven.

They drifted around upstairs for a bit, breathing in the atmosphere and history of the building. Though Tabby felt like she would absorb much more if Henry wasn't standing so close.

He noticed her looking down at the gardens from one of the upper windows. 'Shall we go outside? Sorry, you did want some quiet.'

They retraced their steps back down the staircase and walked into the garden. Tabby tried to ignore Henry's hand brushing against hers on the way down, but it made her shiver.

There were a few people sitting around garden tables in the patio area just outside the door, drinking coffee from big mugs and talking quietly. But Tabby had fixed her gaze on a bench at the back of the garden, propped in front of a wall and almost hidden in an alcove.

They made their way up the path, lined by green box borders that enclosed a variety of medicinal plants. John Hall, Shakespeare's son-in-law, had been a doctor, after all.

Henry sat down first. Tabby became flustered. How close should she sit? Not too close, obviously, but if she sat far away he would think she was being rude. She ignored the voice in her head and sat down. But now she was here, it seemed rather too close.

It's too late to stand back up and move, isn't it? Argh, what should I do? RELAX.

The wood was warm beneath her legs, heated up by the sun. She took a deep breath, feeling the air in her lungs. From this vantage point, she could survey the garden from most angles; there was a sundial directly in front of them, and as she panned her body around to the right she could see the houses she'd admired on their way in over the garden wall. There was so much green staring her in the face – the borders, the trees, the herbs that had been planted.

Tabby thought she should probably say something, break the silence even if it wasn't uncomfortable. 'I'm sorry about before,' she said. It was the only thing she could think to say.

'You don't have to be sorry.' He'd turned his body to face hers. 'Olivia told you that.'

'But you're not Olivia,' she whispered.

'No, but she's right. And you can talk to us. I know maybe you don't like to, but it's what we're here for. You can't expect to take on all our problems and then not feel like we can take on yours too.'

She looked down at her hands in her lap. 'I don't know where to start.' Her words were blown away by the slight breeze. She spoke louder. 'It's not that I don't want to tell you, but things are complicated right now and even *I* can't predict what's going to happen next. Honestly, just having your company is enough. I'm so, so grateful for what you've all done for me, even if you don't realise how much that is. Sometimes we just need to be reminded that we're not alone.'

Her words grounded her, reminded her where she was. She was not alone; she was with Henry, and the way that he was looking at her, so tenderly and with so much emotion and care, hit her in the chest.

One minute Tabby was looking down at her hands; the next she felt herself lean forward, a question in her eyes as she touched her nose against Henry's.

'But you're upset . . .' he whispered, not moving away from her. He took a shuddery breath in, biting his lip.

'Not any more,' she replied. She wasn't sure if what she was doing was sane, if he could hear her heart beating in her chest, but suddenly so much more than their noses were touching and Tabby thought that maybe, just maybe, things were going her way. She tried not to think as their lips softly collided. She closed her eyes, worried about what her hands were doing, what they should be doing, what her lips and tongue and teeth were supposed to be doing, just so that all this would *still* be going her way in a few minutes.

I'M KISSING HENRY. HENRY IS KISSING ME. WHAT ALTERNATE REALITY HAVE I WALKED INTO?! Who am I?!

They pulled apart. Tabby couldn't help but reach her hand up to touch her lips. 'What just happened?' she said, out of breath.

Instead of answering her question, Henry said, '*Finally.* I've wanted to do that ever since Ed's party.'

'And I've wanted you to do that ever since Ed's party.'

I can't believe it.

'Let's go and find the others?' He reached out his hand and she took it, feeling like the female protagonist from a period drama. The first touching of hands was always the most romantic.

'Let's go,' she said. His hand felt soft in hers, and she smiled up at him, taking in his hazel eyes.

She took one last look at the garden, at their little alcove, before they left. *My first kiss*, she thought. *Hopefully the first of many.*

Chapter Twenty-two

The walkway to the church was cool, lined with lime trees that shaded the paved stones and kept out the heat. Tabby had never really taken an interest in churches before, although her dad loved visiting them. As they proceeded to the doorway, Tabby could see what he loved: the feeling of omnipotence as the building loomed over you; the sense of a holy presence, even if you didn't fully believe in a god.

As they walked inside, its sheer scale struck Tabby. She thought it unusual at first, expecting Shakespeare's grave to be outside with all the other weathered headstones, but there it was, inside the church itself. There were a number of rows of pews and the stone floor was worn away from the many thousands of tourists who walked these exact steps each year.

They had to pay a small donation to get into the area where Shakespeare was buried, so Tabby dug around in the bottom of her purse for some spare coins.

'I'll cover it,' Henry said, putting a few coins into the pot.

'No, I'm sure there's something in my bag,' she protested.

'You can pay me back later,' he said.

'Oh yeah?' *What's got into me?*

'I wasn't thinking of that,' he said, quirking his mouth. 'But if that's your preferred method of payment . . .'

She batted his arm. 'You're going to lead me astray!'

He chuckled, leaning closer so that he could whisper, 'I think it was you who kissed me, if I remember correctly.'

She bit back a laugh. 'We're in a church. We should probably behave.'

They strolled through to the burial site, at the far end of the church. Tabby looked up at the magnificent stained-glass window, taking up the entirety of this end of the building. Underneath it lay four stones, each with its own plaque. There was one in particular that everyone was crowded around:

The grave of the poet William Shakespeare
1564–1616

Another plaque lay behind it.

Good friend for Jesus sake forbeare,
To dig the dust enclosed here.
Blessed be the man that spares these stones,
And cursed be he that moves my bones.

Ed walked over to them, grinning. 'Isn't it amazing?' he said. 'It's so beautiful. Apparently, he wrote that himself, so people wouldn't rob his grave after he died. People actually did that back then, you know.'

'We are literally looking at stones covering the ground where dead people are. Skeletons. We paid to see this,' Cassie said, walking up behind them.

'You didn't have to come inside,' Ed said. 'You could have waited outside while we all looked.'

'I wanted to.' Cassie started taking pictures with her phone, presumably, Tabby thought, so she could use them to draw from later. Or for her Instagram.

Tabby walked to the back of the church so she could take a minute for herself. There were a few other people looking about, tourists like them, but it was still peaceful (if she could block out the voices of Ed and Cassie).

She found Olivia sitting in one of the pews, her head slightly bent, her eyes closed. Tabby hadn't thought about religion much, not in the sense of a chosen faith, but she did find it quite comforting being here. It was hard not to feel like there must be some greater being in the universe when you were in a building as breathtaking as this one, so carefully constructed and maintained.

'Did you buy anything good in the bookshop?' A distraction. She needed a distraction. She fought the urge to touch her lips again.

Olivia beamed, lifting up her heavy-looking tote bag. 'Did I ever! I'll show you later. I think I bought five. What did I say about my self-restraint?'

'So giving your purse to Ed was a lost cause then!' Tabby laughed. She was concentrating hard on focusing on Olivia. Anything to stop her looking up to try to find Henry.

'Did you find some peace and quiet with Henry?' Olivia said, her mouth quirking into a small smile.

Tabby looked down at the ground. 'Something like that.'

She wanted to tell Olivia everything, grab her hands and squeal, but here wasn't the place.

'Just wait and see what he's got planned for when we're in Yorkshire,' Olivia said.

'What do you mean?' She didn't like the conspiratorial look on Olivia's face. *What are they up to?*

'No, I refuse to spoil it. You've got to wait.'

Henry joined them on the pew, sitting down next to Tabby and looking up at the stained-glass window.

With a newfound confidence, she decided to ask him outright. 'What's going on with this secret plan of yours?'

His smile fell and he took one look at Olivia before shaking his head. 'Livs, the point of a secret plan is to keep it a secret. That includes the fact there's a secret plan in the first place.'

'Oops! I'm just too excited! Oh, Tabby, you'll love it.'

She shook her head now too. 'I don't know what I'm supposed to be loving!'

'Patience,' Henry said. 'It'll be worth the wait.'

They headed to the park for lunch, which was next to the church. Cassie, Ed and Olivia had picked up sandwiches and crisps from a nearby shop for them all after their trip to Waterstones.

Tabby collapsed on to the tartan picnic blanket Ed had laid out, grateful not to have to sit on the sun-scorched, scratchy grass.

'It's so nice not to have to watch Ed eating dry cereal any more,' Cassie said, stuffing a sandwich crust into her mouth.

Tabby took a handful of Pringles from the tube they were sharing and idly nibbled away.

From her languid position on the blanket, Cassie poked Olivia with her toe. She'd kicked off her gladiator sandals as soon as she'd sat down. 'Hypothetical scenario. If you were stranded on a desert island, what two books would you take with you? You can only choose two and they have to be in two different genres.'

'You can't ask that!' Olivia squealed. 'That's like asking someone to choose their favourite child.'

'Easy,' Ed said, mouth full of ham sandwich. 'I'd take a desert island survival guide and the complete works of Shakespeare. Sorted.'

Tabby felt Henry's finger brush against her wrist. She tried desperately not to look. She could sense the smile on his face without seeing it.

Olivia stepped in. 'I think I'd take *Pride and Prejudice*. No. *Persuasion*. No, it would have to be *Emma*. Or, actually, *Pride and Prejudice* would be better. And then maybe something like *Jonathan Strange & Mr Norrell* because it's so long and so magical and you'd want that if you were on a desert island. But also *Harry Potter*! I couldn't live without Harry Potter. Would I take *Deathly Hallows* or *Order of the Phoenix*, though? Or maybe *Goblet of Fire*. No, I don't like *Goblet of Fire* as much. It would have to be a long one, though.'

'Livs?' Henry said.

'Yeah?'

'I think you're overthinking this.'

Ping. Cassie reached for her phone, her eyes lighting up. 'Another oakavenue52 photo. I wonder what it is this—' She cut herself off suddenly.

'What is it?' Tabby whispered.

Cassie stood up forcefully, grabbing her bag so hard her stuff threatened to spill from the top. 'What is *this*?' The phone was thrust into Tabby's face.

It took her eyes a few seconds to adjust, but once they had it was impossible for her to look away. She could feel the angry electricity pulsing from Cassie, a red halo that would burn if she got too close.

When possums felt endangered, they played dead. They dropped to the ground and froze, tricking the predator stalking them into thinking they were useless prey. This was how Tabby felt, staring down at the screen, frozen to the spot: like she should play dead. Then maybe everybody would lose interest in her and go back to their lives before she turned up and ruined everything.

There, adorning the oakavenue52 Instagram account, were two new pictures.

> **Oakavenue52** *I thought u might want to see this about your 'friend' Tabby, @cassie.artx @bookswithlivs @TheIncredibleEd*

The first picture was a screenshot of a conversation between Tabby and Jess that was dated two days ago. *How is that possible?*

> Tabby: Honestly, they're nobody. Just some losers I met who like dressing up in weird outfits and being huge nerds. I'm only using them because I don't have any other friends here. They're convenient, that's all.

The second picture was another screenshot, this one dated yesterday.

> Tabby: Henry is too quiet and has basically no personality. I just humour him because it's easiest to. And Ed is the kind of person who finds his own jokes funny. Never in a million years.

Tabby looked up into Cassie's venomous eyes, swallowing hard, her heartbeat racing.

'Cassie, I—'

'I don't want to hear it, Tabby. After all we've done for you! You must have known who oakavenue52 was all along, and you never said a word.' Cassie's voice cracked, smashing on the ground as a hot, angry tear rolled down her cheek.

'Cassie, that's not—'

'Seriously, Tabby? There's no way you can excuse this. I was open with you; I was honest. I trusted you and you let us believe this whole time that you were genuine,' she spat.

'What's going on?' Henry asked, not following; he hadn't seen the pictures yet.

Cassie didn't say a word, only handed him her phone for him to look himself. The look of pain that pulled across his face was enough to completely undo any composure Tabby had left.

Jess has won. I've lost everything. She's won and I have nothing and it feels like I'm breaking.

'It's not what it looks like. I promise, I would never—'

'It's never what it looks like!' Cassie screamed. She had no care for the other people in the park, who were beginning to stare. 'I hope you got what you wanted out of this, Tabby. Because you certainly don't have us any more. I'm out of here.'

And with that, she strode away, out of the park, out of sight. But not out of mind.

What have I done? Oh god, why?

'I can't believe this,' Henry kept muttering. 'I can't believe it.'

'Henry.' She reached out to touch his arm but he flinched and pulled it away. 'Please.'

'Was *any* of this real?' He pointed between them.

'Of course,' she said. '*Of course* it was! It *is*!'

'I can't bear to even look at you right now.' He picked up his backpack and followed after Cassie. Tabby tried to grab his shoulder, to turn him back around, but he was gone, and her hand was left hanging in the air.

'But what's going on?' Olivia was saying, high-pitched. 'Tabby, *what's going on*? Ed, text Cassie. See if she's coming back. Tabby, talk to me.'

This can't be happening to me. It's another Tabby. I'll wake up in a minute.

But no. It really was happening. And she didn't know what she could do to stop it.

'Cassie just said to check Instagram,' Ed said as he got a reply. And then added, '*No*.'

Olivia leant over him to look at his phone.

Watching the moment it hit them was like seeing a car crash in slow motion; there was nothing Tabby could do about it but look on in horror.

'But we welcomed you in,' Olivia whispered, 'as if you'd always been here. We treated you like one of our best friends.'

'You know where the van is,' Ed said, not looking at her; his disappointment was worse than any screaming or shouting.

Olivia grabbed hold of the picnic blanket and bundled everything into it, Ed helping. And then she was alone, choking on her own tears as they walked away.

Tabby didn't know how she got back to the car park; it wasn't walking, more like stumbling, trying to stem the tears that fell down her face. The high street passed her in a blur, all noises washed over her. All she could process was putting one foot in front of the other.

Olivia and Cassie leant against the van, their arms around each other. Cassie was stroking Olivia's hair away from her face. They straightened up when they saw her and Tabby recoiled at Cassie's disgusted look, somehow even more malicious than the first time she'd given her the death stare all those weeks ago.

I know you hate me now. I hate me too.

'She can sit in the front with you,' Cassie said to Ed. 'She's not sitting anywhere near me.'

'Cassie—' Tabby said. But there was no hope of even trying.

Chapter Twenty-three

'Can you *please* stop snivelling?' Cassie snapped.

It had been a tense few hours on the road. Ed hadn't even wanted to listen to his audiobook; he'd turned the radio on instead. Henry had his headphones on in the back, Olivia was reading *Pride and Prejudice* and Cassie was aggressively scribbling in a notepad.

Tabby couldn't help the snivelling – every time she looked at them, she was reminded of their faces when they'd seen the messages for the first time.

Motorway gave way to views of moorland, sheep lazily grazing the rough grass and the sky a brilliant blue above them. But even the change of scenery didn't make Tabby feel better. If anything, it made her feel worse.

I've ruined the trip. This was supposed to be one of the best, most memorable experiences of our lives, but now every time they think about it, they'll think about me messing it up.

That wasn't even Tabby feeling sorry for herself; she

genuinely felt awful about the upset she'd caused. But how could she tell them that?

'*Great*,' Ed muttered under his breath, hitting the steering wheel hard.

'What is it?' Olivia put her book down and leant over the seats.

'Took the wrong turning,' he said, and looked frantically around for any road signs. 'You're going to have to get your Google Maps working again.'

Usually, Tabby would have offered to do it. After all, she was in the passenger seat. But she sat quietly, leaning the side of her face against the headrest and looking out of the window.

Olivia worked her navigation magic and they were soon back on track, although the slight detour had added time to their journey. They passed through the towns and villages of West Yorkshire, the architecture so different here to Dorset. The landscape was dotted with old workers' cottages, many dating back hundreds of years when the mills were at their height of production.

Tabby wasn't sure if it was a relief when they finally got to their destination, the campsite they were staying at. What would happen now?

Cassie was the first to jump out, seconds after Ed had cut the ignition. 'We need an emergency meeting,' she said, 'and you're not part of it.'

Tabby waited in the van. She didn't want to look, but she

couldn't help but peek through half-closed eyes at them. Cassie's arms were flailing wildly in the air; Ed's shoulders were drooped; Henry was pacing up and down. Olivia had slumped to the ground and was shaking her head.

They're deciding my fate, she thought. *Why do I have to be so far away from home? It's not like I can even leave of my own accord, for their sakes.*

It seemed to take an age for their meeting to finish. Tabby could just imagine them talking about her. 'We'll just leave her here and go without her,' someone would say. Cassie, maybe? 'She can fend for herself now.'

Would anyone defend her? *Of course not. You don't deserve defending.*

When they were finally done, they split apart, Cassie, Olivia and Henry going off in the direction of the communal toilets.

Ed came over to the van, going into the back and taking something out. *That's my stuff*, Tabby thought.

She opened the door and stood outside. It was good to stretch her legs, but she felt even more vulnerable out in the open.

'You can sleep in the tent,' Ed said. 'Olivia and Cassie said they don't want you in the van with them.'

He chucked the tent down in front of her, and she bent to pick it up, along with her weekend bag. 'Where will you sleep?' she said.

He shrugged. 'It'll be a tight squeeze in the van, but we'll make it work.'

'Could you, perhaps, help me put it up?' she asked, feeling awkward. But there was no way she'd be able to erect a tent by herself. It was too cumbersome.

Ed didn't say yes immediately, his conflicted thoughts playing across his face, but eventually he stepped forward and took the tent bag from her hands. 'All right then,' he said gruffly.

Yesterday we were laughing and joking and poking each other with the tent poles, she thought. But today they had to resort to communicating in one word grunts and hesitant instructions.

When they were finished, Ed rubbed his hands together. 'Well, that's that then,' he said. 'Sleep well. There's a spare sandwich in your bag for your dinner.'

'Ed,' she said before he left. She tried to inject all the feeling she could into her voice – all the pent-up, raw emotion. 'I know you might not believe me, but I promise you, I didn't write those messages. I *promise* you.'

He paused, like he was caught in confusion. He ran a hand through his hair. 'I just don't know what to believe right now, Tabby.'

She was all out of tears. *I don't even have the strength to cry any more.*

Staring up at the roof of the tent, she held her hands over her heart, counting her pulse to try to calm herself down.

I've lost the best friends I've ever had.

She thought back to the moment she'd met the Paper & Hearts Society for the first time, her hesitance to join and fear she wouldn't be accepted. But Gran had been right – they'd been the best possible thing she could have wished for this summer. Though not any more. And she didn't blame them.

I tried too hard to fit in. I should have been honest with them when Jess first appeared; I should never have hidden the truth.

She tossed and turned in her sleeping bag, unable to get comfortable. Maybe there was no use sleeping. What good would it do anyway? She'd only wake up in the morning and feel worse because she was bound to forget for a moment, and then it would all come rushing back to her, ten times stronger.

She reached for her phone above her head and looked back at the photos on the oakavenue52 account.

Why did I say those things to Jess? she thought. *Why was I so insecure that I had to make up a load of rubbish to appease her? She wasn't satisfied anyway and she probably never will be. If only I'd known every time I spoke to her that she'd never keep it to herself. It was too good to resist.*

She wished she'd realised at the time just how much she had to lose.

Angry – at herself, at Jess – her fingernails clutched at her face, tracing red lines down her left cheek.

She managed to snuggle down into her sleeping bag, but she had only shut her eyes for a second when the bad thoughts rushed back in. *You ruin everything in the end. You don't deserve to be happy. Nobody will ever like you.*

The time on her phone read 02:40 when Tabby heard the van door go. She pricked her ears up, heard footsteps move past her tent.

It was impossible to settle back down, so she put her phone's torch on and got *The Bell Jar* out of her bag. She stroked her hand over the cover, picturing the moment Henry had handed it to her.

There'll be no more moments like that. No more smiles, or inside jokes. He hates me now.

She jumped as the tent zip moved, as if by its own accord. A head poked through the opening.

'Ed?' What was he doing here?

'I believe you,' he said, and unzipped the tent the rest of the way. He stepped in, wearing a loose T-shirt and a pair of tartan pyjama bottoms, and looking surprisingly awake.

'What do you mean?' she said, dropping the book to the floor.

'I believe you,' he repeated. 'I know you're not lying about those messages.'

'How?' Tabby asked, sitting upright, springing to attention.

'Because,' Ed said, squeezing in to sit next to her, 'I know bad Photoshop when I see it.'

'Huh?'

'The font wasn't right and neither was the colour.' Ed spoke as if it were obvious, as if Tabby had any clue what he was on about. 'I've spent enough time on Messenger to know what it looks like and that wasn't it. So there's no way those messages are real. I haven't been able to sleep – I was looking back at all the pictures on that account, analysing each one in minute detail. And I just couldn't believe you'd say those things. Then I realised – you didn't.'

'Ed . . .'

'You're my friend. I've known you long enough to know you wouldn't do that to us.'

Tabby opened her mouth to say something, but shut it again, her lips sticking together like glue. *I've got to do this. I have to tell him the truth.*

'I might not have sent the messages yesterday, but I did send them. Just not to you.' She looked into his face to judge his reaction, but it was neutral. 'I can't explain it fully; I don't know where to start. But the messages weren't true. Maybe at first, maybe when I wasn't thinking properly, but this whole thing with you all wasn't meaningless. It wasn't something to pass the time, not when I realised how much . . . how much I loved you.'

He chewed on his bottom lip, not meeting her gaze. She counted each second before he replied, bubbling anxiety rolling in the pit of her stomach as she waited.

'This is such a mess, Tabby. I want to be hurt by what you said, but I also know that messages can be twisted so easily. And I don't want to let this go on and on, missing out on precious moments of friendship. Because friendship shouldn't be conditional, not when it's a friendship like ours. I don't want to lose you because of this.'

She breathed a sigh of relief.

'Give me your phone,' he said. 'There's only one way we can prove this.' She handed it over silently, unlocking it for him, and he scrolled through her apps until he found Messenger.

'Sorry to be so intrusive,' he said, and she watched as he read through her messages to Jess, his eyebrows knitting tightly together as his finger scrolled back and forth. She felt so exposed, watching his eyes dart from side to side, unable to read his thoughts.

Maybe he'll agree with everything Jess said, she thought. *But no. He can't. He's my only hope.*

'Tabby,' he said, breathless, 'how have you let this go on for so long without saying anything? This is *awful.*'

She didn't reply.

'How can somebody treat another human being like this?'

He handed the phone back to her a little roughly, the anger clear on his face.

'I deserved it,' Tabby said pathetically. 'I wasn't good enough to be friends with her. She didn't want me to be friends with her. And then I blocked her and it just made things worse. I shouldn't have maddened her like that.'

Ed widened his eyes. 'Deserved it?! Tabby, nobody deserves to be treated like this. You are an incredible person; you're supportive and kind and funny, and I am so grateful that you are my friend and that you've come into our lives. Why can't you see that?'

'I don't know, Ed. Honestly? I feel broken. I don't feel confident like the rest of you, or like I bring anything to the group other than baggage. I'm just not good at any of this like you are.'

He reached in to bring her closer and squeezed her shoulder. 'Tabby, you *are* good at this. You make us all so happy. God, I never feel confident. I'm making it up as I go along, and that's the same for most people. Who actually feels like they're making the best job of their life?'

'But what am I going to do?' she cried. 'The others hate me! How am I supposed to convince them that this is all a mistake? I *did* say those things, and I can't prove my intentions.'

'You proved them to me,' he said.

She gulped in air, trying to keep calm, but failing. There were so many thoughts swimming around in her head, doing laps of her mind, that she couldn't keep track of them. 'But you're my best friend. And it's easy to talk to you.'

'We can't do anything about it tonight,' he said. 'But we *will* sort this out tomorrow. Trust me, okay?'

How was she supposed to sleep now?

Chapter Twenty-four

Tabby found Ed's half-finished box of cereal outside the tent in the morning, with a note attached. Trust me, remember? X

She sat in the unzipped tent, miserably eating her breakfast. *Seriously, how does Ed manage this? It's practically inedible.* But it did the trick, lining her stomach; she was always more hungry than usual when she was on her period.

Henry walked past her towards the toilets, but it was as if she didn't exist; he didn't so much as glance her way. And it was even worse when Olivia walked by – she picked up her pace, not lingering for a second longer than was necessary.

I've got to trust Ed, Tabby told herself. But how was he going to be able to fix it?

He came over to her after they'd eaten their breakfast, smiling amiably. 'We're going to head to the Brontë Parsonage in a bit,' he said. 'Shall I help you pack the tent up?'

Good riddance to this tent, she thought. *I never want to see it again.*

They dismantled it and Ed took it to the back of the van, leaving her to pick up her bags. Her backpack was unzipped, and the copy of *The Bell Jar* fell out, staring back at her from the ground.

She knelt down to grab it, unconsciously opening it up to her favourite paragraphs. The fig tree. She only looked at the words at first, her brain unable to register them, but then she really focused on each and every one, gazing up at the van when she'd finished.

I can't throw this away.

It was another awkward drive to get to Haworth village, but Tabby fell in love with it immediately, with its sloping cobbles and old-world feel. It was like she'd gone back in time, but with cars and satellite dishes. They skirted Main Street and drove up an equally steep hill, passing under the shade of trees.

When they pulled into the car park, the top of the Brontë Parsonage could be seen. A few days ago, Tabby would have imagined Cassie gasping in awe in this moment, excited to see a place she'd always wanted to visit. But there was no such reaction now – she sat in stony silence until the van stopped.

Cassie jumped out, Henry and Olivia following her, and slammed the door. It was Henry and Olivia's passivity that scared Tabby the most. Cassie was clearly still hurt, but she couldn't read how the other two felt.

'Coming, Tabby?' Ed said.

'Why are you talking to her?' Cassie sneered. 'Don't start feeling sorry for her, Ed.'

The three of them stalked off, leaving Tabby and Ed on their own.

She looked at Ed as he came round to her side and locked the van up. 'We'll never be able to convince them,' she said. 'It'll be a miracle.'

'I have a plan, don't worry. Let's just try and enjoy ourselves for a minute, okay?'

As they walked up the car park path towards the parsonage, the sounds of songbirds in the air as well as some very noisy crows and rooks, a clock tolled the hour. The new cobbled path they joined led directly to the left past St Michael and All Angels Church. But they took the right turning, heading towards the admissions point.

Tabby was about to pull the door open when she felt the weight of it push against her.

It was Henry. He opened his mouth as if to say something but stopped short when he saw it was her.

'Sorry,' she said instinctively. *Curse you and your English politeness, Tabby.*

'Are we going in, Tabby?' Ed said. She nodded and

Henry moved out of the way to let them pass. 'See you in there, Henry?'

'Yeah,' he replied, subdued.

Once Tabby and Ed had paid for their admission tickets, they were able to retrace their steps and enter the museum.

Tabby picked up on the beauty of the Brontë Parsonage instantly. It acted as a barrier between Haworth and the moors, signifying an invisible cut-off point where one met the other. The small garden, separated from the churchyard by a wall, was in full bloom – gorgeous yellow Welsh poppies flowered beneath a stunning purple buddleia, attracting bees and butterflies.

She stopped to capture a picture, gazing in awe. *I could look at this all day*, she thought, and walked side by side with Ed up the timeworn stone steps.

They were ushered in the direction of the first room to their left as they entered. This was where the Brontës would have written, and a large table sat in the centre of the room, watched over by a portrait hanging above the fireplace. It was one of the most famous portraits of Charlotte, drawn by George Richmond and depicting her with soft features and a pretty face.

Tabby had heard the tale of the sisters pacing around the table late at night, reciting the most recent words they'd written as they worked on their masterpieces, the wind soaring around the house, candlelight their only guide.

To the far right of the room stood a chaise longue, the place where Emily had died from the terrible tuberculosis that had blighted her last days, according to the long-standing rumour.

The other rooms downstairs included Mr Brontë's study, complete with an upright piano against the wall. His spectacles and top hat were sitting on the table, as if he'd just popped out and was going to come back later and use them. There was also a kitchen, which had been reduced in size since the Brontës had lived there, and another room that Charlotte had converted when she'd married her husband, Arthur Bell Nicholls, for him to use as a study, which now displayed interesting artefacts about the church.

Tabby felt she could really soak up the atmosphere and history of the place. Of all the locations they'd visited so far, here it was as if she could feel the Brontës drifting behind her; she could picture them working away at their writing desks, see them walking from room to room, hear their literary chatter, laughter, heartache.

The room closest to the stairs used to be the servants' bedroom. Going over to the window, Ed and Tabby looked directly out on to the graveyard. It was remarkable, really, just how close it was; there was the constant reminder of death, both inside and out of the house.

'Ed,' she said, as they stood behind the arch leading to the main exhibition space at one side, an extension to the original building. 'It's going to be okay, isn't it?'

He took her by the shoulders. 'I won't let you down, Tabs, I promise.'

They walked under the arch and Tabby spotted Henry, Cassie and Olivia to their left, looking into a glass cabinet. Cassie was pointing, animation lighting up her face. Tabby's heart panged and she wished, more than anything, that she could walk over there now and it would be like nothing had happened.

But, instead, Ed steered her to the right and they looked in displays of their own. 'Oh my god,' he said, staring keenly at the tiniest paper book with the tiniest spider writing Tabby had ever seen. 'Can you believe that?'

Charlotte and her brother, Branwell, had written hundreds of miniature books when they were children, telling stories of their fictional world of Angria, where heroism, tragedy and intrigue mixed.

Tabby couldn't believe it either. 'How could anyone write that small?'

When she turned to Ed, though, he wasn't looking in the cabinet any more but had fixed his gaze on the others. He grabbed her hand. 'Now's our chance,' he whispered. 'Act casual. Leave this to me.'

He dragged Tabby along, not giving her time to think about what he was telling her. Her heart picked up its pace, sounding in her ears.

Ed stopped in front of them, clearing his throat. 'We need to talk. All of us.'

'No way.' Cassie took a step backwards.

'Do you want to cause a scene?' Ed hissed. 'When you're finished looking around, you'd better meet us outside. This is urgent, and I hold the keys to the van. You'd better remember that.'

Tabby wasn't sure if Cassie would pay any attention to Ed's words, so when they had finished looking around the exhibition and were making their way out through the shop, she was surprised to find Cassie, Henry and Olivia waiting for them.

Olivia put her hand on Cassie's arm, as if to restrain her. 'We're ready to talk,' Olivia said, but she addressed her words to Ed, not Tabby. 'Let's sort this out.'

Ed nodded. 'I have an idea where we can go.'

Chapter Twenty-five

'Are you *sure* you know where we're going?' Tabby said as she followed behind Ed. It didn't look like he did – from the Brontë Parsonage, he'd taken them out of the churchyard, through a kissing gate and up a long path where, peeking through the trees, Tabby realised how high up they really were.

'Yes, I googled it this morning,' he said. 'What did I say about trusting me?'

I won't trust you again if you get us lost, she thought. He took a right turn, climbing up another sharp incline; behind her, Tabby heard Olivia exclaim as she tripped over the messy cobbles.

Tabby's calf muscles were killing her by the time Ed had got them to the top. *Shows how little I've been running recently.*

She hadn't known what to expect, but it definitely wasn't *this*. Tabby took a sharp breath in as she surveyed their surroundings. They were right on the edge of the moors, the rugged landscape reaching as far as her eyes could see. The wind had picked up slightly, adding to the wildness, the bleakness. There was a hint in the air of something so much greater than Tabby could fully comprehend. The landscape had a life of its own.

'Look,' Ed said. 'There's a bench over there.'

They followed a path worn through the scrub. The heather hadn't yet turned purple, as it soon would, but proud rosebay willowherb painted a vivid pink across the scene.

'Watch out for adders,' Ed teased.

'Are you kidding?' Henry said. After that, he paid careful attention to where he was walking.

The bench was parked at the top of one side of a large crater, but no one sat down at first. It took them awkward moments of shuffling to figure out their places: Henry sat at one end, Cassie next, then Ed, and finally Tabby. Ed was the only one who would sit next to her. Olivia sat crossed-legged on the ground, balancing her elbows on her knees and leaning her head on her palms.

'Well, we're here. Start talking,' Cassie said. Her feet were out in front of her, her Dr. Martens crossed over each other. She tapped her fingers impatiently against her thigh.

'We have to be rational,' Ed said. 'No arguing; no shouting. Let's just hear Tabby out, okay?'

He gave her a thumbs up and a smile that she knew was meant to be encouraging. But she didn't find it particularly so – not against the fear pounding through her.

I don't know where to start. I don't know what I can say to make them understand.

'I was with you,' Tabby said, only just able to hear her own words over the whooshing in her head, 'when those supposed messages about you were sent. So you have to know that I didn't send them then. I wouldn't.'

'So what?' Cassie said. 'As far as we know, you could have made it all up and this could be some sick, twisted game for you.'

'We've had a whole summer of amazing adventures and fun. None of that was a lie.'

'So what was?' Henry finally spoke.

Tabby pinched the space between her eyebrows, preparing herself for the final battle. 'Our friendship wasn't. I love you guys like nobody else in the world, and I would never jeopardise that. But before I came here, I had some . . . trouble. And I suppose I just wanted to get away from that, to be somebody completely different.'

'What kind of trouble?' Olivia asked.

'Friend trouble,' she said.

'What does that mean?' Henry asked.

Time for the truth to come out. 'Jess was one of my best friends. One of my only friends, if I'm honest. She was always so intent on us being the *best* of friends, and that meant not allowing anyone else in. But then, at the start of the year, she made some new friends and she changed completely. She'd always helped me train for cross country, but then she decided to join the team and wanted to win at all costs. She made fun of my clothes, humiliated me in front of the other girls. She even sabotaged my chances of winning, just so she could feel better.' Tabby hadn't realised she was crying, but she touched her hand to her cheek and it came away wet. 'It made me feel worthless, and the more worthless I felt, the more I wanted to be worth something. Every time she rejected me, it made me want to cling to her more and more. Because without her, what did I have?'

She had to keep going; the words were pouring out now. 'I thought it would be a fresh start when I moved. I thought I'd never have to see her again. But she wouldn't leave me alone – she was constantly there, on Instagram, on Messenger. I *tried* to push her out of my mind, I really did. But every time she popped up, it reminded me that I wasn't good enough. All I wanted was to feel like I was enough. So when she asked me about you, I panicked. I thought that if I told her the truth, she'd take you away from me.'

'So when *did* you send those messages, Tabby?' Henry said. 'Because it certainly sounds like something like that happened.'

'I did send some,' she admitted, 'but I'm not proud of

it. I wish I could turn back time and take them back, but I can't. I didn't send them yesterday, though. I would never say those things now.'

'It's true,' Ed said. He rested his hand on Tabby's shoulder. 'Get your phone out, Tabby.'

She took it from her bag and handed it over to him; Ed began to read aloud.

Tabby flinched as soon as the sound of Jess's words hit her ears and she could finally hear them for what they were: toxic harassment. Bullying.

She felt the tears trickle down her face and wiped them away scruffily with her sleeve, partly glad that her blurry vision meant she couldn't see their reactions.

Ed kept reading, kept going with the messages until she thought she could feel her heart snap in two. He placed particular emphasis on the dates.

'So, you see, the screenshots we saw on that account make no sense. Why would Tabby be saying that about us when her phone says she was, in fact, telling this Jess to leave us out of it?'

Cassie shrugged.

'So Jess was behind oakavenue52 all along?' Olivia asked. She was so quiet, it was almost scary.

Tabby nodded.

'And you didn't think that we deserved to know about this when she started targeting *us* too?' Cassie said. 'You saw that creepy picture she did of us. You saw her freaking us out by liking all our posts and sending cryptic messages. Why keep lying?'

'I don't have an answer,' Tabby said. 'It wasn't rational. I was petrified. She told me she was going to track me down! I didn't realise how much fear had taken over my life.'

'You didn't need to lie,' Henry said. 'We wouldn't have judged you, you know that. All you had to do was be honest with us.'

'I know,' she said. 'I know that now. And I don't want to just forget about this. I hope that – if not now, one day – you'll forgive me, but this is something I want to learn from.' She hadn't admitted it to herself until now, but . . . 'I need help. And as soon as I get home, I'm going to look for it. Whether that's counselling or therapy, or something else. But I need to sort my head out. I shouldn't feel as broken as this.'

Cassie nodded. 'I think that's sensible. And brave. It's the right thing to do.'

'Do you promise there'll be no more lies?' Henry asked.

'Complete honesty from here on out. I really do mean that.' She covered her heart with her hand.

He nodded, not quite catching her eye but seeming happier than he had been a few minutes before.

'It's not your fault that she targeted you,' Olivia said. 'For somebody to treat you in that way means they have problems of their own, and you shouldn't have to take her problems on too.'

Cassie coughed awkwardly, shuffling the toe of a boot against the dirt. 'And I guess we should say sorry for not believing you. God, if I didn't think social media had done enough damage already, I'd get my phone out and give this girl a piece of my mind.'

Ed stood up and before she knew it, he was tugging on Tabby's arm, then Cassie's and Henry's, and pulling Olivia up from the floor. 'Can we please hug this out? I won't sleep well ever again if we don't have a group hug now.'

Tabby choked on the last of her tears. 'No, Ed, I don't think—'

'No,' Henry said. 'If there's one thing I've learnt, it's that Ed gives the best hugs. So if Ed wants a group hug, a group hug Ed shall have.'

Tabby snapped her gaze to his.

He raised an eyebrow, moved his arms out wide. 'Well?'

How could I ever have been so stupid to align with Jess over them?

Ed and Olivia squished Tabby into Henry's group hug. Cassie was the last to join, but Tabby found she held on the tightest once she was in.

'So I guess that's the end of our road trip,' Olivia said, voice muffled against the group. 'I can't believe that's it.'

'Hold on,' Henry said, and split the group hug up. 'I've got a surprise. But first we're going to need to find somewhere that sells flowers.'

Chapter Twenty-six

What was *Henry up to?*

He sat in the front with Ed, smiling to himself as he looked out of the window. He'd been smiling like that ever since they found a small convenience shop where he ran out and came back with a spray of carnations, ever since he'd got back and handed them to Olivia and made Ed set off down the road.

Tabby watched him out the corner of her eye as he gestured to Ed to turn. The signs indicated that they were passing through Hebden Bridge, and Ed slowed down as he rounded a sharp corner to drive up a steep hill. Not that that was unusual – it was all steep hills around here.

They passed a series of houses and bungalows, finally coming to a stop outside a church, where Ed pulled the van up and turned off the engine.

'We're here,' Henry said, clapping his hands together and bounding out of the van. He quickly slid open the side door, letting Olivia, Cassie and Tabby hop out.

'Where's "here"?' Cassie asked. 'A graveyard? That's a bit morbid for you, Henry. Haven't we seen enough of graves in the past few days?'

'Didn't I tell you to trust me?' Henry stretched his neck out and looked around, popping his phone back into his pocket. 'This is my surprise. It's the place where Sylvia Plath is buried.'

Tabby snapped her head up so quickly that she felt it crick. 'What?' she whispered, not sure if she'd heard him correctly.

'It's the place where Sylvia Plath is buried,' Henry repeated. And more awkwardly added, 'I thought you might like it.'

She looked around, surveyed the area. That he'd think to come here . . .

They crunched along the gravel, following Henry one by one as he led the procession. The car park was stuck between the church to their right, with its own churchyard, and an overflow graveyard to the right where, Henry told everyone, Sylvia Plath's grave was. Tabby had heard the stories of it being removed over and over again after being vandalised over the years; looking out on the hundreds of graves lined up now, Tabby didn't know how anyone could do such a thing in a place where time seemed to stop, where everything seemed so reverent.

'How are we going to find it?' Olivia asked, twisting her body around to take in the entire area.

'I think we'll spread out,' Henry said, 'and whoever gets there first can call out and then we'll all come over. Sound good?'

'It's a plan,' Ed said, saluting Henry and walking off to the far end of the graveyard.

The others nodded and set out along the graves, taking notice of each name before moving to the next.

The grass tickled Tabby's legs and sides as she walked along, the blades reaching up to her waist at points. It felt wrong somehow, she thought, the military precision of them all combing out to find it. Henry was walking along the row on her left-hand side, towards the back of the long graveyard. He stopped dead in front of her, turning around so that she could see his crumpled brow.

'Are you angry I did this without you knowing?'

'Angry? How could I ever be angry? It's *you* that should be angry with me! Honestly, you didn't have to do this. Not after what I did.'

Everyone else was still scouring row after row, occasionally shouting out that they hadn't found 'the one' yet; with the grass so tall, it was hard to see some of the writing on the stones and many had faded or collapsed with age.

'I think,' Henry said and paused. 'I think what you did was understandable. It hurt. A lot. I won't lie about that.

But now that you've explained what was going on, I get it. I just wish you'd spoken up about it, rather than keeping it to yourself. Maybe then we could have prevented all of this.'

She nodded. 'I realise that now. I'd just forgotten how to trust for a while.' *I don't know how we can go back to how we were before.*

'I've found it!' Cassie's voice cut through Tabby's thoughts. She looked across; Cassie was waving her hands in the air to beckon them over.

There was a stab of disappointment in Tabby's chest as she watched everyone congratulate Cassie for finding it. She gazed after Henry with a lump in her throat as he walked away from her.

This was supposed to be her moment. It wasn't Cassie's fault, she knew, but she couldn't ignore her jealousy that she hadn't been the one to discover the grave of her favourite poet. She'd been reading Sylvia Plath's poetry for so long, had absorbed every word of *The Bell Jar* until the pages of her book were creased and crumpled. It was supposed to be her that found it. Henry would have smiled at her like he was smiling at Cassie now and maybe, just maybe, things would have been different.

Tabby was the only one left, so she walked as fast as she could without tripping over her feet towards the grave.

It was situated in the middle of the graveyard, flowers planted in homage on the grassy area in front of the stone. There was purple lavender, Tabby's favourite plant and scent, and another pink flower that looked like a cluster of jester hats atop a long, thin stalk, which she couldn't identify. It touched her, such simple gestures that people didn't have to do but still did anyway. Tabby could just imagine hundreds of other people making the trek up to Heptonstall graveyard to pay tribute to such an iconic poetess.

Tabby stood on the edge of the group, only just able to look on, until Cassie declared that she was returning to the van and pulled Olivia and Ed along with her, exclaiming that if Ed didn't put the kettle on the camping stove for a cup of tea she would abandon them all for the nearest cafe. Olivia had the bunch of flowers they'd picked up in her hand and quickly chucked them at Henry before being dragged away.

'I'd like to see how far you get walking,' Ed grumbled to Cassie, but followed obediently. Cassie winked and smiled at Tabby as they left. Tabby blushed from the roots of her hair downwards.

She shuffled closer to Henry so that they were both standing at the edge of the grave, careful not to trample on the flowers. She was nervous to be this close to him, even though they'd already been closer.

Tabby switched off the part of her brain that whispered bad thoughts repetitively in her ear; she had to live in the moment. Here. Standing in front of her hero's grave, her final resting place.

Tabby bowed her head in respect, closing her eyes and saying a silent prayer.

Thank you, she said. *For your words, your talent, your life, however short it may have been. Thank you for meaning something to me when I wasn't sure if I'd ever feel again, for the times when your words were the only things I had to grasp hold of. I am grateful every day for the emotions you made me experience when I read your words. You may not be here for me to say it to you, but I will remember.*

Henry silently handed Tabby the flowers, pulling them out of their plastic wrapper. She bent down, laying them in front of the grave, and wiped a tear from the corner of her eye.

'Sorry,' she said. 'I shouldn't be so emotional.'

She leant closer to Henry, a movement that felt as if somebody else was controlling her body. He wrapped his arm around her, neither of them saying a word.

They watched in awe at the grave, the setting sun zipping across them and bathing them in ethereal light. Tabby tucked her head in so that it was resting on Henry's shoulder and whispered, 'Thank you.' So softly, so gently, that she felt like it might be taken away by the wind, but he heard and squeezed her shoulders in response.

When he next spoke, his voice was as soft as Tabby's had been. 'I thought you'd like to see it,' he said. 'And, selfishly, I wanted to too.'

'It's peaceful,' she replied. 'Magical.'

He nodded his head against the top of hers. She wondered if the others were watching, but really, she'd stopped caring. It was only she and Henry in this moment. The only two people on the planet, in their own little world, oblivious to everyone and everything else.

'Henry?' she asked, apprehensive.

'Yes?'

'I was wrong, before. So, so wrong.' She twisted her body so that she was facing him. 'I was scared and I panicked and I wish I hadn't said what I did, but you have to know it was all stupid lies. I would do anything to go back and change it now. I guess what I'm trying to tell you is that I really, really like you.'

'Tabby?' he said gently, smiling down at her.

'Yes?'

'I really, *really* like you too.'

This time the question was in his eyes, not hers. She lifted up to meet his kiss, looping her arms around his neck and feeling the soft skin of his lips against hers.

They didn't need to speak after that, only watched over the grave as it had stood for decades. They were not the first to visit and they would not be the last, but it felt special. As if words had the power to bring people together, have had that power for millennia.

Tabby sent another prayer out into the ether to thank whoever was watching out for her, to thank them for her being here, surrounded by people who cared about her and for whom she cared for equally. The magic of it all – that they had found each other and everything had slotted into place perfectly – hit Tabby full in the chest. She took a deep breath to steady herself and looked up at Henry.

'Thank you,' she said again. 'I think your surprises are the best surprises.'

Henry gazed down into Tabby's face, smiling, and kissed her on the top of the forehead.

She didn't want to bring it to a close; she felt so much a part of the moment, so whole and mended, that she felt it would be sacrilege for it to end. Eventually it was Henry who nudged her and asked, 'Ready?'

She nodded and took the first step away. Away from Sylvia Plath and towards something else equally important to her: her new friends, their promised adventures and the future.

She only looked back once – when she got to the open gateway, so that she could capture the graveyard clearly in her mind. This place, where something had changed inside her, where she suddenly felt like it was okay for her to exist, to own the space she inhabited and love every second of it.

Her phone rang furiously from her bag, disturbing the moment. She thought about ignoring it – *Who even cares if it's Jess? No more secrets.* But, as she reached to switch it off, she noticed the caller ID. *Mum.* She rushed to answer it.

'Tabby, love,' Mum's voice said through the speaker. But it wasn't really her Mum's voice – she sounded far too worried. 'I don't want to alarm you, but you might want to come home. Gran's had an accident and she's been taken to hospital.'

Chapter Twenty-seven

'We can get going right away,' Ed said. 'We'll be home by midnight at the latest.'

Tabby was shaken, not sure what to think or what to do. Henry put his arm around her shoulders, keeping her close. 'It will be okay,' he said. 'We'll get home and reassess, but we can't do anything until then. Not until we're back.'

'I don't think I'm worrying for nothing,' she confided. 'What if this is it?'

Gran wasn't getting any younger. Tabby thought of her happiness every time she was with her, how her gran seemed to know her better than anybody else; she thought back to holidays where they would play silly games and spend all their time laughing; she thought of the pleasure on Gran's face when Tabby had told her she was going to be living with her for the summer.

'I'll look after you,' Gran had said. 'I will always look after you, my little Tabby cat.'

And now Tabby was faced with the possibility of life without her, without the figure in her life who had stuck by her these past few weeks without complaint, with nothing but love and affection. Tabby couldn't understand it: Gran was so healthy. She did her OAP aerobics and went for walks and didn't drink or smoke. *How could this have happened?*

Tabby climbed in the van without a word, biting the inside of her cheek to stop herself breaking down; she had definitely done enough of that over the past few days to use up her lifetime supply. Her mascara was close to running out.

Henry buckled up next to her, with Olivia on her other side. Cassie rode up front with Ed.

'Thank you for being here,' Tabby whispered to Henry, as they pulled away.

He stroked her hair back from her face. 'Always,' he said. 'Even if you are a pain sometimes.'

Despite the fear churning around in her stomach, she smiled. 'I've got to keep things interesting, haven't I?'

'Maybe they could stay boring for a little while now?'

'I agree,' she said, nestling down into the seat. 'Boring sounds amazing.'

Ed pulled up into a petrol station to refuel the van, and they took the opportunity to phone their parents to let them know they were on their way back.

Tabby wished with all her might that she could go back in time and give her gran an extra hug before she'd left. She remembered cuddling her, but it hadn't been enough. It would never be enough if she couldn't inhale that lavender scent ever again.

'Back,' Ed said, climbing into his seat and chucking something at Tabby as he put his seat belt on. She looked down and found an extra-big packet of Haribo in her lap. 'I thought they might take your mind off things.'

'Thanks,' she whispered.

She'd been glued to her phone, checking it every minute in case there was any word or update. So far, nothing. *What if it's too late and that's why Mum's not calling me?*

'She probably doesn't want to worry you,' Olivia said, reading Tabby's mind. 'There's nothing you can do until we get home.'

As they travelled through the evening, the sky turning pink and then dark, it was clear Ed was becoming increasingly tired.

'Must stay awake,' he muttered as the sky overhead got blacker still and the lights on the motorway switched on. He'd wound all the windows down and was blasting Justin Bieber from the speakers, much to the chagrin of the others.

The more determined it seemed Ed was to stay awake, though, the more worried Tabby got. *He's going to crash the van and I'll never get home and then my mum will worry even more and her worry will mean Gran won't get better and . . .*

Once one worry popped into her mind, it multiplied, and suddenly she started worrying about all sorts of things she never usually worried about. Like all the people who didn't have anyone to worry about them, who were all alone, or what would happen if they got a flat tyre on the motorway. Her anxiety became worse the more tired she was.

Somehow, Ed managed to stay awake. When they eventually pulled into Gran's housing estate, he got out of the van and opened the side door, giving Tabby a reassuring pat on the shoulder as she hopped out. 'Keep us updated, won't you?'

'I will,' she said. 'Thank you for bringing me back so quickly.' Turning back into the van, and with the most heartfelt tone she could muster, she said, 'Thank you. Thank you so much for being here for me.'

'We love you, Tabby,' Olivia said. 'We'll always be here for you.'

The bungalow was pitch-black as Tabby unlocked the door and pushed her way inside. She looked around the room as if she expected Gran to walk out any minute, a cup of tea in hand and wearing her fluffy slippers.

'Mum?' she called. 'Dad?'

Tabby flicked on the light switch, to find Mum curled up on the sofa, fast asleep. At the blaze of light, Mum's eyes flickered and she was awake, bleary-eyed.

'Oh, Tabby,' she said and jumped up, throwing her arms around Tabby and squeezing tighter than ever before. 'I'm so glad you're home, my darling.'

'Mum,' Tabby said into her hair, 'I'm so sorry I went on the trip without you knowing. I never expected this to happen.'

Mum pulled away and held Tabby by the shoulders. 'Look at me, Tabby. We shouldn't have been so harsh on you in the first place. Gran – god bless her – was right: you are turning into a responsible young woman and we are immensely proud of you. None of us could have predicted this. It may have happened whether you were here or not.'

'But I wasn't here,' Tabby said. *I wasn't here for Gran when she needed me the most.*

'Ah.' Mum smiled. 'That's the thing: I don't know if Gran's mentioned him to you, but the way I found out she wasn't well was through a man called Mr Helstone. Apparently, he lives over the road. He was coming over to visit Gran and when she didn't answer the door, he thought it was strange. He was the one who found her. If he hadn't . . .'

'She's so crafty!' Tabby exclaimed. 'She's had her eye on Mr Helstone all summer. I bet that's the main reason she let me go on the road trip in the first place, so that she could get time alone with him.' But thinking about Gran made her heart ache. 'Is she okay?' she said softly.

'The doctors think she had a stroke. She's broken her wrist, but they can't operate on it because the risk is too high. They said that we should get some rest and go back in the morning. Your dad's just gone out to get us some food because we haven't eaten. I think there's a takeaway open around the corner.'

'But . . . she will get better, won't she?'

Mum smiled, but it didn't reach her eyes. 'Yes,' she said. 'We've just got to wait and see now.'

Chapter Twenty-eight

Tabby watched Gran from the ward window, knowing she couldn't be seen from here. She sat up in the hospital bed, hooked up to wires and drips, snaking out of her arms. Tabby wanted to brace herself first for the sight, wanted to be able to put on a brave face instead of wallowing in her own self-pity; that was the last thing her gran needed. She pushed away from the window and walked in.

Seeing Tabby enter the ward, Gran smiled through cracked, dry lips, and waved the fingers of her unbroken hand. 'Tabby,' she mumbled, her false teeth out on the table beside her, and her face drooping slightly to one side. *I've never seen Gran like this before. What should I do? I don't want to act as if she's not there but maybe she'll feel embarrassed, me seeing her like this.*

'Hi, Gran,' Tabby said. She wished she would jump up from the hospital bed and declare this was just a joke, that she was actually tricking them all and was ready to come home now. 'You weren't going too hard at OAP Zumba again, were you?'

Mum came in then, holding a hot tea and laughing at Tabby's comment.

'No,' Mum said. 'I think it was thinking too much about Mr Helstone that did it. I won't probe you on that now, Mum, but you can bet I will be when you're out of here. Why don't you sit down, Tabs, and tell Gran about your trip? I'm sure she'd love to hear what you got up to.'

Tabby took a seat by her bedside, dragging it closer and holding her bruised hand while careful not to knock any of the drips.

Tabby relaxed as she told Gran and Mum the highlights: the ice cream in Bath and the bookshop; the Elizabethan architecture in Stratford-upon-Avon; the awe of the Brontë Parsonage.

Mum slipped out somewhere in the middle, leaving Tabby alone with Gran. Finally, she told her about the visit to Sylvia Plath's grave and how Henry had planned it specially, because he knew she was Tabby's favourite author of all time.

Gran gasped.

Tabby felt herself blush, tried to stop the grin that was spreading across her face. But she couldn't hold it back. 'Henry and I are kind of a thing,' she said, suddenly embarrassed about telling her grandmother about her love life. 'We . . . Well, I don't know how to put it exactly, but we're going out now.'

Now Gran's face properly lit up.

A nurse came in, smiling at Tabby. 'Is this your granddaughter?' she asked. To Tabby, she said, 'Your grandma is making a remarkable recovery. She'll be as good as new in no time at all, I'm sure.'

Tabby kissed her gran on the forehead, stroking her greying hair. She'd noticed she was getting more tired, her eyes drooping. 'I'll come and visit you again, Gran, and fill you in on everything else. I love you.'

'Love you too,' Gran mouthed.

Tabby blew her a kiss as she walked out of the door, leaving the smell of surgical spirit and cabbage dinners behind as Gran was propped up by the nurse. It hurt her to have to leave her, to have to return home and Gran not be there. It wasn't really home without her.

Tabby and her mum made their way back through all the confusing corridors and out of the main doors to the street. Tabby wiped a tear away. She didn't know if the tears were falling because of the shock of seeing Gran like that, or because it seemed like she was going to be okay.

Chapter Twenty-nine

My entire life, packed up into cardboard boxes.

Mum had stayed with Gran while Tabby and her dad went to finish up the last of the packing. She surveyed her old bedroom, noting the darker patches of paint on the wall where she'd had book posters up, the slight mark on the carpet where she'd spilt nail varnish last year and tried to clear it up. As it turned out, nail varnish remover didn't do the trick.

This is it. I'm really moving.

There was only one thing left to do in Cheltenham – one last thing unsaid, one last piece of unfinished business. The letter was burning a hole in Tabby's pocket and had been ever since she'd written it.

She looked at her room one last time, picked up the last box and left it downstairs with the rest, then called to Dad to say she was popping out for half an hour and shut the front door behind her.

Her hand was in her pocket the entire time, keeping hold of the envelope. It took ten minutes to get to the street, and then she waited at the top of the road, straining her eyes to see down. Just in case she was outside. She felt sick.

But there was no car on the drive, and she knew she had to do this. *For my own sanity. For my own closure.*

Taking the biggest deep breath in she thought she'd ever taken, thinking about Sylvia Plath's grave for courage, Tabby walked forward, and pulled the letter out of her pocket.

This is it.

Dear Jess,

I don't hate you. I want you to know that before I go on. I want to, but I don't. I could knock on your door and scream in your face, hit out, cry, until I was satisfied that you'd felt the pain you've put me through, but I don't have the energy for that any more. I shouldn't have to waste my time on you.

I'm disappointed. Why me? Maybe you won't remember all of the times you called me names in front of everyone else, said that I wasn't good enough, made me feel as if I shouldn't be there. You won't think twice about the time you ruined my chance of winning the big cross-country competition, even after you knew how much I'd trained for it. But I haven't been able to forget. Each incident has been ingrained in my brain like a scar, and scars are permanent. You have to know that your words, your actions, have consequences. They don't just fade away.

Now, I have to rebuild myself.

This summer, I've learnt more about myself than ever before. How resilient I am, how tough I can be, even when faced with the awful stuff you've put me through. It's thanks to you, I guess, that I learnt the importance of being treated fairly, of finding friends who care about me and support me. And so I can't hate you a hundred per cent. Because I know that I am stronger now than I ever was.

Tabby

She pushed it through the letter box and it was gone. Just like that.

Ed: Um what time is the meeting tomorrow?

Olivia: 11am, why?!

Ed: Oh absolutely no reason in the world. Thanks!

Tabby: That does not sound like Ed.

Ed: Hypothetically speaking, if I had accidentally invited someone else to join the book club, how much trouble do you think I'd be in?

Tabby: . . .

Ed: HYPOTHETICALLY SPEAKING

Tabby: It was nice knowing you!

Chapter Thirty

Unlike the first time, Tabby had no reservations about today's meeting of the Paper & Hearts Society in the park. It was another blisteringly hot day, but that didn't bother her.

She picked her way through screaming kids, over picnic blankets and abandoned toys to the oak tree on the other side. Its branches lay unmoving, stilted in the muggy August air; she made out two figures sitting underneath.

'Tabby!' She spun around to find Henry coming towards her, grinning as he leant down to give her a quick kiss.

'Hello to you too,' she said, pushing his glasses up from his nose so they were sitting on his face properly.

'Fancy meeting you here,' he said. 'You don't know of any good book clubs to join, do you?'

She grinned. 'As it happens, I *do* know of a good book club.' She paused. 'Actually, on second thoughts, I'd rather you didn't join. You're too *distracting*.'

'Me?' he said, pointing at his chest.

They walked hand in hand to meet Olivia and Cassie, who were nestled against the trunk of the tree. Olivia was practically sitting on Cassie's lap. Today, Tabby had no worries about Cassie looking cooler than her, because she knew that, no matter how hard she tried, she always would. But Tabby was comfortable enough in her own skin now not to care.

What a difference a summer makes.

'Tabby! Henry!' Olivia squealed, jumping up and pulling at her dungaree straps before enveloping them in a hug. 'You're here!'

'Where else would we be?'

'I don't think you need to be a genius to guess where you'd rather be,' Cassie said to Henry wryly. She turned to Tabby. 'How's your gran doing?'

'Better, thanks. The doctors say she'll be home soon if her recovery continues, which is a huge relief.'

'I bet,' Cassie said, and she smiled. *She smiled.* Tabby still felt unnerved when Cassie did this, as if it wasn't really meant for her.

'To think that this time two weeks ago, we were in Bath,' Tabby said. 'How are summers supposed to be fun after this one? We've used up all the fun for the rest of our lives.'

Olivia snorted, opening a packet of mini doughnuts and handing them around. 'As if I haven't planned out our next road trip. Plus, Tabby, you haven't experienced one of my epic Christmas parties yet; I've already started working out my bookish theme. The proper fun hasn't even begun yet.'

'I did wonder when it was going to be less boring. I should never have come to that first meeting.' Tabby grinned, poking Henry. 'Just think, if I hadn't, I never would have met you.'

'Are you serious?' he said, eyes wide. 'I could have saved myself from being jumped on by you if we'd just advertised it as the most boring book club ever? You could have said before!'

She poked her tongue out. 'You wouldn't be without me now, Henry Gillingham.' He pulled her towards him, looking like he was going in for a kiss, but instead wiped doughnut icing down her face.

'Henry!' Tabby squawked, pouting. He laughed, throwing his head back and leaving him vulnerable for a revenge attack. She got him back, smudging chocolate icing across the frames of his glasses. (Being careful to avoid the glass – she wasn't that mean.)

'Somebody please contain the straight people,' Cassie grumbled, licking icing from her finger. 'They never know when to hold off the PDAs.'

'Where's Ed got to?' Henry asked. 'I thought he'd be first here; he seemed so eager.'

'About Ed . . .' Tabby said. 'Do any of you know what he's up to?'

'Up to?' Cassie said, but she was drowned out by Olivia exclaiming, 'You have *got* to be kidding me,' with her mouth falling open. They all turned around to find Ed coming towards them, a large box in hand.

But it wasn't the box that Olivia was staring at. It was the boy walking alongside Ed, wearing a jumper despite the summer heat and a cold, tight-lipped expression. Tabby wasn't sure if he was frowning because of the sun, or because of the mismatched group he was being dragged towards.

'Hi!' Ed said as he got closer. 'Look what I've got!'

'The box, or the boy?' Cassie said, unimpressed.

He lowered the box for them to see through the plastic – in it sat twelve ring doughnuts, decorated with hundreds and thousands atop white icing. Ed licked his lips. 'So what did you guys bring?'

'What do you mean?' Tabby frowned.

'I mean that these are mine. What did you all bring to eat?'

'Doughnuts too, you doughnut,' Henry muttered.

Ed cracked up laughing. 'You call those mini doughnuts real doughnuts? You guys don't know how to have a good time.' He placed the box on the ground between them, sighing in contentment. 'So, what bookish theme are we talking about today?'

Tabby and Cassie exchanged a look. *What the hell is going on?*

'Hello, Felix,' Olivia said, her tone even but determined. 'What are you doing here?'

'Oh,' Ed said, patting Felix on the shoulder, 'Felix wanted to join the Paper & Hearts Society. That's okay with you, isn't it?'

More looks were exchanged.

'Of course!' Olivia's voice had risen to a dangerous level, bordering on hysterical. 'It was so lovely of Ed to invite you, Felix. The more the merrier! I'm so glad the society is finally taking off!' The laugh that accompanied this lasted a fraction too long. 'Why don't you introduce yourself to everyone? I don't think we're all acquainted. You don't know Tabby, do you?'

'*That* Felix?' Cassie hissed at Henry. He nodded, not taking his eyes off Felix.

This can't be a good sign, Tabby thought.

'Usually we share a bit about our favourite books. Y'know, to get into the book club spirit,' Olivia continued.

They all awkwardly shuffled into seating positions, Olivia with a strained smile glued to her face.

'Felix,' Felix said abruptly. 'My favourite author is Ernest Hemingway, but my favourite book is *War and Peace*. Have any of you read it?'

'Only used it as a doorstop,' Tabby said jokingly, knowing that the Leo Tolstoy book had over a thousand pages. Henry laughed, but the joke fell flat on Felix.

He sniffed. 'I didn't expect you to understand the nuances of Tolstoy. Some of us have moved on from *young adult fiction*, you know. You have to grow up at some point.'

'Is that supposed to be an insult?' Cassie narrowed her eyes.

'Just an observation.'

'Actually,' Tabby said, feeling anger well up inside, 'the Paper & Hearts Society is about celebrating *all* books, not shaming them.'

'Well,' Ed said, passing a doughnut to Felix. 'I'm sure we're all going to have *lots* of fun. See, we already get on like a house on fire.'

'And you're burning inside it,' Cassie muttered.

Tabby had to grab a doughnut to distract herself from saying something she'd regret.

'Yep,' Olivia said. '*Fun*.'

'We're next-door neighbours, you know, Felix and me,' Ed said to Tabby, motioning towards Felix. 'What a coincidence that two book lovers live next to each other.'

Cassie murmured, 'You might not be living much lon—' but Olivia shot her a glare and she stopped.

It hit Tabby then: it had started with the books, that day in the library when she'd felt so out of control, so desperate to get her gran off her back, and it would end with the books. And most importantly, with friends.

Besides, if there was one thing she'd learnt this summer it was that everyone had a story. As the saying went, 'You should never judge a book by its cover.' Maybe it was best not to write Felix off quite yet.

As long as she had Olivia, Henry, Ed and Cassie by her side, Tabby thought she could conquer the world.

THE END

(For now.)

Olivia: ED EASTFIELD I AM GOING TO MURDER YOU IN YOUR SLEEP

Ed: I accidentally maybe might have mentioned it to him and he said he wanted to come!!! What could I do?!?!

Cassie: say no perhaps?

Olivia: I swear to god, Felix is your responsibility, Ed, and if he continues to be a nuisance it will be your fault. I can't believe you!!

ACKNOWLEDGEMENTS

The first thing I turn to when I pick up a new book is the acknowledgements. I've dreamed of writing my own for years and when writing The Paper & Hearts Society felt like the most difficult thing in the world, it's been imagining this moment that has made me even more determined. So this is very surreal!

First of all, I have to thank my parents who have had to put up with more cries of frustration, tears, and midnight meltdowns than any parents should have to put up with. Thank you for supplying me with chocolate when I needed it most, celebrating with me, and telling everybody you meet that they should read this book. I think you could get a job in publishing after this! I really couldn't wish for more supportive parents and I LOVE YOU!

Also to the rest of my family – Grandma and Grandpa, for their continued love and support, and for passing onto me their love of books; Auntie Kim and family; Uncle David and Sarah; and everyone else. There are too many of you to mention personally, but I certainly am very lucky to have you all.

Behind every good author is an amazing agent and Lauren Gardner is a SUPER-AGENT. I'm always joking that the way authors talk about their agents is like they've fallen deeply in love with them, but I really did know as soon as I spoke to Lauren that she was The One. Lauren, knowing how much you believed in me and The Paper & Hearts Society gave me the confidence and courage I needed. Also, thank you for the Mini Eggs enabling. You're the BEST!

I'd also like to thank Sophie Clarke, the most stylish agency assistant in publishing, who always appreciates a cute guinea pig picture (and who I may be a little bit obsessed with). And to everyone else at Bell Lomax Moreton – thank you!

Bringing a book baby into the world takes an entire team of people who work tirelessly behind the scenes.

Thank you, most of all, to my editor, Polly Lyall Grant, who championed The Paper & Hearts Society from the beginning and who made my dreams come true when she offered on the series. I can't wait to write more adventures for The Paper & Hearts Society with you!

From PR and marketing, I'd like to thank Katy Cattell, Emily Thomas, Naomi Berwin and Natasha Whearity, who have helped to deliver a campaign I'm so proud of; and from Sales and Rights I'd like to thank Katherine Fox and Nic Goode, and Valentina Fazio. I'm in awe of their amazing work.

Alison Padley and Sarah Baldwin have designed the most gorgeous cover, which made me burst into tears as soon as I saw it. Thank you for bringing Tabby to life!

More of my biggest thanks go to Ruth Alltimes and Hilary Murray-Hill, for welcoming me into Hachette Children's Group.

I also owe a huge amount of gratitude to my Brontë Parsonage Museum family, especially Rebecca Yorke. Being Brontë Society Young Ambassador has been the biggest dream come true and has given me more confidence than I could have imagined possible. Getting to work with the entire team – the museum staff, the volunteers, and everyone who makes things run as smoothly as possible behind the scenes – has been such a privilege and I couldn't have wished to meet a nicer, more passionate and knowledgeable group of people.

I've been part of the online book community since I was 12, and by far the biggest advantage has been getting the opportunity to meet and make friends with so many wonderful people.

Lauren James is my number one author inspiration. She's been invaluable in the writing of The Paper & Hearts Society – she listened to me discuss it in the early days, offered encouragement along the way, and wrote many amazing blog posts filled with writing advice that guided me through. Thank you for being you, Lauren!

Thank you to the Nineteen Newbies, for the advice, jokes, and group chat names that can never, ever be revealed outside of the group for fear of scandalising the entire publishing industry. An extra big shout-out to Aisha Bushby and Yasmin Rahman, for the ramblings, rants, and general awesomeness. I'm very lucky to have you both.

To the #UKYAChat community – thank you for the friendships, the laughs, and the fun every Friday night. When I started the chat in July 2013, I didn't imagine it would ever turn into what it is today, and you really are a special bunch. I hope you'll enjoy my book, too! And of course, to everyone who has supported my blog, my YouTube, and various other ventures. You are the best bit!

There are too many bloggers and authors to mention you all by name, but special thanks have to go to: Stacey Croft, for being the awesomest and one of my longest friends; Katherine (Writing Hideout), Ross (The Royal Bookshelf), Helen Harvey, Rosie Threakall, and everyone else who sprinted with me; Sarah J Harris, for being one of the loveliest authors in publishing; Rachel Ward, for the words of encouragement; and Kit Berry, who made me believe that one day I could become an author too.

And finally, to Izzy, Daisy and all the guinea pigs, especially Hazel and Saba. Because would it really be *my* acknowledgements section if I didn't acknowledge how much my animals mean to me?